DANIEL MIGNAULT & JACKSON DEAN CHASE

— AS SEEN IN BUZZFEED AND THE HUFFINGTON POST —

Praise for TITAN: The Gods War, Book I:

"[Co-authors Daniel Mignault & Jackson Dean Chase have] stepped up to the plate with gusto...[a] diligently crafted debut novel..."
  — The Huffington Post

"[*Titan*] succeeds in taking fiction to a whole new level."
  — TheBaynet.com

"Irresistible... a heart-pounding story full of suspense, romance, and action!" — Buzzfeed

"Excellent... *Titan* is a beautifully crafted story that braves all odds."
  — Medium.com

"...[loaded with] suspense, romance, and action thrills."
  — The Odyssey Online

"A delectably great experience... [gives urban fantasy] a new twist."
  —ThriveGlobal.com

"...will keep readers guessing until the very end."
  — WN.com

ALSO BY JACKSON DEAN CHASE

USA TODAY BESTSELLING AUTHOR

BEYOND THE DOME

Science Fiction Series

- Book 1: *Drone* (releases August 3, 2018)
- Book 2: *Warrior* (releases August 10, 2018)
- Book 3: *Elite* (releases August 17, 2018)
- Book 4: *Human* (releases August 24, 2018)

JON WARLOCK, WIZARD DETECTIVE

Urban Fantasy Series

- Book 1: *Warlock Rising* (releases Sept. 14, 2018)
- Book 2: *Warlock Revenge* (releases Sept. 21, 2018)
- Book 3: *Warlock Reborn* (releases Sept. 28, 2018)

ALSO BY DANIEL MIGNAULT & JACKSON DEAN CHASE

THE GODS WAR

Urban Fantasy Series

- Book 1: *Titan* (releases July 13, 2018)
- Book 2: *Kingdom of the Dead* (releases July 20, 2108)
- Book 3: *Gift of Death* (releases July 27, 2018)

TITAN

THE GODS WAR — BOOK 1

DANIEL MIGNAULT
JACKSON DEAN CHASE

WWW.DANIELMIG.COM
WWW.JACKSONDEANCHASE.COM

First printing, July 2018

ISBN-13: 978-1978023666 / ISBN-10: 1978023669

Published by Jackson Dean Chase, Inc.

TITAN

PUBLISHER'S NOTE

For the dreamers, the doubters, and the doers:
You made this happen.

CLIMB!

To those who dream:
    those who dare are watching,
    waiting for you to join them
    high above it all.
    The climb is hard,
    but it begins for you
    the same way it began for them:
    by seizing the first rung of the ladder,
    by never giving up,
    never letting go.

Is your grip secure?
    Have you packed your courage?
    Good.

Now climb!

— Jackson Dean Chase

TITAN

PART I

CRONUS IS WATCHING

1

ONLY ROOM FOR ONE

I AM THE MOUNTAIN.
   I am one with it.
   I am one with the earth.

CHILL WIND BLASTS MY FACE. I'm hanging off the side of Mount Olympus, thousands of feet above the ground. The sky is dark and streaked with lightning. I dig my fingers into the stone, finding cracks, crevices. Handholds that keep me hanging on. My shoes scrabble against the wall, dislodging dirt and rocks that have been here for centuries. I look down and grin, watching the rocks fall, knowing I could fall just as far, just as fast. But not today.

Thunder booms. Adrenaline courses through me. I pull myself up, muscles burning, blood pumping. I don't stop. I keep climbing. My body knows what to do, but my mind is racing. Wild with exhilaration, with triumph! I am so close now, and if I can do this, I can do anything. And if I can do anything...

My toehold breaks away, knocking me off-balance. I scrabble, quickly find another, then pause to catch my breath. This mad joy I feel needs to be controlled. I must focus my mind as easily as I focus my body. It's not easy. The storm isn't just around me, it's *in me.* I take a moment to breathe, feeling my fingers dig into the stone, and close my eyes.

Darkness.

The sound of the storm dies. I no longer feel the cold. A sense of calm comes over me. I open my eyes and climb. Smarter, not harder. It's not about how fast I get to the top, only that I get there, and when I do...

"Hey, Andrus! Move your ass!"

The voice is sudden, unexpected. Mount Olympus is replaced by the rock climbing wall of the Axios Academy. I'm not thousands of feet up, just thirty. There's no palace of the Gods waiting at the top, only a red flag.

Blake Masters clambers up beside me. He's eighteen, a senior like me. Hard-muscled, tanned, with the hungry smile of a wolf. "Daydreaming again?"

Before I can reply, Blake kicks me, causing one of my hands to come loose. I swing wildly away as he climbs past me, straining for the top. Bastard! I should have seen it coming. There are no rules except winner take all. I see the upturned face of my teacher, Mr. Cross, and the other students in the gym below. Watching. Waiting for me to fail.

I swing back and find another handhold. I'm pulling myself after Blake, but now there's no joy, no calm. Just rage. He sees me coming and climbs faster. I don't like the feeling that's coming over me. It's a deep down, bottomless rage and it scares me, but it's all I've got.

I reach out and grab Blake's ankle, yanking hard. His whole body tenses, then he's lashing out with his other foot, trying to dislodge my grip. I grab his other ankle as his foot comes toward my face. Now I'm hanging onto him instead of the rock wall.

He grits his teeth, struggling to hang on.

"Get off my mountain!" I snarl, and I say it with such hate, I can't believe it. It doesn't feel like me. It feels primal. Ancient. And Blake can't hang on anymore, not with our combined weight. We're falling,

but the harnesses we're wearing save us from splattering on the gym floor. Instead of broken bones, we've got broken dreams.

As we hang there, Blake mutters, "Good going, moron. Now we both lose."

That means Mr. Cross will have to punish us. I get the feeling our gym teacher enjoys punishing more than teaching, though he never calls it that. He calls it "correcting." Mr. Cross is a stern man, middle-aged, with a military crewcut that's more salt than pepper. Rumor has it he got a "Section 8" from the Army before the Gods War ripped our planet apart. I don't know if he really is crazy, but I do know he's the kind of teacher you don't mess around with.

I guess you could say we have a love/hate relationship, and I can already tell what kind it's going to be today. Most of the time, I'm his star pupil, a model warrior, but that just means he's that much harder on me when I fail.

From below, a familiar whistle shrills. Mr. Cross yells, "Andrus! Blake! Quit fooling around and get down from there." After we're back on the gym floor, he tears into us in front of the whole class. "What was that?" he demands, not waiting for an answer. "You do know there's only room for one winner, right?"

"Yes, sir," Blake says. "I know it, but I'm not sure Andrus does." Snorts and laughter come from the class.

"Quiet!" Mr. Cross demands and the whole class shuts up. Our teacher paces back and forth, scowling, and I know he's about to let us have it. I'm not wrong.

"Preventing your opponent from winning is not the same as you winning," he spits. "To be a winner, you must win! No mercy, no compromise! War is not limited to the battlefield or the classroom. War is the struggle you face each day, from the moment you wake, to the moment you fall asleep. War is everything! It is not just glory and honor, it is survival. Those who do not survive, do not win!"

There are nods and murmurs of agreement from the class. Mr. Cross waits for his message to sink in, and I know where he's going with it. It's where he always goes, and he doesn't disappoint me.

"Andrus," he asks, "can you tell us what our world would be like if Cronus and Zeus had destroyed each other in the Gods War?"

A lot of answers come to mind: Happy, normal. Not living in fear of monsters—or failure. But I know better than to say any of that. Instead, I say what the teacher expects me to say: "Lost. Alone. Without guidance. Without protection. Worthless."

Mr. Cross nods. "That's right, and that's exactly what I saw from you and Blake today. I saw weakness!" He says it like a dirty word. "I saw tragedy! I saw two of my best students fail. And do you know why you failed?" His flint-gray eyes flash under the harsh overhead lights. "It's not because you lack passion. It's because you lack focus. Winners use their passion; they do not let their passion use them. This isn't the Old World. This is New Greece! The Titans only want the best to serve them. That's why you're here at Axios! And what does 'Axios' mean?"

"'I am worthy,'" Blake says.

Mr. Cross shakes his head. "I can't hear you."

"I am worthy!" Blake repeats, and this time, I join him.

"I still can't hear you," Mr. Cross says, then turns his attention to the rest of the class. "I can't hear any of you!"

"I AM WORTHY!" the class yells.

"Again!" Mr. Cross shouts. "Louder!"

We all yell, and we keep yelling until it becomes a chant, until we feel it in our bones, our hearts, our souls. We are worthy—or at least, we've been given a chance to be, which is more than most people in the New Greece Theocracy get.

Finally, Mr. Cross raises his hands to stop us. "Very good, class. We all need a little reminder now and again why we're here. Why we must survive, and never forget." His eyes skim over the students, then hold on me. "Some of you may feel I'm being too harsh, that I'm training you too hard. It's easy to lose sight of your goals, to think you've got it safe and easy because you're here. But you're not. The Titans are watching. And the mightiest Titan, Cronus, sees you! He sees all. You are his children, in a way, and like his children, he will devour you unless you can prove you are strong enough to survive, to serve him. It doesn't matter who we were before we came here..."

He pauses, and his eyes go unfocused and far away before coming back to us. "The truth... The truth is we must train hard because we must *be* hard. Always. We are the future priests and warriors of this world. We get there by proving ourselves, by giving glory to the Titans, and by making sacrifice. So unless you want to end up in Cronus's belly, you'll climb that damn wall. You'll climb, and you'll win!"

Blake and I glare at each other, our eyes punching the hate our fists can't.

"Blake!" Mr. Cross says. "Andrus! Because you both failed, we're going to have a little rematch on Monday."

Blake smirks and whispers to me, "You're gonna lose."

"We're going to have a rematch," Mr. Cross repeats, "but not like you think. What is the penalty for failure?" He addresses the class and two dozen kids shout, "PUNISHMENT!" Most of them mean it. Most of them *want* to see us fail, because we're the top students in the class. Blake looks as happy about the idea of punishment as I do, maybe even worse.

"Punishment," Mr. Cross agrees. "But what kind of punishment?"

"A duel!" Vince Garber suggests. "Swords and shields at twenty paces!" Vince is a dick and just psycho enough to suggest the worst and rarest form of punishment our school has to offer. That's because no one can die anymore.

Death doesn't exist since Hades, the God of the underworld, was defeated by the Titans and imprisoned in the depths of Tartarus. You'd think not being able to die would be a good thing, and that's how the Titans sold it to us, but they can magically heal themselves and never grow old. Humans aren't that lucky. So if you get injured bad enough to die or be crippled, you just have to suffer. *Forever.* And if you can't do your job anymore? If you get too hurt or too old? Maybe you get fed to Cronus, or put on display in the Museum of Failure as a lesson to others.

I've been to the Museum. I've seen the wretches hanging on hooks and on poles or pinned to walls like butterflies in some madman's collection. I've heard the screams, the moans, the cries for mercy. Every year, our history teacher, Mrs. Ploddin, takes us on a class field trip, and every year, she warns we could be the next exhibit. She says it with a wink, almost as if she hopes she can show one of us being tortured there to next year's class. I think I'd rather be eaten by Cronus than put on display. At least then, my suffering would be private.

The idea of a duel makes me nervous. I'm a good fighter, but so is Blake. He also fights dirty.

Fortunately, Mr. Cross shakes his head at Vince's suggestion. "No, there will be no duel, though I am sorely tempted. Do you know how many nights I wish I could just arm you all and set you loose on each other?" He chuckles, but no one sees the humor in it.

"If it won't be a duel," Vince asks, "what will it be?"

Mr. Cross smiles. "What do the Titans enjoy more than bloodshed?"

"A contest," I say. "A battle of brains and brawn."

"That's right," Mr. Cross agrees. "And it seems to me that I can use your failure to make a point—not just to you, but to the rest of the class." His withering gaze falls on Mark Fentile and Brenda Larson, the two lowest-ranking gym students. "Mark, Brenda! You're going to partner with Andrus and Blake for the rematch. Mark, you're with Andrus, and Brenda, you're with Blake. You'll be harnessed together as a team and both of you must make it to the top of the wall. It's Friday, so you have the whole weekend to train."

"What happens if both teams fail?" Blake asks.

Mr. Cross shrugs. "Then it's swords and shields, except only one of you will have a sword, and the other a shield, and you'll be tied together. Probably something you want to avoid, so you focus on training your teammate and do not fail. Class dismissed!"

"Ha!" Blake snorts. "You got stuck with that Loser? Looks like I've as good as won." He grabs Brenda by the arm and practically drags her out of the gym. He's already whispering strategy in her ear (or more likely, threats).

Mark stands there, looking miserable. He's bookish and skinny, a better candidate for the priesthood than the warrior class. I know he's smart because I've seen him ace history tests and get straight A's in everything that doesn't involve gym. "I'm sorry," he says. "I don't want to let you down, but I'm not sure how good I can do. That wall is pretty high, and —"

Before I can say anything, Mr. Cross shuts him up. "That's Loser talk, Mark. Do you praise the Titans with that mouth? Get out, and you better not disappoint me Monday."

"Come on," I tell Mark. "We can train after school."

"Not here," Mr. Cross says. "The school's putting in some improvements to the gym. Construction zone. Off limits and all that."

Mark and I turn to leave, but the teacher stops me.

"Andrus, stay here. I'd like a word with you. In private."

"Yes, sir," I say. "Mark, I'll see you in history class. We can figure out where to train afterward."

Mark nods and heads for the exit.

"What did you want to talk to me about?" I ask Mr. Cross.

He doesn't answer until the gym door closes behind Mark. "I saw you up there, Andrus. You were winning! You were whipping Blake's ass, and then something happened."

"Yeah," I say. "He kicked me."

"No, before that."

"I'm not sure what you mean, sir. I was climbing."

"No, you were *daydreaming*. I'm not sure about what, and I don't care. You slowed down, acted like you had all the time in the world. That's how Blake caught up. That's why you failed, and I don't understand it. This isn't the first time this has happened. What's going on?"

"Nothing."

"Nothing, my ass!" Mr. Cross says. "Look, you may think I'm a bastard, you might even think I'm stupid. I'm no priest, I can't read omens, but I can read my students. I know a winner when I see one, Andrus. You could be number one. You *should* be number one, not Blake. Kids like Blake are a drachma a dozen. They're tough, they're cunning, they may even be charming, but they're not hero material."

"And I am?"

"You could be," Mr. Cross says, "someone has to be, and I have to train them. Contrary to the Vince Garbers of this world, I don't get off on blood and guts even though I have to act like it sometimes. I don't want to see my students fail, even the weak ones like Mark. But he will fail if you don't train him, and *you* will fail if you do what you did up on that wall today. Know yourself. Gain focus. Get control."

"Yes, sir. I won't let you down."

Mr. Cross puts his hand on my shoulder. His fingers dig into me like my hands on the rock wall. "No more dreams, Andrus. You must take action instead. Dreams without action will destroy you."

2

A SINKING SHIP

"ONCE UPON A TIME," Mrs. Ploddin says, "all was Chaos." She pauses, looking over our history class through her horn-rimmed glasses as if waiting for one of us to disagree. I'm sitting in the back of the room, paying more attention to Mark than to the teacher. He sits two rows ahead and to the left, and I wonder if he's thinking what I am: How we're going to beat Blake and Brenda in Monday's rematch. If he is, Mark doesn't give any sign. He sits there, scholarly as ever, as if what Mrs. Ploddin is saying is the most interesting thing in the world. And maybe it is to him. After all, Mark is destined for the priesthood... if he doesn't get us both fed to Cronus first.

Mrs. Ploddin drones on: "From primal Chaos sprang Gaia, the Earth Mother, and Ouranos, the Sky Father. From the holy union of heaven and earth came their children, the immortal Titans. But Ouranos grew jealous of his children and cast them into Tartarus, the vast and terrible underworld. There, the Titans languished until Cronus, the youngest and most daring of them, escaped. Cronus defeated Ouranos, and there was much rejoicing as the Titans were reunited with Gaia. There was a Golden Age of peace under the rule of Cronus, King of the Titans, and his queen, Rhea. But when Rhea became pregnant, Cronus knew he could not let his children usurp him as he had usurped his own father. And do you know what happened next?"

Mark raises his hand. "Cronus devoured his children. One after the other: Hades, Hera, Hestia, Demeter, and Poseidon. But not Zeus."

"No," Mrs. Ploddin agrees. "Not Zeus. Rhea had had enough of her children being devoured when she became pregnant with Zeus, so she had him hidden away and substituted a rock disguised to look like a child in his place. Cronus ate the rock, and it joined the children in his stomach who were still alive. And can any of you tell me *why* they were still alive?"

"Because they were immortal," Mark says. "And immortals cannot die."

"That's right! The children of the Titans were a new race, a lesser race, called Gods, but they could not die. So mighty Cronus swallowed them, not only to ensure they could never escape, but also to absorb their power and add it to his own..."

"Except for the rock," Mark adds.

Mrs. Ploddin sighs. "Yes, Mark, except for the rock."

The class laughs, but Mark looks at them strangely, like what he said wasn't supposed to be funny.

The teacher waits for the class to settle down, then goes on, "Zeus decided to overthrow Cronus. Zeus was a cowardly, deceitful creature who lacked the power to challenge his father directly. He knew he could never do it alone, so he poisoned Cronus, which caused him to vomit up his imprisoned brothers and sisters. The Gods went to war against the Titans and after ten long years, managed to imprison them in Tartarus. And Zeus, the youngest of the Gods, became their ruler, much as Cronus had when he overthrew Ouranos..."

The story isn't holding my attention. I drift into a daydream. I'm climbing the rock wall again, only this time I'm beating Blake. I'm leaving him far behind, except there's something waiting for me at the top. A shadow. Someone—or some *thing*—watching me.

Waiting.

I snap out of my daydream as Mrs. Ploddin holds up her hands. "Yes, class, we all know Zeus was a pretender! He and his fellow Gods thought they could rule better than the Titans, but they could not. Because they had been held so long in Cronus's stomach, all the Gods except Zeus needed the psychic power of others. So the Gods created mankind to worship them, and they made us in their own image, but they knew better than to make us immortal. They thought that we would worship them forever, and for a time we did, in many countries under many names, but the Gods grew complacent and eventually, our faith waned. That waning faith is what caused the locks imprisoning the Titans in Tartarus to weaken. And as the locks weakened, what happened?"

Mark raises his hand, but the teacher ignores him. Instead, she does the worst thing possible and calls on me. "Andrus! Andrus Eaves, if you're not too busy, can you tell us the answer?"

I clear my throat. "Uh... bad stuff happened?" The class laughs and I smile, at least until I see the look on the teacher's face. "Um, I mean wars. Climate change. Natural disasters. That sort of thing."

"Exactly," Mrs. Ploddin says. "And then the locks broke and the Titans were released, igniting the Gods War. A war the Gods could not win, and when they refused to surrender, they were responsible for why so much of the world was destroyed. The Titans won, and rather than make the mistake of keeping them all in Cronus's stomach again, the Titans had the Gods killed, all of them except Hades."

"But there was still the problem of man to deal with," Mark says.

Mrs. Ploddin nods. "Yes, and in their mercy, the Titans created the New Greece Theocracy and allowed mankind to live to serve their infinite glory. All hail the Titans! All hail the NGT!"

The class cheers and raises their fists in salute. I join them.

Mrs. Ploddin says, "Now I bet some of you are wondering why I'm telling you all this..."

The class murmurs in agreement. We've all heard this stuff since childhood, even before coming to Axios.

"Well," she continues, "it's to illustrate a point. After all, you're seniors and will be graduating soon. You'll become priests and warriors and many of you will be put in positions where you'll have proximity to power, to those in command, and to others like you. Not all of those people will be happy in their roles. Some may be stupid, greedy, or impious, placing their own needs above the Titans. Some may even think they can blaspheme or rebel. These foolish few may argue that as the Gods once rebelled against the Titans and won, that man can rebel..." She gives each of us a soul-piercing look from behind her horn-rimmed glasses. "But men are not Gods. Even the Gods themselves lost in the end. The Titans are invincible! And they have chosen you to serve them, to train here with the best of the best."

The class cheers.

"You will graduate in a few months and take your place in the world. As you do, keep your eyes and ears open! Report anyone suspicious or incompetent, and most of all, watch for rebels and heretics! Only through your vigilance can New Greece prosper."

There are more cheers. The bell rings and Mrs. Ploddin dismisses our class. School is done for the day, but it brings no relief. I join Mark in the hallway and watch as the rest of the students go by. Some give us sad looks, others grin cruelly.

"Word gets around fast," Mark says. "How do you want to handle this rematch thing?"

I shrug. "Train. We can use the Harryhausen gym downtown."

"Good idea. You really think we can do it?"

"Yeah. Blake's overconfident, plus he's got Brenda."

"Are you kidding? Brenda did better than me! She may be terrible, but she's not hopeless."

"And you are?"

Mark sighs. "Maybe. I'm not into all this athletic stuff. I work out with my mind. You don't need to climb rocks to be a priest."

"True," I admit, "but it can't hurt. That's why they stick us in all these different classes, isn't it?"

"Ah, the benefits of a well-rounded education," Mark muses, but it's obvious he takes no pleasure in it. "The time I spend in gym could be put to better use in the library."

"And the time I spend in the library could be put to better use in the gym. Guess we're both in the same boat."

Mark smirks. "I think our boat's sprung a leak then. Hope we don't go down with the ship..."

3

HIT AND RUN

THE PARKING LOT is full of kids eager to get away from the pressure cooker of the Academy. Most of them probably don't have a care in the world, and if I close my eyes, I can almost pretend I don't either. Time seems to stretch, the way it always does on a sunny Friday afternoon. It's telling me that tonight and two days can last forever. Normally they can. My parents are rich and let me do whatever I want, so most weekends I'll work out, maybe go climbing or caving. I do those last two whenever I need to get away, which seems to be more and more lately. It's the only time I really feel at peace, whether I'm clinging to a cliff or slipping into darkness...

Mark nudges me, knocking me out of my daydream. "Hey!" He points across the lot. "Isn't that Blake?"

It's him, all right, and he's not alone. He's got Brenda with him, and they're getting into his black Lexus. Well, his father's black Lexus. "Yeah, that's him. Looks like they have the same idea we do. We better get going."

"Great," Mark says. "Where's your car?"

"I don't have one."

He frowns. "What do you mean? You're richer than Blake! How'd you get to school? Your parents' limo drop you off?"

"No, I walked. It's only a few miles."

"I don't get you, man. You're rich, and you could be rolling in style, even if it is your parents' ride. Why would you walk to school? Is it part of your warrior training?"

"No. I don't know... I just like to have my feet on the ground as much as possible. It's not just a health thing or a 'it gives me time to think' thing."

He gives me a funny look, so I awkwardly try to explain. "It's more than either of those. It's a *connection* thing, a feeling I'm part of something greater than myself, you know? That I'm one with the earth."

"Wow," Mark says, "if I had to walk 'a few miles' in my neighborhood, I'd be toast. But you Rich-O's really can do whatever you want, can't you?"

"I guess." I'd forgotten how poor Mark is. He's only at Axios because he passed the Gifted exam and got here on a scholarship. Otherwise, he'd be stuck doing whatever lousy job his family does. It's also probably why he tries so hard to prove how smart he is and why he doesn't have any friends.

I'm trying to think of something diplomatic to say when I notice a strange girl watching us from across the lot. She's half-hidden in the treeline, not moving. Black hair. Dark eyes. I don't think she goes to our school, but there's something familiar about her. Do I know her? I raise my hand to wave, then realize how weird that is. You don't wave to strangers in New Greece, especially not ones hiding in bushes.

Even if they are girls.

Mark coughs on purpose, and I turn my head to look. "I thought you said we were going to catch the bus? Standing here staring into space isn't helping me train. Not that I'm excited or anything, but I understand how important this is. I'd like to avoid losing Monday, 'cause I'm no better with swords and shields than I am at scaling walls, so I think—"

"Hold on. See that girl over there?"

"No. What girl? Where?"

"In the bushes, over by that group of trees."

Mark shrugs. "I don't see anybody."

"She's right there!" As I raise my hand to point at her, the downtown bus pulls up, blocking the view. By the time we pay and take our seats, the girl is gone.

"Was she hot?" Mark asks.

"Yeah, I think so, but she was pretty far away."

"Then how do you know she was hot?"

"Just a feeling... Forget it."

Mark looks like he wants to ask something else, like maybe why I space out all the time or see things that aren't there, but I shut him down with a steady stream of what we're going to do at the gym. The truth is, I wouldn't know what else to say about me or the girl. I'm not even sure she was real. She could have been another of my daydreams, or a hallucination from all the stress I'm under. Maybe Mr. Cross was right, and I'm losing it.

The streets flash by, the green hills and mansions slowly giving way to the glass towers of downtown Othrys. It's named after Mount Othrys, the birthplace of the Titans in old Greece. Before the Gods War transformed much of the landscape, Othrys used to be called Los Angeles. The sidewalks are bustling with people, rich and poor, warriors and priests, tradesmen and slaves. Despite the differences in wealth and rank, everyone dresses in the style of ancient Greece: light linen or silk tunics that either fall to the ankles or are cut at the knee for greater mobility. Slaves wear black tunics, but free citizens wear white. Citizens who can afford it add decorative trim or wear cloth of different colors. Some wear cloaks fastened at the shoulder. Warrior cloaks are blood red and priests wear azure blue, but other colors can be worn by anyone.

Before the Gods War, people could dress as they pleased, but the Titans put a stop to that. They said too many choices were what had caused men to stray from the path of honoring their creators, and they would not make the same mistake the Gods had. Fashion wasn't the only change they made, of course, but it is the most noticeable. It makes it easy to know who you're dealing with and where you belong. Plus, the Titans' magic changed our climate to a Mediterranean one, so wearing lighter clothes makes sense. It's some of the other rules that bother me...

Mark says, "Hey, wasn't that the gym?"

I look back, curse, then yank the cord to stop the bus. It pulls over and we get out a few blocks past where we should have. We move to the crosswalk and wait for the signal. Traffic zips by. It will get worse soon with rush hour and the nightfall curfew. The light changes from green to yellow. An old man on the other side of the street begins to cross.

"You OK?" Mark asks. "You seem kind of spacey."

"I'm fine, it's just—" Before I can finish, there's a shriek of brakes and a high, thin scream. A green sedan hits the old man and sends him sprawling into the gutter. Mark and I rush to help, but the man's legs are broken, the bones sticking out at crazy angles. There's nothing I can do. The driver gets out, a middle-aged man in a gray business tunic. His face pales when he sees the old man's injuries.

He says to us, "You're witnesses, right? The light was yellow."

"You should have seen him," I growl. "Do you have any idea what you've done?"

The old man groans and tries to say something, but coughs blood instead.

"His fault," the driver says. "He's old! I've got a son to raise, same age as you. You gotta back me up, OK?"

When neither of us answer, the driver curses.

A crowd gathers. Everyone wants to know what happened, but no one is doing anything to help. The old man's not going to die, but if the hospital can't fix him, what then? He'll be sacrificed to Cronus's hunger or put on display at the Museum of Failure.

I sit in the gutter with the old man and squeeze his hand. "You're going to be all right," I tell him, and I want to believe that's true. I look up at Mark, who is looking almost as scared as the old man.

"We shouldn't get involved," he whispers. "We should go. Come on, man!"

"No. We're staying."

Mark swears and starts pacing. If he wasn't depending on me to train him, there's no doubt he'd run—which sounds lousy, but I'm not sure I can blame him. Priests and warriors have a tendency to enslave the poor for the slightest infraction. Even taking the wrong side in a situation like this could be bad for him. But the rich have a way of getting out of trouble no matter what we do. The Titans say it's because we contribute more, so we're valued more. Judging by the driver's car and appearance, he's somewhere in-between. That's why he's nervous.

A red and white Day Patrol car pulls up, sirens blaring. The slogan on the side reads, *"To protect or punish."* Two warriors get out, red cloaks flapping in the breeze. Since guns are outlawed, they're armed with swords and shields. The younger one presses the crowd back with his shield while the older warrior comes up to me. His trained eyes seem to take in the situation all at once, and he keeps a hand on his sword hilt. "The ambulance will be here soon. What happened, citizen?"

Before I can answer, the driver steps forward. "The old fool crossed against the light! He didn't give me time to stop. These two boys are witnesses."

The warrior looks from me to Mark. "Is that true, son?"

"Y-yes, sir," Mark says. "The light was yellow."

I point at the driver. "He was going too fast trying to beat the light. He wasn't paying attention to anything else."

The warrior's eyes narrow. "Are you related to the victim? What's your stake in all this?"

"No, I'm not related. I'm just telling you what I saw."

"What's your name, citizen?"

"Andrus Eaves. I go to Axios."

"The Academy, huh? You training to be a warrior?"

"Yes, sir."

"Good lad. Well, then, Mr. Eaves, let me tell you something. Warriors have to judge situations like this all the time. By your own admission, the driver didn't mean to hit anyone, and he's still got a lot of good years left in him. Now he can serve the Titans in one of two ways: in his present skilled capacity as a free citizen, or as a slave. You tell me which it should be."

I stare at the driver. He's wringing his hands. Sweat drips down his forehead. He sees me watching him and forces a desperate smile onto his face. A smile that says he wants to go back to his office job and forget this ever happened. Just like I want to go back in time to gym class and beat Blake. Only I didn't ruin anyone's life, except that isn't entirely true. Mark has the same pathetic smile on his face, hoping I will make this new pain go away.

The ambulance pulls up. I squeeze the old man's hand one last time and tell him how sorry I am. Then I tell the warrior to let the driver go back to his family.

"That's the right call," the warrior says. "You'll make a fine addition to the force someday."

I'm not so sure about that. I'm not even sure there was a right decision to be made. I'd been excited to be a warrior, proud to be put into a position where I could help people, but now I'm left to wonder if the only chances I'll be given will be to choose the lesser of two evils. It doesn't feel right.

The warrior offers me his hand. I take it, careful not to jostle the old man as I get to my feet. The old man gives me a hopeless look, one that haunts me, but then the warrior is pulling me up and I turn toward the crowd. There's a face in it that's familiar. *That girl!* The one hiding outside school.

"Hey, you!" I yell. "Wait!"

The girl runs, which is something I'm pretty sure hallucinations don't do. I chase after her, but the crowd gets in the way. I try to push through when a strong hand falls on my shoulder.

"You can't leave," the warrior says. "I need to get your information for my report."

"I'm sorry, I just thought I saw someone I knew, that's all."

"A girl?"

"Yes! You saw her?"

He chuckles. "No, just a guess. A pretty girl is about the only thing that could make me move that fast when I was your age."

We return to his patrol car where Mark and the badly-shaken driver are giving the other warrior their information. The paramedics load the old man onto a gurney; a tall priest is with them. He's got cold eyes set in a cruel face.

"Will he be OK?" I ask the paramedics.

They look at each other, then the priest. Something passes between them, because neither answers. They load the gurney into the back of the ambulance. The priest brushes his blue cloak back over his shoulder and steps forward. "I'm sorry, did you say something, citizen?"

"Yes, I asked if that man's going to be all right."

"And you are?"

"Andrus Eaves. I'm a witness. I just want to know if you think he'll be OK. The hospital can fix him, right?"

"Hospital?" The priest smiles thinly. "Do not fear, citizen. The old man will be taken care of."

"What does that mean?"

"That means I have answered your question. Unless you care to ask another?"

I hesitate, then think better of it. "No," I say. "No more questions."

The priest's smile widens, but doesn't get any warmer. "Then bless you, citizen, and remember, Cronus is watching!"

4

BE THE MOUNTAIN

I DON'T MENTION the girl again to Mark. He'd just think I was crazy, and that would undermine his confidence in my ability to train him. So I shove it aside as best I can, shove her and the old man and everything else to focus on the only thing I'm sure of. The only thing I can control.

We walk to the Harryhausen gym and I pay our admission. Inside, there are all kinds of people working out or wrestling on mats. Greek wrestling has become popular again, as you might expect, and even *pankration* is big. Pankration is a Greek word that means using all your power. It's like mixed martial arts combined with boxing and wrestling, with lots of takedowns, chokes, and joint locks. There are only two rules: no eye-gouging or biting.

Warriors use pankration to arrest people who resist—that is, the ones they want to question. Otherwise, they just use their swords. As you can imagine, there's a lot less crime when you know the law is likely to chop first and ask questions later.

Since I'm training to be a warrior, I have to take a second gym class, one that teaches pankration. Mr. Cross teaches that class too and he says I'm pretty good. It's harder for me to daydream in that class. I tried once, and the next thing I knew, Blake had me in a head-lock. That was pretty embarrassing.

"Looks like Blake and Brenda beat us here," Mark says, pointing to two figures working their way up the rock climbing wall.

We watch them. Mark sucks in his breath and I can tell he's not happy with how well they seem to be doing. As for me, I try to look beyond that to see any weaknesses we can exploit—both in how they work as a team and where Brenda's skills are. As Mark said, she's not very good, but she's not hopeless. What surprises me is how well Blake and Brenda work together. For once, Blake isn't being a jerk. He's actually trying to teach her. No yelling. No anger. Just smiles and encouragement. I glance over at Mark. He's staring at the wall like it's a Titan, maybe Cronus himself.

I wonder if I can teach him in time. I'm not exactly known for my patience, and I'm so much better at climbing than him that I don't know if I can even relate to where he's at. Then I get an idea...

Wrestling and pankration taught me grappling, which helps with climbing. I mean, instead of grappling some guy, I'm grappling a mountain. And I know I can't just "tap out" to end it. When I'm hanging off a wall, I can't let go. I have to keep going or fall.

"Come on," I tell Mark. "I've got an idea that might help."

He sighs in relief. "Great! I'm not exactly eager to tackle that wall, especially with Blake and Brenda watching. I don't want to make a fool of myself."

"You sure? Because if you mess up bad enough in front of them, they might get overconfident." I say it like a joke, but now I'm wondering if maybe that's not such a bad idea. After all, any edge could make the difference. But no, I can tell by the way Mark reacts, he's not ready. It'll be better if I get his confidence up first.

We go to an empty wrestling mat and I explain the basics of my plan. How learning pankration helped my climbing skills, and how he needs to learn to fight to hold on.

"I don't know," Mark says. "You sure this will work?"

I shrug. "Look at it this way: At least if you fall, you won't have far to go." That gets a laugh—a nervous one, but better than nothing. I teach him the proper stance, facing me with right leg bent and his hands raised. "Now turn your body slightly left."

"Why?"

"You'll see in a minute. Raise your hands higher, like this." I raise mine so that the tips of my fingers are level with my hairline, and my left arm is almost fully extended, while keeping my right bent. "Now lean forward, just a bit, and put your weight on your right foot." Mark does as I ask. "OK, now the ball of your left foot should be touching the ground." Once he's in position, I tell him, "The reason the left foot is like that is so it's ready to attack or defend, like this!" I lash out at him with a low kick, which he fails to block.

Mark crashes to the mat grabbing his leg. "Ow, man! What the hell?"

"Sorry! I'm trying to teach you to be ready for anything. Not just in combat, but climbing. You have to be ready to make a split-second decision. Come on, let's try again. I'll go slower this time."

"You promise?"

"Of course. The point's not to hurt or humiliate you. It's to train your reflexes. That first kick was just to get your attention." I help him up and we get into position. "So I'm going to kick you again," I warn, "but in slow motion so you can see it coming, all right?"

Mark nods and watches as I come at him with another kick. "Now block," I tell him.

Mark raises his leg just in time to make contact with mine. It's a weak defense and I could easily overpower him if I wasn't holding back. "Good," I say, "but you need to do it faster, with more force." I lower my leg and resume my stance. "Again."

We run through it a few more times, going a bit faster until Mark gets it. Then we try it with punches, then a combination of kicks and punches until I'm satisfied he's built up a little confidence. "OK, now let's grapple." I move in, stepping around or knocking aside his blows until I'm close enough to grapple. Mark's pinned to the mat in seconds. "See how I'm holding on?" I say. "You've got to do the same to the wall. Never let go."

I let him up and then we go through it again. And again. Finally, I let him practice grappling me. Where to hold, how to hold, and how long. "You have to become an immovable object," I explain. "You have to be the mountain."

A male voice says, "Ooh! Nice form, ladies!" I look up and see Blake sneering down at us. "You two going to prom together?"

"Shut up." I easily break free of Mark's chokehold and jump to my feet. I'm in Blake's face in seconds. "It's a confidence building exercise."

Blake chuckles. "Well, don't let him get too confident, or you'll be the one wearing the dress."

I shove him, but Blake just grins and holds up his hands to show he doesn't want to fight. "Easy, tiger! I'm going. The wall's all yours since you guys were too chicken to face me and Brenda." He swaggers off and joins her, putting his arm around her as he steers her toward the exit. Brenda looks back at us with a mixture of pity and disdain.

"What a dick," Mark says once they're out of earshot. "I can't believe that guy."

"Tell me about it. You ready to tackle that wall?"

"In a minute. You really think I can do this?"

"It doesn't matter what I think. Do you think you can?"

Mark looks from me to the wall. There's some steel in his voice when he says, "Yeah. Let's do this!"

5

THE NIGHT PATROL

THE SUN DIPS on the horizon as we finish training. I have a much better idea of what Mark can do on the wall and what he can't. The good news is he can take direction, the bad news is he likes to ask a lot of questions instead of just relying on his instincts. I learn by doing, by throwing myself into something new. I don't care about making mistakes or looking stupid because I don't really care what anyone thinks. But Mark does, and that's a problem. It's slowing me down, forcing me to explain every little why, when all he really needs to know is how.

Just do this, I want to scream at him. *Don't hesitate, don't overthink it.*

But that's all Mark does, and at first, I get really mad until I realize being a teacher is hard. I used to think Mr. Cross had the easiest job in the world, but it's clear now he doesn't. The trouble is, I don't know how to teach Mark the way he wants to be taught. I can only teach him the way I know how, and I don't know if he can, at least not in time.

A female voice comes over the loudspeaker: "Attention, citizens! Attention! The time is now seven p.m.; the Harryhausen gym is closing. You have one hour until curfew. Please return to your homes, stay safe, and remember, Cronus is watching..."

There's no time to shower, no time to go over our strategy for tomorrow. The employees want to be home before the Night Patrol comes out, and so do we.

The Day Patrol are all humans, but monsters make up the Night Patrol—monsters created by the Titans to serve them. Weird hybrids of man and beast made by magic: centaurs, harpies, and worse. The only thing the Titans forbid the monsters to do is enter the homes of law-abiding citizens.

"How did I do?" Mark asks as we make our way onto the street. People hurry by, casting nervous glances at the setting sun.

"You did good," I tell him. It's not exactly true, but I figure the lie will help him more than the truth. When he raises an eyebrow, I can tell he's not buying it. "Well, not too bad," I say. "You had to start somewhere."

Mark shakes his head. "Damn. Tell me at least I made some progress."

"You did. You've got nowhere to go but up."

"Up," Mark echoes. "That's where I've been trying to go my whole life. First, up from my caste to the Academy, now up that damn wall. You know I'm only at Axios because of my scholarship, right?"

"Yeah." I look at my feet rather than him, kicking a loose stone into the street.

"My family's poor. I can't hide it, but the more I try to prove I belong in your world, the more the other kids hold it against me."

"Maybe you're trying too hard. Maybe you should be yourself."

"Myself?" Mark laughs. "I'm not even sure what that is. I don't fit anywhere. The other poor kids resent me for being smart, for daring to want more, and especially for having the chance to achieve it. For the longest time, I thought all I had to do was get into Axios and I'd finally find my place. But once I got there..." He shrugs, and I can almost feel the weight on his shoulders.

"Hey, I get it. Believe me, I don't fit in either."

Mark stops walking. "You? You're Mr. Popularity compared to me! I always see you talking to people."

"That's because my family's one of the richest in New Greece. I'm sure some of them like me for me, but I'm not always sure which ones. So I've got the opposite problem: You're too poor, and I'm too rich. Plus, I'm adopted. I mean, for all I know, if my parents hadn't given me up, you and I could've been neighbors."

"I never knew you were adopted."

"It's not something I like to talk about."

"Do you know who your birth parents are?"

"No. They didn't want me, that's for sure."

"Maybe they wanted a better life for you than they could give. That's possible, isn't it?"

Now it's my turn to shrug. "Come on," I say. "We're gonna miss your bus."

Mark gets the hint and falls silent as we head for the bus stop. It's just a few blocks, but feels like forever. It feels even longer as we round the corner and see the bus pulling into traffic.

"Wait!" Mark calls, chasing after it. "Hey, wait! Stop!"

We're too late, and the bus disappears into the pre-curfew rush. It feels like everyone is going somewhere but us. I scan the oncoming traffic, hoping for a taxi, and spot one.

"There's a cab," I say. "Everything's gonna be all right." I step into the street to hail it, but the taxi already has a passenger. It flies by, blasting its horn, and almost hits me. That's when I look down and see the greasy red smear on the pavement. This is the exact spot the old man got hit. I can see him in my mind, lying broken and doomed in the gutter. That could have been me. Quickly, I step back onto the sidewalk and try not to seem too shaken. "So, um, where do you live?" I ask Mark.

He looks away, not wanting to meet my eyes. "The east side."

"East Othrys? You mean Loserville?" I frown, not believing it. I knew Mark was poor, but I didn't know he was *that* poor. Most slaves live better than the people there. Now I remember Blake calling Mark a Loser and Mr. Cross telling him his lack of confidence was "Loser talk." But I just thought they were using the term in general, like an insult. That's pretty much the worst thing anyone at our school can call each other. But I didn't know Mark was literally a Loser with a capital "L." I'd never met one before, never thought I would. Real Losers were about as close to my social circle as monsters.

I must be staring, because Mark sneers. "Yeah, man. You didn't know? I'm a Loser. Losers live in Loserville." He says Loserville with the same contempt as the kids at the Academy, but without the smugness. There's anger in his voice. Shame. Despair. And more than a little fear. "But I won't be one for long."

"No," I say. "Of course not. You're a smart guy."

"You mean for a Loser?" His eyes flash defiance.

"I didn't say that."

"You didn't have to. But that's OK. And I *am* smart, only not smart enough, or I would have learned to climb walls and avoid this mess. I thought I could get by on my brains. I should have known they'd never let me. And now..."

"Look, I told you it's going to be all right." I reach out to pat his back but he cringes away.

"No, it won't! Nothing will be all right!"

"Hey, Mark. Listen, Monday's a long way off. We've got two more days to train and—"

"It's not Monday I'm worried about! It's tonight. Don't you get it? I'll never make it home in time. I can't be caught out after curfew. Do you know what the Night Patrol does to Losers?"

I do. They enslave them if they're lucky, and devour them if they're not.

"What are we going to do?" Mark's voice is shrill, tainted by despair. "If I'm not home on time, it's all over for me! At least with the rematch, I had a chance!" He checks his watch and shudders. "But now, there's no way."

"I'll walk with you. Maybe we can hail another cab, hitchhike, or something."

I've never been to Loserville, so I have no idea how far it is. East Othrys is one of those places rich people rarely talk about, and then only to make fun of. Hardly anyone I know has actually been there, and the ones who have only went to make trouble. "Slumming," they called it. They get drunk, break things, then bribe their way out if they get caught. While warriors have been known to take bribes, monsters have no use for money, and social status doesn't impress them. All the drachmas in the world can't save you if you get caught by the Night Patrol. About the only thing that can is to flash them an Amulet of Safe Passage.

The amulet is a gold disc stamped with the glaring eye of Cronus. For a fee, the Temple of the Unblinking Eye issues the amulets to the wealthiest families in case they get caught after curfew. It's not something you're supposed to use to break the law, but if you show it to a monster, it can't eat or enslave you. It even has to escort you home, but you'll be reported to the Temple and can expect a visit from the priests the next morning.

An expensive visit.

I pull my amulet out from under my shirt and show it to Mark. "Relax. You know what this is?"

His eyes grow wide. "Whoa, is that thing real? I'd heard stories, but I thought it was something people made up."

"It's real."

"That's great for you," he says, "but what about me? I don't have an amulet."

"No, but you're with me. I can explain that if we get caught."

"And that will protect me? You're sure?"

I nod, but the truth is, I have no idea. It's not like this situation has ever come up before. Instead, I say, "We should hurry." I hope Mark will take it to mean he'll be safe, but also so we don't waste time arguing.

"All right," Mark says. "Maybe we should have focused on exercising my legs today instead of my grip." He says it with a half-smile, one that makes me think he's covering his doubt with humor and hoping for the best. It's not like he has a choice. Neither of us do.

Twilight paints the horizon harsh red. Hell-red. The color of an open wound. The streetlights switch on. As we walk, the frantic traffic dwindles, each driver desperate to get home. The Night Patrol never comes out until after dark because monsters can't stand sunlight. The priests say that's because they were trapped so long by the Gods in Tartarus, where it's always night.

A raven croaks from a streetlight above us. It's a large, black-eyed brute with a beak the size of a small knife. The bird cocks its head and flaps its wings, warning us to hurry.

We quicken our pace, but it isn't long before it feels like we're being followed. Of course, that's crazy. It's not sunset yet. That means it can't be the Night Patrol... but it could be that weird girl.

I stop and peer into the gathering gloom behind us. The street is empty.

"What's up?" Mark says. "Why are you stopping?"

"Nothing. Let's keep moving, only we better jog the rest of the way."

We pick up the pace. After several blocks, Mark is gasping. He slows, then stops to catch his breath.

"I need a minute," he says.

"We haven't got one."

"I need one anyway." He's sweating worse than in the gym, and the smell is acrid. It's fear, paralyzing fear, and it's coming from his pores in waves. "I don't think I can make it," he says, wiping sweat from his forehead. "Maybe we should just hide somewhere? Hole up till morning?"

"I'd rather not. Besides, hiding makes you look guilty. Not of breaking curfew, but something worse."

"What's worse than breaking curfew?"

"Treason. Think about it from the monsters' perspective: only rebels and traitors would hide when they could use an amulet instead."

"Good point."

"Yeah, that's—" I let my sentence trail off because there's a loud flutter overhead. I look up in alarm, expecting a harpy, one of the hideous bird-women who haunt the skies after dark, but it's just another raven. Or maybe it's the same one.

Mark laughs nervously. "Man, you really jumped! You thought it was a harpy too, huh?"

"Come on," I tell him. "It's just a few more blocks."

"More like ten."

"Fine, so it's ten. You ready?"

He doesn't look like it, but he shrugs. "As ready as I'll ever be."

"We might have to run," I warn, then add, "I mean, part of the way, but not if we get caught. If we get caught, stay behind me and let me do the talking."

We start jogging again. The sun is sinking lower now, the evening sky purpling toward black.

"You ever talk to a monster?" Mark asks.

"No. Have you?"

"Once."

"Seriously?"

"A harpy, when I was little. I'd left my favorite toy outside, and the monster must have heard me begging my mom to let me go get it, because she was waiting in the tree outside my window when I went to my room. The harpy told me it was safe for me to come outside. That she wouldn't hurt me, and that she understood the pain of having toys where you could see them, but couldn't touch them."

"What did you do?" I ask. "I mean, you didn't believe her, did you?"

"Almost. I was pretty young, maybe ten, and I really wanted that stupid toy. It was a priest action figure. It represented everything I wanted to be, and I was worried if I didn't keep it near me all the time, my dream would never come true."

"So what'd you do?"

"I asked the harpy to get it for me." She did, but then she held it just out of my grasp. '*If you want something bad enough,*' the harpy told me, '*you just have to reach out and grab it.*' I almost did, but I knew if I put even one hand outside, I'd be breaking the law. And I didn't like the way she was looking at me. The way she snapped her beak and flexed her claws..."

"What happened?"

"I explained it was my dream to be a priest someday, so I couldn't break the law, not even for my favorite toy, not even because she said it was all right. She got mad and destroyed my action figure. And I never forgot what she told me right before she flew away. She said, *'You can't eat dreams, boy.'*"

"That's horrible!"

"Yeah, but she was right. I'd just been dreaming about being a priest before. I didn't have a plan. I got one after that. I found out everything I needed to do to turn my dream into a reality."

"Oh, that's why you're so driven. That explains a lot."

"Yeah. I still get scared I'm not gonna make it sometimes, but when I do, I remember that harpy's hungry face, and her words, and that pulls me through. I don't think she meant to help me, but she really did. Crazy, huh?"

"Not really. One thing they teach us in warrior class is your enemies make you stronger. They force you to do better, to think bigger. Defeating them brings you glory. Without them, you'd have no reason to push yourself."

"They teach us pretty much the same in priest class," Mark admits. "Only they say our enemies are a test from Cronus, and also a gift."

"A gift?" I'm not sure I like the sound of that.

"Yeah. You know, for sacrifice. The bigger the enemy, the better the sacrifice." He makes a stabbing motion with his hand.

"OK... I, uh, never thought of it that way, but change 'sacrifice' to 'glory,' and maybe priests and warriors aren't so different."

"Maybe," Mark says, but doesn't sound convinced.

I'm not sure I am either. There's a rivalry encouraged between the two groups, one I've bought into. But even before Axios, I'd never been fond of priests. They always creeped me out with their talk of magic and metaphysics, telling us to obey this, obey that, but never to question why. You never saw them in the streets helping people like warriors. You never saw them in physical contests or doing normal things. Just preaching and making blood sacrifices.

I start to ask Mark if he knows what priests do for fun, but I never get an answer. That's when all the streetlights switch off. Which is a very bad sign. The lights only come on a half hour before curfew and once they're off, that means curfew has begun.

"Run!" I shout to Mark, and I don't have to tell him twice. My breath rasps in my throat. The amulet bangs against my chest. Every muscle in my body is in motion. The slap of our sandals against the pavement is loud in our ears, but not as loud as the clatter of hooves behind us.

6

COWARD

THE MAIN STREET is a death trap. There's nowhere to hide. Every-thing's dark, far darker than it should be, because the buildings block out the moon. It's a night-black forest of brick and stone. No neon, no lit up signs, nothing. Not just because monsters don't like light, but because they don't want anything to help curfew-breakers see where they're going or know where they are.

The hooves behind us get louder. I know what that means: centaurs. Not the kind of handsome half-human, half-horse most people would have imagined before the Gods War, but vicious brutes: part-man, part-horse, part-ram. That means they're fast. It also means they're bad-tempered and stubborn. They carry long barbed harpoons in their clawed hands; each weapon tethered to their utility belts by a rope. They stick the harpoons into you, then break into a gallop, dragging you behind them. But that's just for fun.

The centaurs are infamous for doing something far worse, and that's what gives them their other name: Skull-crushers. They're called that because centaurs have a nasty habit of grabbing victims by their necks, lifting them up to watch them strangle, then head-butting them to crack open the skull. That's their favorite way to punish curfew-breakers, and it's effective. One good head-butt and you're brain-dead forever.

The priests say it's so when you see curfew-breakers wandering around with their brains spilling out, you'll know why you need to obey the law. I've seen a few people like this, and it's not pretty. They become "zombies" that wander around moaning, and no one's allowed to do anything to help. There's no way I want to end up like that, and I can't think of a worse punishment for a guy like Mark.

That's why I'm glad I've got the amulet. But what if it doesn't work? What if it can't keep Mark safe? Should I try to hide him, then confront the centaurs myself? I could lead them away, get them to escort me home, but that would leave Mark out on the street, still blocks from safety. It would have to be a good hiding place, one Mark could stay in overnight. Because if the centaurs find him...

I glance around, panic rising. There are no cars to hide under because no one leaves them outside after dark. Anything outside a legal residence is fair game for monsters to attack: cars, bikes, pets, people. But not dumpsters. I mean, monsters *could* attack them, but why? They're big, heavy, and hard to roll over. They don't scream or explode or do anything fun. And they're full of garbage. I've never heard of one being ruined by monsters. A dumpster might be Mark's only chance.

We need to find an alley fast. But there's nothing, just more tightly-packed buildings. I hear braying laughter behind us.

"They've found us," Mark whispers. "Skull-crushers!" To his credit, he doesn't sound half as scared as he should be. "Break out your amulet. We'll be fine, right?"

"Um..."

"You said it would work!"

"No, I said I thought it *might* work."

"So it still could?" Mark asks.

"Do you want to find out?"

"Hell no! I mean, not if I don't have to. What's Plan B?"

I see a shadow between two stores that's blacker than the rest. It has to be an alley. I grab Mark by the arm. "This way!" We veer off the sidewalk into a narrow, trash-strewn alley.

"Slow down, I can't see!" Mark complains. He trips over a pile of debris and goes sprawling.

"We hear you, humans!" one of the centaurs shouts, then laughs and adds, "You better run!" Soon, his bleating taunt is taken up by the rest of the Night Patrol: "RUN! RUN!"

I help Mark up and half-lead, half-drag him deeper into the alley. There's a dumpster up ahead and I tell Mark to hide in it.

"What are you going to do?" he asks.

"The only thing I can do. The centaurs know someone is on the street. That doesn't mean they know there are two of us. I'm going to show my amulet and get them to take me home. All you have to do is stay hidden until the sun comes up. I'll meet you at the Harryhausen gym tomorrow, eight a.m."

Mark curses, but goes along with the plan. The stench of moldy food is strong as he opens the dumpster, climbs in, and closes the lid.

I head out of the alley into the street. I take off my amulet, then bend down as if looking for something. Three monstrous shadows clop forward to surround me. The centaurs smell like wet dog wrapped in musk. Their shaggy-cheeked faces are gray, wild-maned, with glaring yellow eyes, sharp teeth, and long, curling horns set atop a high, hard-ridged forehead. Their hooves paw the pavement in anticipation.

It's show time. I rise up and present my amulet. I hold it so the centaurs can see the symbol stamped on it. "My name is Andrus Eaves," I say in my most confident voice. "By Cronus, and by the authority of the Temple of the Unblinking Eye, I request you grant me safe passage and escort home. That is your duty! That is the Titan's command."

The leader steps forward. He's larger than his fellows, meaner-looking, but hopefully not smarter. he introduces himself in a low rumble, "I am Captain Nessus of the Night Patrol. Give me that amulet. Is it yours? I want to see if it's real."

I start to hand it to him, then remember Mark's story about the harpy, and snatch it back before the captain can grab it. "It's real," I tell him, "and it's mine, but if I give it to you, I won't have it anymore. The law says you can't attack me as long as the amulet is in my possession."

Nessus's black lips pull back from his ivory fangs in a sneer. "The law? Who are you to quote the law?"

"I'm a student at Axios. I'm training to be a warrior."

"A warrior," Nessus muses. "Perhaps you'd care to test your training against one of us?"

That gets a round of enthusiastic grunts and growls from the other centaurs, but I know better than to accept.

"No, thank you. As I said, I'm a student, and only human. It wouldn't be a fair fight, and I'm sure you would prefer a challenge."

"What we would prefer, coward, is to drag you screaming through the streets, to bash your brains in, and..." Nessus pauses to sniff the air, then looks over my shoulder toward the alley. His eyes narrow. "Democ! Ruvo!" He addresses the other centaurs. "Do you smell that?"

The other monsters sniff the night, nostrils flaring.

I step forward to draw their attention back to me. "No offense, you guys, but the law's the law. Are you going to take me home or not?"

Nessus twists his mouth into something that resembles a smile: an awful, sinister one full of sharp teeth. "In time, human. First, we are going to search that alley for your companion."

"What companion?"

"Do not lie to me, boy! We can smell him. His scent... is different from yours. He reeks of fear, while you..." Nessus sniffs again and frowns. "You smell familiar. Have we met before?"

"I don't think so. I mean, I'm sure I would have remembered it."

"Hmm," Nessus says. "Curious."

"What about the other human?" Democ interrupts.

"We'll find him," Nessus replies, "and when we do..."

"We'll crack him open like an egg," Democ cackles. "Crack him! Scramble his brains."

Ruvo raises his harpoon and shouts, "Crush him! Drag him through the streets!"

"Enough, brothers!" Nessus motions his fellow monsters to be silent. "Democ, go around back to close the trap. Ruvo, you seal off this end. I shall remain here to 'protect' this strange-smelling coward. When you flush out his friend, be sure to bring him to me."

"In one piece or two?" Democ asks with a sadistic edge in his voice.

"One, but save enough fight in him so there's something left for me."

Democ and Ruvo start toward the alley. Not fast. The centaurs want to take their time. After all, they have all night.

My fists clench. "I'm no coward."

Nessus snorts. "So you say, yet here we stand while you do nothing. I assume your friend is not fortunate enough to possess an amulet, or he would be with you. Correct?"

"OK, yeah. You're right. He doesn't have an amulet, but it's my fault he's out past curfew. He missed his bus. He's under my protection. Doesn't that count for anything?"

"For one so fond of quoting the law, you know little. Your amulet protects you, not him! Unless..."

"Unless what?"

"Unless you'd care to give the amulet to your friend. That would spare him."

"But not me?"

"No, not you. Giving your friend the amulet would prove you are no coward. Then we could fight! Such blood! Such glory! What do you say? Will you trade your friend's life for yours?"

When I don't say anything, Nessus shakes his shaggy head. "You disappoint me, like all your kind. You humans hiding behind your priests and amulets! You think you can command us? We are the true children of Cronus! We are his blood. And you, you are nothing! A miserable, half-formed wretch born of dust and clay. There is no magic in your bones, no might! If we cannot punish you, then my brothers and I will take it out on your friend while you watch." He levels his harpoon in my direction. "Unless you dare to stop us?"

At the mouth of the alley, Ruvo turns back to watch me, and I get the crazy idea that if I can distract him and Nessus long enough, maybe Mark can slip past. Maybe. So I take a step forward.

The captain's eyes widen—not in fear, in hope. The hope I will break the law by attacking him. My amulet won't do me any good then.

I take another step forward, my face set in defiance. Out of the corner of my eye, I can tell Ruvo is still watching me, not the alley. This is a stupid plan. Reckless. What if Mark already got away before Democ could get in position? But I can't back down. Not yet. Every second I buy gives Mark another chance to escape.

"Come, little man!" Nessus says. "Fight me!"

I take a third step. The barbed tip of the captain's harpoon pokes my chest. We lock eyes and stare at each other for what seems like forever. There's a rage building in me, vast and deep. I want to fight. I want to prove how brave I am. But slowly, painfully, I remind myself that no, that's not why I'm doing this. This is a front, a stall, a bluff.

Come on, Mark. Run!

But Mark doesn't run, and Ruvo remains where he is. At the far end of the alley, I don't hear Democ shouting an alarm or galloping after Mark. Either he's already gone, or he's still in the dumpster.

"You going to stand there all night?" Nessus taunts. "Is this all you've got?"

I step back and hold up my amulet. "You're trying to goad me, captain. First, into giving you my amulet, then giving it to Mark, but you said the amulet only protects me. If I give it to my friend, it won't protect him, will it?"

"I said it would spare him," Nessus answers, but his tone is evasive. He glances over at Ruvo, noticing his brother is paying attention to us instead of his duty. "Ruvo! Do you think I can't handle this human?"

"No, brother!"

"Then watch that alley, not us!"

Reluctantly, Ruvo turns away. Whatever chance Mark had is gone.

I see Nessus about to bark another order, so I stop him by saying, "You meant the amulet would only spare my friend until you finished with me, right? You wanted to get our hopes up, only to dash them one after the other. That's what monsters do."

Nessus laughs. "It seems you are neither fool nor coward, but I think you've delayed our fun long enough. Ruvo!"

The other centaur snaps to attention. "Yes, brother?"

"Get in that alley and catch us our dinner!"

7

MONSTERS

I'M OUT OF TRICKS and out of time. As Ruvo slips into the alley, I swallow my pride and plead with Captain Nessus, appealing to whatever slim shred of mercy might be hiding in that monstrous brain of his. "Please," I say, "You don't have to do this."

Nessus looks at me. Feral. Gloating. It's in his hungry smile, his alien, unfeeling eyes. "Please? Please?" He mocks. "Of course I don't have to do this! I *want* to do this."

"But why? Because it's your job?"

He stamps a hoof in disgust. "You ask the wrong question. Better to ask why the hawk eats the dove? Because he must! That is his nature. *That is my nature*, and I give in to it freely, just as Cronus does. Have your teachers taught you nothing?"

"They taught me your kind were created first, then cast aside by Gods and man. Is that why you hate us? Even though we worship the Titans now, the same as you?"

The captain's eyes flash, full of malice. "There is your mistake! We hold true to the Titans, yes, but do not presume to think we worship the same. They are our true parents, our family. You humans are adopted bastards at best, made by renegade Gods in their image, not ours. There is no shared blood, no common ground. Humans are worse than nothing! You are the stain that reminds us of our down-fall; a stain that can never be removed all at once, but only one drop of blood at a time."

His gray-bearded face comes closer. Close enough to smell his brim-stone breath, to feel the flecks of sour spittle spray across my cheek. He grabs my tunic with one clawed hand and drags me close as his voice rises. "Do you see the truth now? Have your eyes been opened? That is why we hate you! That is why we will *always* hate you. You could not even stay true to your own Gods, your own family! Why Cronus and the other Titans allow your kind to live is beyond me, but I honor my father's wishes. And I honor my brothers by killing your kind whenever the law allows." He snarls, wide enough I can see the gristle between his fangs.

I wonder if it's the flesh of some other boy like Mark. Like me. I know now I underestimated Captain Nessus: his intelligence, his hate. The anger is building in me again, born of helplessness, born of fear, and this time, I'm not sure I can keep it in check. "You're a monster," I say, and then because I can think of nothing else, I add, "You don't know any better."

Nessus chortles, an ugly sound. "Really? That's what my kind says about you."

The earth trembles. The buildings shake. The alley, already dark, grows darker still. Nessus lets go of me as a flock of ravens pour from the alley's mouth. Ruvo drops his harpoon and throws up his hairy arms to protect his face. He's pecked and clawed badly until he bolts, hooves clattering on concrete. A handful of black birds trail behind, cawing loudly, but the bulk of the flock flies straight at us. Nessus and I both duck, hands over our eyes. Then the birds are gone, swooping skyward. The earth stops shifting.

Nessus glares wildly in all directions, as if expecting an attack, but only distant caws greet him.

Alarmed, I shout, "It's an earthquake!"

Nessus doesn't seem so sure. "No. It's an omen."

I don't know what he's talking about, or why the captain suddenly looks so worried. New Greece was founded on the ruins of old California. We get earthquakes all the time, and I have no idea why he would think this was any different.

"We should get going," I urge, hoping he'll forget about Mark. "There could be aftershocks."

Nessus ignores my advice, turning to face the other two centaurs as they return. I'm not happy to see Democ or Ruvo, but breathe a sigh of relief because neither has captured Mark.

"What of our prey?" Nessus demands.

Democ shrugs. "I searched, brother, but there was nothing. No sign of him, not even a scent."

Ruvo doesn't say anything. Instead, the wounded centaur pulls a cloth from his utility belt and holds it against his scratched and bloody face. His blood is black and oily, almost tar-like. He mutters curses under his breath.

"And what of you, Ruvo?" Nessus snaps. "Report!"

Ruvo pulls the cloth away from his cheek and inspects it before answering. "I didn't see him either. I checked the dumpster. It's as Democ says. There was no scent, no evidence."

Nessus scowls and paces back and forth. "I know he was there! I smelled him. *We smelled him!* He couldn't have completely vanished, not without leaving a trail."

Democ points his weapon at me. "Maybe we could eat this one," he suggests hopefully.

Ruvo grins and wipes a thread of drool hanging from his beard. "The boy looks chewy enough..."

Nessus hesitates, seeming to consider their words.

"Think on it, brother!" Democ argues. "If we get rid of this one, who can contradict us? We won't even need to mention failing to catch the other human in our report—or those damn birds."

"Less questions mean less paperwork," Ruvo agrees. "Less paperwork means more time to drink and rut."

"You forget who commands here," Nessus says. "I decide what is worth reporting. Go now! Widen the search."

His brothers grumble but move toward the alley, Ruvo first

pausing to pick up his harpoon. The wounded centaur casts a backward glare in my direction.

"We have all night," Nessus assures me. "Your friend can't hide forever."

No, I think to myself. He can't. Unless he got away during the earthquake using the birds for cover. Which seems awfully convenient, and I'm wishing now I'd used that distraction myself, but it was like I'd been rooted to the spot at the time. Not from fear, from something else...

Before I can think what, Captain Nessus says, "You have won a small victory, but no triumph! The Titan's justice will not be denied. If we cannot find your lawbreaking friend now, then you will give me his name. A feast delayed is a feast to be anticipated all the more."

"I won't."

Nessus takes a threatening step toward me.

"I mean, I don't know! I can't tell who he is because I just met him. I've never seen him before."

"Lies!" Nessus growls. "Do you mistake me for some dimwitted harpy? I know something is wrong, and either you or your friend is responsible. What just happened was magic! I know, because *I am magic*. I can smell it, the same way I can smell you..." He pauses to sniff the air. "I cannot put my hoof on this mystery—not yet—but when I do, rest assured I am going to crush it. I pray you will be the guilty one, Andrus Eaves! I pray it shall be your body to be ground under, broken open, and your clever brain my feast!"

"I had nothing to do with it," I protest. That's the one thing I'm sure of, maybe the only thing. "Besides, I have an amulet. You can't harm me."

Nessus considers that, then breaks into a sly smile. "I can if you're guilty of the right crime." His grip on his harpoon tightens. He prods the weapon forward so I have to shrink back from it.

"No, you cant! All I'm guilty of is breaking curfew. The amulet protects me from being punished."

Something dark and terrible shifts behind the centaur's eyes. "Does it?"

"Of course it does! You saw it."

"Did I? Funny, I don't remember you having an amulet, only that you said you lost it."

I hold up the amulet as if that can save me.

Nessus knocks it aside with his harpoon. "The name," he growls. "Give me the name, or I eat your brain. Here, now!"

I can't give Mark up. Desperate, I look to each side, but there's nowhere to run the centaur can't catch me.

"If you won't tell me with your mouth, then I'll tear the name from your brain with my teeth!"

I scramble back, but the centaur presses forward, raising his right arm, the one with the harpoon in it, the one he's going to destroy me with...

Time slows, my pulse races. There's a thunderous flapping, a croaked battle cry from a hundred black beaks. The ravens return, and a girl's voice whispers in my mind. It's one word, the only one I need:

"Run!"

Adrenaline crashes through me. There's no girl by my side, no footsteps except my own, but that doesn't matter. I run, leaving Nessus to fend off the ravens. His hooves strike the pavement in a wild, confused dance. He's not following. For now.

The darkness takes me. My vision strains, seeking cross-streets, alleys. If only there were streetlights. If only the buildings didn't blot out the moon.

I have to find Mark. I have to get home.

Two conflicting goals that war in my head. There's what a hero would do, and what a sensible person should. My parents can protect me. The walls of my house and the money that built them can protect me. But Mark has none of these things. If I save myself, can I live with the consequences?

Give it a few more blocks, I tell myself. *If I can't find Mark by then, I can go home. No one can accuse me of not having tried... well, no one but me.*

But that's not good enough. I have to do better. I have to find

Mark. But how? He could be anywhere! And it's not like I can just start shouting his name—not without alerting the centaurs.

How did Mark escape? Did the ravens help him? Or was it that girl? Or maybe he bailed before all that. Not like me. I'm just a rich idiot.

I slow and try to get my bearings. The buildings are shadows, but if I look closely, they aren't as tall or modern as when I started. I have to be close to Loserville. And that's good, because Mark will come this way if he can.

There's a light in the alley ahead. No, not a light exactly. More like a gray fog. A girl-shaped cloud with one wraith-like arm extended toward me. Beckoning.

It could be a monster trying to trick me, but it could also be her—the girl who saved me. I hesitate, but only long enough to hear the distant galloping of angry centaurs. The Night Patrol are heading in this direction. I can't stay on the street, so I run toward the alley.

The cloud becomes less girl-shaped as I get closer, and when I pass through it, I smell fear and pain and death, the rotting sadness of a million years and a million more to come.

And then the smell is gone. I'm through the cloud, and when I cast a wary backward glance, the cloud has taken on my form. It's moving away, out of the alley, into the street, picking up speed.

What the hell was that thing?

Not that it matters, because whatever it is, it's not after me. At least not anymore. I head down the alley, having to pick my way carefully between dumpsters and debris.

"This is the most messed-up night ever," I mutter.

"Tell me about it," a voice says from the dark. "I've been waiting for you."

8

SAVED

A SHADOW DETACHES from the alley wall.

I take a step back and raise my fists. "Mark?" I whisper. "Is that you?"

The shadow stops in a thin sliver of moonlight. It's him, all right—even more nervous and pale than usual. "She told me to stay here. That she'd bring you."

"She? You mean the cloud-girl?"

"Yeah," Mark says. "Whatever she is, she also told me to get out of the alley just in time. The centaurs—"

"*Ssh!*" I hiss. I cock my head, listening. Hoofbeats drum by. They're heading away from us. We both breathe a sigh of relief. "That was close," I say. "I think they're chasing the cloud. She took on my form."

"She did more than that," Mark says. "She took on your scent. That's why the Night Patrol will keep chasing her, not us."

I look back over my shoulder, listening for hoofbeats, but the night is quiet. "Is your house far?"

"No," Mark says. "Come on, I'll lead the way." And with that, he leads me into Loserville.

The first thing I notice is the stench. It's awful, an airborne soup of burning tires, sweat, and urine that gets in my nose and tries to strangle me. The streets here are narrow and trash-filled, the buildings old. They're hanging on, but barely. Crumbling. Powerless to change or grow, like the people who live in them.

All my life, my parents told me, "There's no escape from Loserville. Those people belong there because they don't know how to live in our world and couldn't, even if we let them. They're not blessed by Cronus. They exist to serve."

"Like slaves?" I'd asked. Our family had many slaves. They made life easy, and the more you owned, the more status you had.

My parents had looked at each other, smiling. "No, not like slaves," my mom said, "They're different. They don't know their place. And that means they're dangerous. That's why you must avoid them, Andrus, and promise you'll never go to Loserville, even though a lot of your friends might."

My father had given me a sly wink, adding, "Slumming might seem fun at first, but the thrill quickly fades. Some Losers will do anything *for* you, but others will do anything *to* you if they think they can get away with it. They'll rob you, injure you, anything to make their squalid little lives better, even for a moment. They don't understand our lives are worth more than theirs."

Mom nodded. "It's sad, really. Sometimes, I think they'd all be better off as slaves. At least then they'd be taken care of. They wouldn't have to fight for scraps... but who am I to question the will of the Titans?"

When I'd asked why the Losers weren't all slaves, Dad sighed. "The Titans need people like us to worship them, but they need Losers to feed to the monsters. Without them, the centaurs and harpies would have to eat people like us, and then who would be left to worship the Titans?"

That answer had satisfied me at the time, but that was many years ago. Before I met Mark. Now I'm not sure if Mark is an exception or if it's all a lie.

What if everyone deserves something better, or at least a chance?

Mark leads me to a broken-down shack at the end of a broken-down street. "This is it," he says. Even though it's after dark and after curfew, even though the Night Patrol could find us at any moment, Mark seems reluctant to invite me in. His head hangs down, his shoulders slump, and he stands there, helpless in the moonlight. "It isn't much," he explains. "Now you know why I spend so much time at the Academy, why I stay in the library as much as I can."

"Look, I know you don't live like I do. I get that. But this shame you feel? There's no time for it. Not now."

As if to make my point, there's a distant scream, followed by animal-like cries of pleasure. The scream is definitely male, so it can't be the cloud-girl the Night Patrol has caught. The scream comes again, closer.

"What are you waiting for?" I demand. "You want them to find us again?"

Mark swallows hard, fear fighting shame, until fear wins. He knocks on the door. Softly, repeating a certain pattern: one long, two short. He does this three times, then stops.

We wait—what feels like forever—then we're greeted by the sound of locks un-clicking. A lot of them. The door opens, just wide enough to show the face of a haggard, middle-aged woman behind a rusty metal chain. Her hair is thin, gray, and wiry. It hasn't been brushed in weeks. Her eyes are bleary, red-rimmed, and I'm not sure which she's been doing more: drinking or crying.

"Mom!" Mark says. "Quick! Let us in."

"Who's that?" she shrills, and her eyes latch suspiciously on me. "He's not a monster, is he? He's not making you trick us to get inside?"

"No, Mom! This is Andrus. He's a friend from Axios. He was helping me get home when the Night Patrol found us. We barely got away."

From inside, another female calls out, "Who is it? Is that Mark?" This voice sounds much younger.

Mark says, "Mom, we don't have time for this. I swear this isn't a trick. Andrus is just as human as you and me."

"Prove it," his mom says. She tosses a small paring knife out. "Cut him. Let's see if his blood is red or black."

Mark bends down and picks up the knife, staring at me apologetically. The blade glitters in the moonlight. "Humor her, OK? Monsters have black blood, like oil. She'll see yours is red, and then everything will be fine."

"What the hell, man? I'm not letting you cut me! You've seen me in the daylight. You know I'm not a monster."

"I know that," he says, "and you know that, but my mom... Look, let me just make a little cut." He steps toward me.

"Are you crazy?" I back away. Everything my parents ever told me about Loserville flashes through my mind, and even though I know Mark isn't trying to hurt me, I can't let him do this.

Mark stops, then reverses the blade and holds it out to me. "Fine, cut yourself. Just enough to show her you're human."

I take the knife, but make no move to use it.

Behind the door, the two women argue. The younger one wants to let us in, the older one says it's not safe, that she won't lose another child to these damned monsters.

"I'll do it," I say. "Just tell them to shut up before they alert every monster in the neighborhood." I raise the knife, holding it over my forearm, letting the blade hover.

This is stupid, I think to myself. *I shouldn't have to prove myself to Losers. They're crazy!*

The chain rattles and the door flies open. There's a girl there. Blonde. Beautiful. Wearing a simple pink tunic, and not much younger than Mark and me.

"Get in!" she says.

Mark rushes in.

When I hesitate, she adds, "You too!" She motions me inside, then slams the door behind me. The chain clicks into place, then she busies herself resetting the rest of the half-dozen locks.

I look around the house. No wonder Mark was embarrassed. It's a dump: dingy, mismatched drapes and carpet, rickety furniture. A bottle of cheap wine sits on the table with two clay cups. One of them is chipped and bears the inscription, WORLD'S BEST MOM.

Mark's mother gets up from the floor with a resentful look on her face. "You didn't have to hit me!" she says sourly. "I had to keep us safe, didn't I? It could have been a trick..."

"It's not a trick," I say, then stare at the knife in my hand. "I'm not a monster." I give the knife to Mark. I'm grateful he doesn't hand it back to his mom.

"This is my sister, Lucy," Mark says. She comes over and gives her brother a fierce hug, then turns to me as he introduces us. "Lucy, this is Andrus Eaves. We have classes together at the Academy."

Lucy's blue eyes light up. "It's a pleasure to meet you, Andrus. Mark never brings friends home. I was beginning to think he didn't have any."

I almost correct her that Mark and I aren't friends, that we barely know each other, but after all we've been through, maybe we are. Even if we aren't, I'd be a jerk to say otherwise. So I smile and say, "Sorry to bother you at this hour." Which seems like the polite, proper thing to say, the kind of thing I'd be expected to say if I'd gone to one of my neighbor's houses. Only it sounds ridiculous after being chased by centaurs. "Um." I clear my throat and try again. "I mean, thanks for letting me in. It's kind of dangerous out there."

"It's dangerous in here," their mom mumbles. "Opening the door to strangers..."

"Mom!" Mark snaps.

"I didn't say nothing," she protests. "Nobody listens to me anyway." She moves away, pretending great interest in picking at the stray threads of her mud-brown, shapeless tunic.

"Don't mind Mom," Lucy says, and motions me to the table. "She's like that with strangers."

"With family too," Mark adds glumly.

I take a seat and Lucy pours me a cup of wine. I try not to gag when I taste it. It's sour and strong, not like the wine my parents serve.

"You're very brave," Lucy says, picking up the other cup. "Thank you for bringing Mark home. I don't know what we would have done without you."

"Hey," Mark says. "What makes you think *I* didn't save him?"

Lucy smirks. "What did you do, little brother? Hit a monster with one of your books?"

"Well, no," Mark says. "Of course not! But I helped Andrus get here, didn't I? That counts."

Lucy raises an eyebrow.

"Fine," Mark says. "We saved each other! Happy now?"

She laughs. "Is that what happened, Andrus?"

I look from her to Mark, then back again. "Yeah. Your brother's braver than you think."

"Really?" Lucy takes another sip of wine. "I always knew Mark had courage in him, I just wasn't sure he was going to live long enough to find it."

"It takes a lot of guts to do what he does. It's not easy at Axios. The Academy's tough on everyone, but it's even tougher on kids like Mark."

Lucy snorts. "I wouldn't know. The priests said I wasn't special enough to go."

"I'm sorry." I want to tell her in a way she's lucky, that just because Mark gets to go to Axios doesn't mean he's going to survive it, but I take another drink of wine instead. How am I going to tell his family that it's my fault we were almost eaten by centaurs? That it's my fault Mark and I are going to compete Monday against Blake and Brenda? And worse, that Mark might not make it home if we don't win?

But Mark saves me the trouble. "Mom, Lucy," he says. "There's something else Andrus and I need to tell you. It's about school..."

9

WELCOME TO LOSERVILLE

LATER, Mark and I are in his room, which is about as big as my walk-in closet. There isn't even a bed, just a rolled-up sleeping bag and pillow shoved in the corner. He sits at a small desk by the window, digging through a dusty book on monsters.

I sit on the edge of the desk, peering through the thin gray curtain into the back yard. It's dominated by a dead tree, the branches almost close enough to scratch the glass. This must be the same tree Mark told me about—the one he saw the harpy in. I glance up at the sky, half-expecting to see a legion of harpies dive down, but there's only the moon.

"Your sister seems nice," I say. "I mean, she took the news about the rematch well. Better than your mom."

Mark mumbles something that sounds like he agrees, but his eyes never leave the book.

"What are you reading?"

"Research," he says, not bothering to look up. "I'm trying to find some mention of that cloud-monster. Just because it saved us doesn't mean it's friendly. What if it did something more than take our scents?"

"What do you mean?"

"Not all monsters feed on flesh and blood. Some of them eat memories and some eat souls."

I shiver, remembering Captain Nessus saying he was going to pull Mark's name from my memories after eating my brain. "I think we're fine. I don't feel soul-less and my memory seems OK."

"Me too. But I've never heard of a monster that eats scents, which is what's making me nervous." He stops to sniff his armpit. "I think mine's starting to come back. You should check yours."

I make a face.

"Seriously?" Mark says. "After all we've been through, that's where you draw the line?"

Feeling dumb, I raise my arm and take a whiff. It's faint, but it's there. "Mine's coming back too. Maybe the cloud was some kind of magical deodorant."

"It was more than that," Marks says. "The cloud acted on us in different ways. It didn't take on my scent; it absorbed it, made it disappear. But with you, it used your scent to lead the centaurs away."

I get up from the desk and lean against the wall. "And that matters why?"

"Because we don't know why she did what she did. Was she helping us, or was she helping herself? That's the age-old question, isn't it?"

"I guess."

"Fine, let's drop that line for now. Do you remember anything else about tonight?"

"Yeah, man! Ravens. A whole flock of them attacked the centaurs. That's how I got away. And I heard a girl's voice in my head telling me to run."

"That must be the same voice I heard telling me to get out of the dumpster."

"You know what? Those weren't the only ravens I saw today. There was one watching us from a streetlight after we left the gym. And then there's that girl, the one I saw earlier in the bushes, and at the accident."

Mark snaps his fingers and points at me. "Good thinking! If that girl is the same one we heard in our heads, then she's not a monster."

"Right! Because both times I saw her, she was in daylight."

"Exactly." Mark puts the monster book away and pulls out one on magic. "That means the ravens, the cloud, and the girl are all related. She must be some kind of witch or something. They're rare, but they do exist. Or maybe she's just a girl who found magic items left over from the Gods War. They warned us about that in priest class."

"You mean like Zeus's lightning bolts?"

Mark nods. "Or Poseidon's trident, or the golden swords of Ares. But I'm thinking something less flashy, something more along the lines of Hermes's winged slippers, since she's using it to move around. Some kind of transportation magic."

"What about the ravens?"

"That could be part of it," Mark says, "or something completely different. But these are all guesses. That's the problem with magic: there are too many unknowns. Let me do some more research and see what I can find out."

I leave Mark and head back to the living room. Drunken snoring comes from his mom's bedroom, but Lucy is camped out on the living room floor in a sleeping bag.

"Sorry," I say. "I didn't know anyone would be in here."

Lucy sits up. There's a butcher knife in her hand. She grins and sets it aside. "It's OK. I was keeping watch."

"What for?"

She looks at me like I'm stupid. "For burglars."

"Burglars?"

She sighs. "You're really not from around here, are you?"

"No," I admit. "Don't the monsters keep the burglars off the street at night?"

"Some of them, sure. But monsters also keep people from paying attention to what's going on outside, and they damn sure keep people from coming to help if burglars do break in." She gets up and we both sit at the table. Frankly, I'm not sure what burglars would want to steal from this shack, but I guess desperate people do desperate things.

Lucy picks up the bottle. "More wine?" she asks.

I hold out my cup, but as I do, there's a high, feminine scream from somewhere outside. Somewhere not too far away. I jump a little, but Lucy doesn't flinch, doesn't even look over her shoulder toward the sound, and her hand stays steady as she pours.

"Screams are pretty common after dark," she says. "During the day too. It's not like we can trust the warriors much more than the monsters to keep us safe. Day Patrol or Night Patrol, it's all the same."

"But aren't you worried that scream could mean monsters are coming here?"

She shrugs. "Not really. It means they probably *aren't* coming here because they're busy with whoever made that noise."

"So screams make you feel safer?"

"Usually. Unless those screams are coming from the other side of the door, or one of our windows. Then I get scared, because if that person were to break into our house, the monsters would follow."

"But I thought they can't enter homes."

"Not normally. Only if you break the law, or if they're pursuing someone who has."

"But why should you worry? If the monsters are only after the lawbreaker, they can't hurt you."

Lucy shakes her head. "That's where you're wrong, Rich-O. The monsters will attack everyone inside, claiming we allowed the criminal in. That we're harboring a fugitive."

I remember how Nessus lied about not seeing my amulet, how he was going to eat my brain and get the information he needed. Totally illegal, but who was going to dispute his word? Certainly not me without my brain.

I take a sip of wine, wiping my mouth with the back of my hand. It doesn't taste as bad as before, though I'd hate to think I was getting used to it. "So, um, your mother mentioned not wanting to lose another child..."

Lucy looks down at her cup. "We—we're not supposed to talk about that."

"I'm sorry," I say, realizing that's the third time I've apologized to her in the past hour. "I didn't mean to upset you."

"You didn't know." She drains her cup, then pours another for her and me. "It's OK, Andrus. Mom's asleep. I can tell you."

"Not if you don't want to. It's just I've never met anyone who's lost someone before. Where I come from—well, I kind of live a sheltered life, you know?"

"Really?" Lucy mocks. "I never would have guessed. Welcome to Loserville." She raises her cup in a toast.

"Hey, it's not like that. I'm not looking down on you. I'm not some jerk slumming for thrills. I want to understand."

She sets her cup down, a troubled look on her face. "I'm sorry. I'm being a bad hostess, but frankly, I'm not sure you *can* understand, and even if you can, I don't know what difference it makes. You'll go back to your palace—"

"House," I correct her.

"Call it what you want. But after tonight, you'll go back there and tell your Rich-O family and your Rich-O friends all about your little adventure in Loserville, and they'll all laugh and make rude comments. Maybe you'll laugh with them, or maybe you won't. Maybe you'll even feel bad or tell them to shut up. But it won't matter, Andrus. It won't change things for my family, for anyone I know. Things will just keep on going the way they always have. The screams will be just as loud, just as many, only you won't be able to hear them in your castle, and eventually, you'll forget."

I don't know what to say, so I don't say anything. I reach out and place my hand over hers. She doesn't try to take her hand away. She just stares at me, and I stare at her, wanting to take her pain away.

Lucy wets her lips, swallowing nervously. "Andrus, I don't think this is a good idea—"

I lean in, never taking my eyes from hers. Her breath quickens. Her lips part, just a little, and mine do the same. And then we're pressing them together, lightly at first, then harder, our hands snaking out, winding through each other's hair, urgent with need.

Lucy finally pulls away, the soft pant of her breath making her breasts rise and fall beneath her pink tunic. "Andrus," she whispers. "That was wrong." I start to apologize, but she waves it away. "No, it's just as much my fault as yours. I *wanted* you to kiss me. I wanted... "

"What?" I take her hands in mine.

She laughs ruefully. "I don't know. To feel special, I guess—to know I was just as desirable as any Academy girl. But more than that, to feel I had a chance to escape this life. To have a shot at something more, like my brother."

"You do," I say. "I mean, you can."

"No," she says. "Not that way. I'm not going to sleep my way out of Loserville. I know too many girls who've tried, and they just end up right back where they started, or worse, with a baby in their belly or working the streets."

"That's not what I meant," I begin, then try again. "I wouldn't do that to you."

"Maybe not, but your parents would. They'd buy me off, or have me killed, or enslaved, or eaten by monsters, even sacrificed. They won't let their son be with a Loser. You know that."

I know my parents, and I know she's right. "OK, but what if I could get you to take the test again? Get you into the Academy?"

"That won't work."

"Why not? Mark and I can help you study. It's hard, but it's not that hard."

Lucy takes her hands from mine and reaches for more wine. "I know that! I'm not stupid. I'm just as smart as Mark, maybe smarter."

"Then why didn't you get in?"

She purses her lips, almost like the words are too painful. "I did," she says. "I mean, I passed, but the priest said there was one more test, one he wanted to give me in private..."

It takes me a second to get it, but then I say, "Oh."

Lucy nods. "I refused, of course. So then the priest told me not only was I not getting a scholarship, but neither was Mark." She pauses to knock back her wine, then glares at the table. "So I slept with him. I'm not proud of it, but I made that sacrifice for my brother."

I reach out to comfort her, but she pulls away.

"Mark doesn't know," she says. "And he never will. You can't tell him. It would break his heart, and he'd do something crazy to that priest, and then I'd have done what I did for nothing. Promise me you won't tell him."

"I won't."

"Good. I don't know why I told you. I never told anybody, not even my mom." She reaches for the wine again, but I move the bottle out of her reach.

"You don't need more wine."

Lucy gives me an angry look, then slumps back in her chair as if the effort is too much. "It's all I have! It dulls the pain."

"Like it does for your mom?" I don't mean it like an accusation, but she stands up and walks to the window, keeping her back to me.

I go to her, putting my hands on her shoulders. I expect her to tense, but she relaxes into them instead. "You think I don't know that?" she says. "You think I *want* to be like her? I don't have a choice."

"We all have a choice. I haven't known you very long, but I know you're better than this. Stronger. I know you can make something of yourself."

"And how do you know that?" She says it without much fight, and I can sense she's on the verge of tears.

"Because you already have. You saved your brother before, and you saved him again tonight. And me."

"I'm no hero," she says. "I just did what I had to do."

"I've been thinking maybe being a hero isn't about saving the world. Maybe it's about the small stuff, saving one person at a time. Including yourself."

Lucy turns around, coming into my arms. Her eyes are wet, her lips trembling. And we kiss. There's heat in it, passion, but like everything else today, it's crazy. We let it linger, knowing that once it ends, we're going to be right back where we started. And that's not a place either of us is eager to get back to.

When it's over, Lucy says, "That was nice, but it doesn't have to mean anything."

I hold her tight, loving the soft warmth of her melting against me. "The truth is, I've never really felt *connected* to anyone before. Don't laugh, but I've always felt more connected to things. Well, rocks mostly."

"Rocks?" She frowns, unsure if I'm joking.

I clear my throat. "You know: stones, gems, geodes. I collect them. I even dream about them, about going into caves or climbing mountains. Ever since I can remember... especially Mount Olympus."

"Really? Even your dreams are rich! I only dream about getting out of Loserville."

"You will."

She sighs. "We should probably get some rest."

I look down at her sleeping bag. "Um, sure. Do you have an extra one of those or should we just..." I let the words trail off on purpose.

Lucy grins, but points at Mark's room. "You can sleep in there. And try to dream of something other than rocks for once."

"Like what?"

Her grin widens. "Like me."

It's a nice thought, but it doesn't happen. Instead, I dream of scaling snow-swept mountains. Alone, as always. The rocks are solid beneath my fingertips, comforting.

They don't change, like people.

They don't change, like me.

10

CHANGED

I'M UP EARLY the next morning. I don't stay for breakfast because I don't want things to get awkward with Lucy, plus I know my parents will be worried. I want to get home fast. Which means another trip across town, but at least now there won't be any centaurs in my way. Still, it's going to waste a lot of time—time Mark and I could be training.

My parents told me that before the Gods War, everyone had these things called "phones" that they could use to talk to each other from miles away. Unfortunately, the stuff that made them work got destroyed in the war, and the Titans didn't think such things were worth rebuilding. I guess since Titans can magically appear anywhere they want or talk to people in their minds, the idea of phones seems pretty dumb.

Their mom is still asleep, so I say my goodbyes to Mark and Lucy. I tell Mark to meet me at the Harryhausen gym at noon. There's a moment's weirdness as I thank Lucy, one where we're not sure whether to hug or what, so we just sort of smile stupidly at each other and hope Mark doesn't notice.

Stepping into the sunlit street, it's hard to believe last night even happened. When I look back at the house, Lucy is watching through the window. She waves, and I wave back, then she's gone.

I walk on, remembering last night—the good part, the part where she was pressed up against me and there were no monsters, no magic, not even the threat of Monday hanging over my head. What I wouldn't give to get back to that moment, or to have a thousand more just like it.

My rosy glow is wrecked by the sight that greets me a few blocks down. There's a victim of the Night Patrol—a brainless zombie—shuffling toward me. Half her face is gone, the skull cracked open. There's blood crusted to the front of her dress, some of it still wet. She's not much older than Lucy. She even looks like her—the part of her that hasn't been eaten. The zombie shambles forward, her remaining blue eye glassy, unfocused.

Who is she? Why was she out past curfew? Was she meeting her boyfriend and lost track of time? I'll never know, and I doubt she even remembers.

The zombie moans and staggers by. I can't help but wonder if it's my fault this happened to her, if having led the centaurs to this part of town caused her to get caught instead of me. There's no way to know, and I'm ashamed at the relief I feel it was her and not me, or Mark, or Lucy... but it could be. If not last night, then tonight, or the next.

Because that's the world we live in.

I watch the living dead girl, feeling even sicker as a pair of feral, bone-thin kids in rags run from behind a nearby shack. The brother and sister surround the zombie and laugh, pelting her with stones.

"Half-face! Half-face!" the skinny girl yells. "You're a stupid freak!"

"Yeah! Take that, ugly!" her brother shouts. He throws a fist-sized stone toward the gaping hole in the zombie's head. Only the stone doesn't connect. It just veers away from the target into my outstretched hand.

"Get out of here," I growl. "Now!" I'm angrier than I should be, angry at a world where so much is so wrong.

The Loser kids shriek and run. The zombie wanders on, as she will for all eternity.

I want to think I've done some good, but I haven't. I haven't changed anything for her, or those kids. I haven't changed anything for anyone but me.

I stare down at the rock, still not sure what happened is real. The rock is a flat, smooth gray, perfect for throwing. It doesn't look magic, though it feels slightly warm to the touch. I think about tossing it away, but put it in my pocket instead.

Above me, a raven caws, circling the blood-red sky.

I HAIL A TAXI when I get to the better part of town. The cabbie is a pudgy guy with a thick red beard. He asks me where to, then whistles when I tell him.

"Fancy!" he says. "That's a long trip. Sure you can pay?"

I jingle my coin purse at him.

"OK, buddy, you got yourself a ride. Say, you look beat!Rough night?"

"Sort of."

He puts the taxi in gear. "I heard that! Every night's a rough night when you're young. Why I remember this one time when I was your age, I met this girl and—"

I cut him off. "No offense, but I'm pretty wiped. How 'bout a little music?"

"Sure thing. You're the boss." He turns on the radio. The sound of Greek folk music fills the cab.

I lose myself in the cheerful strings as we pull away from the curb. Saturday traffic is light this early. We're making good time, but before we get out of downtown, traffic snarls. Ahead, a sanitation crew is hosing down the blood-stained street—someone's life swirling into the gutter.

The black-clad slaves finish hosing the pavement, then go at it with brushes as a bored overseer cracks his whip. "Move it, you lazy dogs!" he barks. "Move your asses!"

People walk past the spectacle, pretending not to notice, or too busy to care. *That can't happen to me,* they think, *as long as I play by the rules.* Or maybe they even think whoever that happened to, they must have deserved it. But Mark and I didn't deserve it. That zombie in the street outside his house didn't deserve it. It's funny how people can rationalize even the worst forms of cruelty as long as it doesn't effect them. It's easier not to fight. To give in and give up. Especially when you're rewarded for it.

Like my parents.

They're rich, and that's an understatement. They struck oil on their land when I was young, one of the largest veins ever found in the NGT. That oil allowed them to move to the big house we have now, on the well-manicured land far from the problems of the city.

Until today.

I have no doubt Captain Nessus is going to report me to his commander, who will report me to the Temple, who will send some annoying priest over to reprimand me in front of my parents. That should worry me more than it does, but I have so much going on right now, I really don't have room for it.

My main problem, the one I have half a chance of solving, is can I really train Mark in time? I'm going to have to. Then there's Lucy, but that's such a huge question mark it makes my head hurt worse than the rematch. It doesn't help that she keeps pushing herself back into my thoughts just as soon as I think I've pushed her out.

Is that love? It's lust, for sure. I mean, I like her. Maybe because Lucy's exactly the kind of girl I shouldn't like. The kind I can't be with that makes me want her more. And she needs me, but she doesn't seem *needy,* if that makes any sense. She's smart and strong. I know if she could just get into Axios, she'd be fine. Better than fine. Or, if not the Academy, then some other opportunity. In business, perhaps. It's not like my family doesn't have connections.

I'm not going to solve the Lucy question right now, anymore than I'm going to solve the Mark one. What I need to focus on is what I'm going to tell my parents about last night. But that's not what my mind wants to do.

I pull the rock from my pocket. It's not warm now. I stare at it, trying to sense if it's magic, but nothing happens. Then an idea hits me:

What if I'm magic?

"That's it," the cabbie says.

Startled, I look up and realize he means we're parked outside the gated driveway of my house. It's funny how I wanted to be here so bad last night, but now I wish I was anywhere else. I push the rock back into my pocket.

"You want me to drive up?" the cabbie asks, "or you want out here?"

"Here's fine. How much for the ride?"

"Fifty drachmas."

I tip him an extra ten.

He thanks me, then says, "Hey, it might be none of my business, but if this is your house, it doesn't matter how rough last night was. Why, if I owned a place like this, I'd—"

I don't wait for him to finish. I get out and stare at the wrought-iron gate as the cabbie drives away.

I'm home. So why doesn't it feel like it?

11

IT'S COMPLICATED

I TAP IN THE SECURITY CODE on the gate panel and step into the wooded driveway. It's a half mile to the house from here. I could have had the driver take me, but I'd rather walk. After all, the sun is out, the birds are singing, and there's a soft breeze. The ground under me feels familiar, welcoming. I've always felt safe here.

Protected.

But am I? Couldn't it all be ripped away from me the second I stop playing the Titans' game? No wonder so few resist.

My house looms into view, and it's like I'm seeing it for the first time. I can see why Lucy called it a palace or castle. It's neither of those things, but it's a lot closer than I'd care to admit. The front of the two-story house is supported by ornate columns in the Corinthian style, topped with fancy scrollwork. Everything is white except the ocean-blue shutters and trim. It's a big house, far more than we need, with dozens of rooms. Some of the rooms I've only ever been in once or twice.

There are slaves washing my dad's red Ferrari. Slaves tending the flowerbeds. Slaves cutting the grass. I remember an old history book in Dad's library. It was written in English, not Greek, so I don't think he was supposed to have it. From what I could make out from the pictures, before the rest of the world was destroyed and the USA became the NGT, people only kept slaves of one color. I never understood that. Our slaves are every color, just like they used to be in ancient times.

The Titans don't care about skin color. To them, a human is a human, and humans are only good for three things: work, worshipping, or food. Anyone can become a slave, just like anyone can rise or fall to any station in life. The priests say that makes it fair, but I'm not so sure. People like me seem to have things more "fair" right from the start.

The slaves pause in their tasks to look at me. There's relief in their eyes, and a few wave or shout greetings, but I'm not sure if that means they're glad I'm home or glad my parents can stop taking out their worries on them. My parents don't beat them or anything, but sometimes they get mad and say mean stuff. I could never bring myself to do that, even with my temper, because I figure the slaves have things hard enough already.

I move past them, returning the waves, nods, and hellos. After seeing how people live in Loserville, it feels weird. Maybe because I'm not the same as when I left yesterday. I'm different, more aware of how others live. My eyes have been opened to the cruelty and injustice of this world, and I don't know what to do about it.

No ideas come to me as I walk up the front steps, through the double doors, and into the foyer. Paintings and photographs greet me: my family, our oil business, landscapes, cityscapes. People I barely know and places I've never been. Greek vases on pedestals line the walls. A grand staircase sweeps up and away in all its polished glory to the bedrooms on the second floor. My room is up there. My sanctuary. But it will have to wait.

James, the white-haired old butler, hurries forward in his black tunic with the gold striped sleeves that signify his position as head slave. James practically raised me because my parents were so busy being rich they didn't have time.

"Master Andrus!" James says, "We were all so worried when you didn't come home last night. Are you OK?"

"I'm fine. I lost track of time and had to spend the night in the city."

"But your amulet! The Night Patrol should have granted you safe passage."

"Yeah, well, they would have, only they didn't want to extend the courtesy to my friend, so I had to improvise."

He gives me a worried look. "You got into trouble, didn't you?"

"A little." I try to blow it off with a shrug, but there's no fooling James. He knows me too well. "It's complicated. The important thing is nobody got hurt." I can't help but shudder, thinking of the zombie and the screams I heard last night. With a heavy sigh, I say, "I guess I better tell my parents what happened. Where are they?"

"At breakfast, sir. Shall I have a place set for you?"

"Nah, I'm not hungry."

"Forgive me, but I've never known you *not* to be hungry. Why don't I have a tray sent up to your room?"

My stomach growls and I break into a grin. "Fine." It's not that I don't want to eat, it's that I don't want to eat with my parents. Things are going to get awkward fast, and I'd like to be able to digest my food in peace.

He leads me to the dining room and pulls back the sliding wooden door to reveal my parents.

"Master George," James says, "Mistress Carol! Master Andrus is back, safe and sound. Nothing to worry about, just a boyish misadventure, that's all."

"We can see that," my father says gruffly. "That will be all, James."

The butler frowns, clearly expecting a less frosty reaction. He presses a hand to my shoulder. It's a gesture telling me to be strong, one he's given me many times before. I nod to him, thankful for it. James backs out of the room and slides the door shut.

My mom opens her mouth to say something, but Dad stops her. "Well?" He leaves the question hanging like a knife between us.

"I'm sorry."

My father takes a sip of coffee, watching me squirm. Finally, he says, "Sorry? You were out all night! I think you can do better than sorry."

"George," my mom begins. "He's safe. I don't think—"

But my dad is already holding up a finger to silence her. It's not his middle one, but it might as well be.

"Go on," my father tells me. "Let's hear all about your latest 'misadventure.'"

"Promise you won't be mad?"

My father's cheek twitches in annoyance. "No, but I promise I will be if you don't start talking."

I shuffle my feet. "Well, something happened yesterday at the Academy... I, uh, lost to Blake Masters in gym class at the wall climbing event."

Dad is pissed. "You lost? But that's your best event!"

"I know. I didn't lose by much, and only because Blake cheated. Anyway, Mr. Cross says we have to do a rematch Monday and he made it a team challenge. So he assigned each of us one of the weakest kids and we have to train them, but he said we couldn't use the school gym and—"

"Does this story have a point?" my father interrupts.

"Yes, sir." I realize I've been talking too fast, like I always do when he's grilling me. "I'm sorry, there are a lot of details, and I didn't want to leave anything out."

"Details are important," he agrees. "Continue."

I clear my throat. "Like I said, I have to train Mark—he's the partner Mr. Cross gave me. He's there on scholarship."

My parents exchange a worried look.

Dad says, "Mr. Cross stuck you with a charity case, huh? Well, at least he didn't put a Loser on your team."

"Actually, Dad, Mark is a Loser—I didn't know that either at first—but he's a good guy. He's going to be a priest."

"Of course he is," my father says dryly. "That's the only way his kind will ever make any money, by extorting 'donations' from honest, hard-working citizens like us!"

"George..." My mother lays a hand on his arm. "Let's not get worked up over that again."

My father has always had a thing against priests and goes off about them in private every chance he gets. He calls them blood-suckers and leeches, snakes and perverts, saying you can't trust them, how all they care about is lining their own pockets and they'll ruin you every chance they get.

Mom's grip on Dad's arm tightens. He sighs, not wanting to back down, so she moves her hand to his, locking them together. Some of the anger drains out of him. Enough for me to keep going.

"The thing is, since we couldn't train at the Academy, we had to go to the Harryhausen gym downtown. And Mark needs a lot of help, so we trained really hard and the time got away from us. Since I had an amulet, I offered to walk Mark home."

"To Loserville?" Mom asks in a horrified whisper.

"Yes. Only we got chased by the Night Patrol—centaurs—but I was able to hide Mark just in time. The centaurs looked for Mark, but couldn't find him, and I said we'd just met, so I didn't know his name or where he lived. That's when they got mad and pretended I didn't have an amulet. They were going to eat my brain."

"That's outrageous!" my father snaps. "What was their captain's name?"

"Nessus. He seemed to think he could get away with it."

"Maybe," my mother says, "you shouldn't have lied about Mark."

"But they would have tortured him!"

Mom shrugs. "I know this is going to sound harsh, dear, but after all, Mark is a Loser, and you're an Eaves. You have your family to think about, your future."

I don't know what to say to that. Don't know how to tell her that she's wrong when she's saying this horrible thing out of love. I'm her son. I matter to her. Mark doesn't.

When my father speaks, it's not about me or Mark, it's about money. "I paid good drachmas for that amulet," he grumbles. "Archieréas Vola himself swore it was proof against monsters! That they had to obey and grant you safe passage. If the high priest's word isn't good enough..." Dad pauses, his hawklike face flushing with renewed anger. "I mean, who do those centaurs think they are? They're monsters, not lawyers! They're not allowed to interpret the law or the whole system falls apart. I tell you, I don't know what this world's coming to!"

There's no point arguing with Dad when he's like this, so I don't even try. It's better for him to be angry at priests and monsters instead of me.

"But the centaurs let you go?" Mom asks.

I hesitate before answering. "Not exactly. I escaped."

"There's no way you outran centaurs," my father says. "You're fast, son, but not that fast."

"I know. I didn't."

"Then how did you get away?" he asks.

"I'm not sure. One minute the centaurs were going to eat my brain, the next there was this earthquake and a swarm of birds attacked them."

"Harpies?" Mom wonders. She's right to ask, because even though the monsters were all spawned by the Titans, that doesn't mean they like each other. Harpies and centaurs are well-known rivals.

"No, not harpies," I say. "It was ravens. I can't explain it. Anyway, I ran and met Mark a few blocks later. We made it to his house. Since the centaurs didn't know who Mark was, they didn't know where to look. I spent the night with his family, then took a taxi here. I know I wasn't supposed to run, but the centaurs weren't supposed to go against the amulet, so we were both in the wrong."

"You did what you thought was right," Mom says, "which is more than I can say for those monsters! But what you did was foolish, risking yourself and our good name for that boy, that Loser! What were you thinking?"

"That nobody deserves to walk around for all eternity with their head smashed open. I had to help Mark; it was my fault he was out past curfew. I would have done the same for anyone, Mom. I would have done the same for you and Dad."

"Don't be ridiculous! Your father and I both have amulets. You wouldn't need to."

"Still," I say, "if you were ever in any kind of trouble, I'd do whatever I had to to keep you safe."

Mom's smile is slow in coming, like melting snow, but I know I've touched her, reached through the frost of upper-crust nonsense that traps her, that traps all of us. Even Dad seems to have a new respect for me.

"I suppose they'll report it and send a priest," he says. "And you can bet he'll come knocking with his hand out."

"Probably." I shift from one foot to the other. "Hey, I'd appreciate it if you guys left Mark out of anything you say to the priest."

"Of course we will," Dad says. "You never admit anything to a priest you don't have to. That's part of the whole confession racket; it gives them evidence to blackmail you with later."

"OK. Thanks, Dad."

"Just to be clear, I'm doing this favor for you and for us, not Mark. Now go to your room and get some rest. Your mother and I will handle the priest."

"Yes, sir."

My father nods, dismissing me. It's as close to an "I love you" as we get.

12

WARNINGS

I SLIDE the dining room door shut. James is waiting outside the door, a familiar guilty look on his face. We both ignore the fact he was obviously listening to my conversation. He walks beside me, neither of us speaking until we're well away from the dining room.

"How did it go?" James asks, as if he doesn't know already.

"About what I expected."

James makes a sympathetic sound. "They love you."

"I know."

"They were worried. I've never seen them so rattled."

"They sure didn't show it. My father seemed more concerned about wasting money on my amulet."

"Your father..." James begins, then lowers his voice. "Your father expresses his love in a different way than most people. His business has made him cold, hard to the outside world, even to family. But I've been with him since the beginning, just like I've been with you. He built all this for you. So when he complains about losing money, or priests interfering with his business, he really means he's worried about you. *About your future.* You'll inherit all this someday."

"I don't care about all this, or the future! I may not even have one."

James frowns. "Don't say that, sir."

"It's true! Anyway, why should I care about money and things when I can care about people?"

James doesn't reply, just waits for me to continue.

"Something happened last night," I tell him. "Something I can't explain. I wasn't sure I'd feel the same today, but I do."

"Is it a girl?" James asks as we head upstairs.

"What?" I say. "No! I mean, yeah. There's a girl, but that's not it. Well, not the main thing."

James smirks. "I see."

I feel my cheeks redden. "Damn it! I wish it was that simple, I really do. There's way more going on than just a girl."

"If you'll pardon my saying so, your first one is never 'just a girl.'"

"We didn't—I mean, we kissed, that's all."

He raises an eyebrow. "I was referring to falling in love, sir."

"Oh! Well, I wouldn't say it's gone that far. It probably won't. I may never see her again."

James nods, but the smirk is still on his face, telling me he knows better.

I check to see if there are any other slaves around, but we're alone. Still, I keep my voice down. "Even if I do see her, there's the fact she's from Loserville. My parents would never accept her. No one would."

"Love is rarely convenient..." James gets a wistful look on his face, no doubt remembering some girl from his youth. "Would you like my advice?"

"Definitely."

The wistful look goes away, replaced by concern. "Sometimes love is best kept to oneself. Especially if it will harm the one you love more than it will help."

I chew on that as we walk down the hall to my bedroom. James must mean what Lucy warned me about last night: How my parents would stand in the way, how everyone would, and yet... I really don't want to be alone anymore.

James says, "Love is a wonderful thing, but it's also selfish. It can destroy happiness as easily as it creates it."

"So you're saying I *shouldn't* love this girl?"

"No, I'm saying *if* you love her, be sure the consequences won't leave her worse off than before she knew you."

"Thanks, James. That helps."

He nods. "As to the rest of what's going on, I wouldn't worry. You've always done well in physical challenges. It's that Blake fellow who should be worried." When he sees that doesn't cheer me up, he adds, "Did something else happen? Something you didn't tell your parents?"

I can trust James with my secrets. I've shared things with him in the past and he's never let me down, but how do I share that I might be magic?

"What do you know about ravens?" I ask instead.

He looks puzzled. "Ravens, sir?"

"Come on, James. I know you were listening at the door."

He shrugs. "They eat the dead."

"Yeah, but do they ever attack in swarms?"

"I've never heard of them doing that. And I have no idea why they would attack centaurs, of all things! That seems rather odd."

"Have you seen any ravens hanging around?"

He wrinkles his forehead in thought. "I spend most of my time in the house, so I wouldn't know about what goes on outside, but come to think of it, one of the maids *did* report she found a bird in the house yesterday. A great big black one! In your room, in fact."

"What was it doing?"

"I'm afraid it was gone by the time I got there. I had the maid tidy up and saw no need to report it. It was just a bird, after all."

"Was it?"

"Was it what?"

"Huh? Oh, nothing. I was just thinking aloud."

James smiles. "Very good, sir. Will that be all?"

"Yes. No. I mean, if you happen to notice any more ravens hanging around, like in the house, or outside the windows, could you let me know?"

"Of course. You should rest up now, all right?"

I nod, then open the door to my room. It's exactly the same as I left it—the normal teenage room of a normal teenage boy: desk, chair, bed, lamp. Framed pictures of mountains and caves on the wall. Posters of warriors in battle and athletes in competition. And then there's my rock collection, the many geodes and crystals glittering in the morning sun. I run my hands over them and instantly feel better.

The next thing I do is look out the window at the perfectly land-scaped backyard. You could fit a hundred shacks in it, maybe Mark's whole neighborhood. A bird flies by, but it's not a raven. I know I'm being paranoid, but I lock the window just to be safe.

James has left a breakfast tray for me, loaded with a fluffy ham and cheese omelette, side of bacon, buttered toast, and orange juice. I sit at my desk and wolf the meal down. An image comes to mind of Cronus devouring the Gods, but it's one I quickly shove to the side along with the now empty tray.

I pull the stone from my pocket, setting it on the desk next to my collection. I pull out my rockhounding kit and busy myself cleaning and polishing it. Nothing happens, no mystery reveals itself, and certainly no magic. It's just an ordinary rock, not even worth iden-tifying.

That means I'm the one that's magic, and that thrills and terrifies me because it's crazy. Only the Titans and monsters are magic... except for the old Greek Gods. But I'm not any of those things. I'm normal. Aren't I? I have to be. I may be adopted, but my parents were human.

That means I'm human.

I have to be sure. I push back my chair and stand up. I back away from the desk a good five feet, then hold out my hand. Palm out, fingers splayed. I concentrate, focusing on the stone. Willing it to fly into my hand.

Nothing happens.

"Come on," I hiss. *"Move, damn you!"*

Sweat pops out on my forehead. I squint my eyes and grit my teeth. My muscles tense, fingers tightening into a claw. I reach out to the stone with my mind. Trying to make a connection. Trying to make it understand:

I am the mountain.

I am one with it.

I am one with the earth, and we are brothers...

I can't be sure, but I think something is happening. I think I see the stone move, just the tiniest bit.

There's a sharp crack at my window. Startled, I turn to see a raven on the windowsill. It pecks the glass again, then cocks its head and croaks at me. Black bird. Black eyes. It flaps its wings and is gone.

Downstairs, the doorbell rings.

13

THINKING

THE PRIEST SITS across from me in the living room. He's not wearing the usual azure cloak, but one of midnight blue. It marks him as a member of the Inquisition, the Temple's special investigative arm. That means he's not here to reprimand me. Any priest could do that. No, he's here to check for crimes against the state:

Blasphemy.

Treason.

Magic.

A leather folder rests in his lap, and there's a golden mace—a ceremonial club with a blunt metal head on the table next to him. Its head is in the shape of the Eye of Cronus. The inquisitor's face is carefully composed in a neutral, almost-friendly way, but the smile never touches his eyes, which are sharp and gray. He's middle-aged: thinning black hair, slight paunch, entirely unexceptional. His azure robe stands out against the white cream of the couch.

"I am Inquisitor Anton," the man says. "Your parents were just telling me what an exceptional young man you are."

I smile blandly, trying not to look nervous. "I do all right at Axios, if that's what you mean."

He nods, reaching for the folder. He opens it, eyes flicking over the documents inside. "Your reports from the Academy give you high marks for physical ability. Your gym teacher, Mr. Cross, says you have the makings of a fine warrior. You're one of his top students."

"I am, praise Cronus." Maybe this won't be so bad after all. I must look good on paper, even if I'm a mess inside.

"However, your academic instructors are a bit less enthusiastic," Anton continues. His expression hasn't changed, but his gray eyes seem sharper. "Why is that? Are you having problems at home?"

"No." The only problem is my parents didn't get rid of this guy. But no one, not even my parents, can throw an inquisitor out. Not without consequences.

If Anton notices my discomfort, he doesn't react. Instead, he asks, "Problems at school, then?"

I hesitate, thinking of Monday's rematch, then shake my head. "Nothing I can't handle."

"Spoken like a true warrior." Anton flips to another page, taking his time to reread what he must have already memorized by now. "Tell me, Andrus, what would make a fine, upstanding, citizen such as yourself break curfew?"

"The Academy gym is being remodeled, and I wanted to work out, so I had to go to the one downtown."

"The Harryhausen gym on 81st Street?"

"Yes, sir. That's the one."

"Mm-hmm. And after?"

"I wanted to take a walk to clear my head. I wasn't paying attention and got lost. I didn't break curfew on purpose."

"No? Why am I not surprised? Young man, you should know intent is irrelevant in the eyes of the law. One is either guilty or one is not. Surely they teach you that much at Axios?"

"Y-yes, sir. They do! But they also teach us there are exceptions, and not every sentence deserves the harshest penalty."

Anton studies me before slowly nodding his head. "And they said you weren't a scholar! Answer my questions then, and we'll see how lenient I can be."

"I'd be happy to."

"No, boy! No one is 'happy' to answer my questions, but they answer all the same. Now, let us return to the events of last evening: When you went for your walk, what were you trying to clear your head from?"

I scratch my head. "I don't remember. It was nothing important. You know how it is."

"No, I'm not sure I do. Were you unhappy?"

"Unhappy?" I swallow. "No."

"But you must have been concerned about something, correct? Something big enough to make you forget curfew."

"No, I just daydream sometimes. That's all."

"Interesting. About what, may I ask?" Of course he can ask. He's an inquisitor; that's what they do. And after they're done asking questions, that's when the real torture begins... When I don't answer, he says, "Daydreams indicate you are unhappy about something in your life, not merely 'concerned.' Tell me, Andrus, what could a boy like you be unhappy about?"

"Nothing! It's just I'm excited to graduate and become a warrior. I can't wait to put in my service to the state. I feel like I could be doing more. You know, like you. You've got all your training behind you and an important rank now. You're happy, right? Happier than before you graduated?"

Anton's half-smile falters. "We're not here to talk about me."

I'm not sure what to read into that, or if I should bother trying. I was hoping to draw a comparison between us, to compliment him and make him empathize, but it feels like I've touched a nerve instead.

"Sorry," I tell him. "I was just thinking that—"

"Oh, you don't want to do too much of that." Anton cuts me off. "Thinking too much is what gets people into trouble. They *think* they have the money and resources to avoid arrest. They *think* they're too important, that they can do anything they want. Is that what you think, Andrus? Do you *think* you can talk your way out of this?"

"No, sir."

Anton snorts. "That remains to be seen. Now then, in his report,

Captain Nessus says you were apprehended breaking curfew south of the Harryhausen gym—the opposite direction of your family's estate."

"I guess so. I'm not sure where I was. I was lost."

"Were you alone?"

"Yes." The lie comes quickly, since technically I was alone when the Night Patrol found me.

"Really? There was no one else around? Any other witnesses who can corroborate your story?"

"I can't say for certain. It was dark." I'm determined not to bring Mark into this, not if I can help it. I know my parents didn't mention Mark, and there's a good chance the centaurs didn't either. It would make them look bad for not catching him. Since I know my father will have mentioned it, and am eager to change the subject, I say, "Captain Nessus didn't want to honor my amulet."

Anton sighs. "According to the captain's report, he says you had some trouble producing it, which escalated the situation."

I sigh and look away. "Oh, it escalated, all right."

"Andrus, if the captain failed to honor the amulet, then you are well within your rights to file a complaint. The Temple takes such allegations quite seriously."

"My father hasn't filed one?"

Anton shakes his head. "He wanted to, but it was not his amulet in question. It was yours. It's up to you to file charges. Is that something you would like to do?"

"What will happen to Captain Nessus if I file?"

"He will be reprimanded. It will go on his permanent record and be factored into any future promotions."

"That doesn't sound like much."

"I'll be candid, it's not. You could request a formal hearing. Archieréas Vola himself will decide—"

"The high priest? Really?"

"Yes," Anton says, "and if Archieréas Vola finds in your favor, you will have the right to challenge Captain Nessus to trial by combat in the Temple Arena. As the accused, he would be allowed to choose the weapons for both of you."

As much as I'd like to fight Nessus, I don't like my odds. "No, thanks."

Anton looks disappointed. "So you agree with the captain's claim you had trouble producing the amulet? And that the captain acted appropriately?"

"Yes."

Anton pulls out a pen and makes a notation on the page as he mutters, "Regarding amulet... Citizen Eaves agrees with Captain's report... no charges filed." He then hands the pen and page to me, pointing to a blank line. "Sign here, please."

I sign and hand it back to him. "Is that it?"

"Almost." Anton leans forward. "Tell me about the ravens."

"The ravens, sir?"

"Yes. Tell me about the ravens and the reason you ran."

"Um..."

"Come now, Andrus! The question's not too hard, is it?"

"No, sir." So I tell him as much of the truth as I dare, leaving out the part about the girl, the cloud, and how the birds had been following me all day. I finish by saying, "I think the earthquake must have startled them; that's why they attacked. There was nothing I could do, so I ran."

"I see. What do you think caused the earthquake?"

"Uh, the normal reasons? Earthquakes happen all the time."

"They do," Anton admits, "but sometimes, they happen for *unnatural* reasons."

"I'm sorry, I don't understand."

"You don't? Are you sure?" His eyes take on a dangerous, fanatical gleam. "I'm talking about magic."

"It wasn't magic! At least I don't think so. If it was, what could have caused it?"

"What indeed?" Anton muses. "Let's forget that for the moment. You say the ravens attacked. Were you injured?"

"No, I was lucky." The inquisitor frowns, so I quickly add, "I wasn't the only one who ran. One of the centaurs did too. Ruvo, I think his name was. I figured if the monsters couldn't protect themselves, they couldn't protect me. I know I shouldn't have run, but I panicked."

"I see," Anton says. "Normally, fleeing from the Night Patrol would be a serious offense, but I am prepared to accept that there were extenuating circumstances in this case."

"Extenuating?"

"Yes, to remain might have endangered your life. And just between you and me," he adds, "I might have run too."

"Thanks," I say. "I knew you'd understand."

"Oh, I understand a great deal. I have to in my line of work: truth from lies, an honest mistake from a deliberate crime, everything all the way up to blasphemy and treason. That's really all the Inquisition is interested in. We exist to keep the world safe. It's not a pleasant job, it's not a pretty job, but without the Inquisition... There are cracks, Andrus. Cracks in loyalty and devotion. Men like me are the glue that keeps the NGT together."

I want to say, *you mean on its knees*, but give him a nod instead. "You're doing an important service."

"Yes," Anton says, "I am." He files his papers in the leather folder, then stands up. I stand too, and offer my hand. He shakes it, his grip firm, not letting go. "After you ran," Anton asks, where did you go?"

"Nowhere." I can't help but feel shifty when I say it.

The inquisitor's grip tightens. "Surely, you must have gone somewhere. To Loserville, perhaps?"

I pull my hand back, scowling. "I don't know. I knocked on doors and tried to get some people to let me in, but no one would help. I'm not proud of it, but I ended up hiding in a dumpster. I thought maybe the centaurs would find me, but they must have lost my scent because of the trash. It was pretty smelly in there."

"That's entirely possible," Anton says. "Would you mind showing them to me?"

"Show you what?"

"Your clothes—the ones you were wearing in the dumpster."

"Sure, but the slaves have washed my tunic by now. It wasn't that dirty, you know. It was more the smell."

"The cab driver didn't mention any smell."

"Cab driver?"

"Yes, the one you hailed downtown this morning."

"Maybe he didn't notice. I was in the back seat with the window rolled down. Why does it matter how bad I smelled?"

Anton grins, but it's cold. Menacing. "Oh, it's not how bad *you* smelled that concerns me. It's how bad your story smells." He picks up his folder, then his mace, giving it a casual swing. "Do you know what this is, Andrus?"

"It's a mace."

"That's right. But do you know what I use it for?"

"No."

"Truth-getting. Pain can be a powerful motivator. Even just the fear of pain can work wonders! But sometimes, fear isn't enough. Some people respond better to greed, some to hate, and some..." He chuckles, hefting the weapon, then brings it down on a nearby vase. "Some are stubborn! And if they want to keep their secrets badly enough, I let them. Only I make sure they can't share them with anyone else. Not ever."

I shudder as the zombie girl flashes through my mind. I see her shattered skull in the shattered vase, the white shards shifting between ceramic and bone.

The inquisitor loops the weapon to his belt. "I trust we understand each other. Keeping secrets always has a cost—one most are unable or unwilling to pay. That's where I come in." He heads for the door, then turns to face me. "Cronus is watching, Andrus. *I am watching.* If I discover you had anything to do with that attack on the Night Patrol, or that you lied to me, all your family's wealth and privilege won't save you."

14

THE PROBLEM

AFTER INQUISITOR ANTON LEAVES, I thank my parents for not giving up Mark. I know they did it out of wanting to protect me and the family name, but the fact is, they still saved his life.

"Once the rematch is over," my father says, "We want you to promise you won't hang out with that boy again. We recognize you need him now, but you have to understand no good can come from associating with a Loser in the long run. It's not just dangerous for you, it's dangerous for him. Our classes... well, they aren't meant to mix together."

"We're not saying it's right," my mother adds, "but it's just the way the world is. We only want what's best for you. You understand that, right?"

There's no sense arguing. Maybe it's not a question of whether I'm better off without Mark or Lucy, but that they're better off without *me*. I've already endangered them in more ways than I know. And just because I've been able to protect them so far, doesn't mean I can do it forever. "Fine," I say. "I'll ditch Mark after the rematch."

Dad offers a rare smile.

Mom hugs me. "We know it's hard, dear, but you'll see we're right someday." She kisses me on the cheek.

"Hey, before I go, can I ask you guys something?"

"Of course," Dad says. "What is it, son?"

"Remember how I told you about the earthquake and those ravens? How they attacked the centaurs?"

"Yes," Dad says. "What about it?"

"Well, the inquisitor was really interested in that part. He seemed to think it was magic and that I had something to do with it. I told him it wasn't true, that I had no idea what he was talking about. That's right, isn't it? Humans can't be magic."

"No, son. They can't."

"So why would he think I had anything to do with it?"

Mom and Dad exchange a look. Something weird passes between them, something I can't quite place.

James appears, announcing the car is ready to take me to the gym. I look to my parents for an answer, but Dad is silent and all Mom can say is, "Have a nice time, dear. We'll send the car to pick you up at six o'clock sharp."

"Six? But that's three hours before curfew!"

"We don't want to take any chances after last night," Dad says. He moves to the bar to pour himself a drink, and I notice it's not just one drink he's making, but two.

Mom smiles at me so hard I think her face might break.

I walk with James toward the front door, but then an idea pops into my head. I tell James to wait, then run upstairs to my room and get my favorite book on climbing. Mark likes to learn by studying, so I should let him learn his way as much as possible. The next few days are going to be tough on him, but the book should help. I know it helped me back when I first started climbing. I mean, I was always a natural, but my technique needed work, and that's what this book teaches.

Look at me, I think to myself. *I'm becoming a regular Mr. Cross. All I need now is a crewcut and a whistle.*

When I come downstairs, I follow James out of the house, blinking as my eyes adjust to the noonday sun. The limo is parked nearby, the driver standing at attention, but I don't make any move to go to him. I know James wants to talk, so I pretend something in the sky fascinates me, shielding my eyes and looking up. It's bright blue. Lazy clouds, as white as my butler's hair, drift by.

"I take it everything went well with the inquisitor?" James asks. He keeps his voice low, his expression neutral. To an outside observer, he could be asking about the weather, but I hear the love in his voice.

"I'm still here, aren't I?"

James nods. "Please don't joke, sir. If anything were to happen..."

"I know," I say. "Trust me, everything will be fine."

"Of course, sir. Good luck with your training. I know you'll do—" James never finishes his sentence. Instead, he stares at something on the roof.

It's a raven.

I TRY TO ENJOY the limo ride downtown, try to imagine the workout routine. But I can't focus. I keep craning my neck, trying to see if the raven is following me. Between the sun's glare and limited angle, there's no way to tell. Finally, I can't stand it anymore. I have to know. I open the sun roof and stand up, ignoring the driver's urgent warnings to sit down.

Trees whiz by. Mansions behind hedges, behind stone walls and iron gates. Locking the world away.

I look up and there it is: a speck of black against the blue. The raven! "What do you want?" I yell. "Why me?"

The raven dips lower, cawing, and I can almost understand it, almost hear what it's trying to tell me. Reality seems to shift and sway, the woods replaced by rock walls and ceiling, the black road becoming a black river that winds its way deep into the earth, oozing like blood through a monster's veins.

The limo rounds a corner, jostling me. I lose sight of the bird. The world is normal again. I wait for it to reappear, but we're racing downhill, leaving it far behind.

By the time we get to the Harryhausen gym, I've got my head on straight. Ready to teach, ready to train. Mark is waiting on a bench outside. He doesn't seem happy.

"Hey, man," I say. "What's up?"

"Bad news."

I look around nervously, but just see ordinary people on the street. No priests, no warriors, and definitely no raven.

"The trouble's not out here," Mark says, jerking a thumb over his shoulder. "It's in there."

I walk to the front door. It's locked. "What the hell? They're supposed to be open Saturdays!" That's when I see the sign taped to the inside of the glass. It reads, GYM CLOSED FOR PRIVATE PARTY. WE APOLOGIZE FOR THE INCONVENIENCE AND WILL RE-OPEN MONDAY MORNING.

I press my face against the glass, using a hand to shield my eyes from the sun reflecting off the door. I expect to see a children's birthday party or some crap like that, but the gym is empty. Well, almost empty. There's the usual slaves standing by, but that's not who catches my eye.

Freaking Blake Masters is inside with Brenda Larson. She's working the rock climbing wall while he watches. She's actually made a lot of progress since the last time I saw her. That's not good.

Almost as if he knows I'm there, Blake turns his head in my direction and smiles. He swaggers to the front door, taking his time, and motions one of the slaves to unlock it. He stands in the open doorway, filling up the entrance with his stupid ego. "Andrus! Hey, buddy. Great to see you. You and your lady came to work out, huh? Get a little one-on-one time in the sauna?"

A rage builds in me. Everything I risked, everything I suffered to be here now, has all been thrown away. I take a menacing step toward Blake.

He holds up his hands in mock-defense, that same contemptuous smile plastered across his face. "OK, OK! Don't get steamed." He chuckles at his joke. "Or maybe do, but not here. Guess you two love-birds will have to practice climbing each other somewhere else."

"You had no right to do this," I begin, but Mark grabs my shoulder to hold me back.

"Andrus, don't!" Mark says. "It won't do any good."

"Yeah, Andrus! Listen to your Loser friend. You're just mad I thought to rent out the gym before you did. You would've done the same thing to me."

"Actually," I snarl, "I wouldn't have. I want to beat you fair and square."

Blake shakes his head. "Wow, you're dumber than I thought. Fair and square, huh? Seriously? You think that's how this world works? Get real!"

I twist out of Mark's grip and punch the smile off Blake's face, forcing him back into the gym.

The slave rushes to lock the door as Blake scrambles backward. He wipes the blood from his split lip. I see the hate blaze in him, but then he smirks and turns away. He thinks he's won. Maybe he has, but at least I gave him something to remember me by.

15

GETTING WARMER

FIFTEEN MINUTES LATER, Mark and I are drinking coffee in the Medusa Café. The usual weekend shoppers stroll by. It's a perfect day for everyone but us.

"So what are we going to do?" Mark asks. "If we can't use the gym here or at school, where are we going to train?"

"There's only one place I can think of, but you're not going to like it."

Mark raises an eyebrow. "Oh, yeah? Where's that?"

"Bronson Canyon."

He spits out his coffee. "Seriously?"

"Yeah, it's not like we've got another choice."

Bronson Canyon is in Griffith Park, just outside Hollywood. They used to film old TV and movies there. It's always had a reputation for being haunted, but no one could prove anything until a bunch of caves opened up during the Gods War. Some of those caves led to Tartarus, the Greek Underworld. A lot of ghosts and monsters got out and caused problems until the Temple put a stop to it. The priests say everything is fine now, and the park's open. Well, most of it. Some sections are still sealed off, and the place has a sinister reputation.

That hasn't stopped me. I've been to the park a few times and never seen anything weird.

Mark sighs. "I guess it won't be so bad as long as we stay outside the caves."

"Here's the thing..." I say, watching Mark's frown deepen. "The canyon's no good for climbing. Bad rock. It crumbles too easy. We're gonna have to go caving."

Mark covers his face in his hands and makes a strangled sound somewhere between a sob and a laugh. When he pulls his hands away, his mouth is set in a grim line. "Fine. Why not? I mean, if we get eaten by monsters, at least we won't have to get humiliated Monday."

I take a sip of coffee. "Listen, it's gonna be all right. I've been caving there before. The priests sealed the monsters up real good. Trust me."

I see a flash of blue, and my heart skips a beat. A priest walks by, cloak flapping, but it's not Anton, and he doesn't even look our way. Still, I don't like it.

"Come on," I tell Mark. "Let's get out of here. I gotta do something first."

I spend a few drachmas hiring a messenger service to tell my parents we can't use the gym and to have the driver meet us at Bronson Canyon instead. I don't want to take any chances breaking curfew again, and I know it makes Mark feel better.

We stop to buy some caving gear and backpacks, pick up a few drinks and snacks, then hop a bus to Griffith Park. During the ride, Mark keeps looking at me funny. When I ask him why, he rolls his eyes and looks out the window.

"Fine," I say. "Don't tell me."

I reach into my pocket and pull out the stone. I don't know why I brought it with me. Holding it helps. Holding it, I'm not alone.

"I know about you and my sister," Mark says. "I know she likes you. She *begged* to come with us today."

"Oh yeah?" I fake cough and look away. "Maybe she's taking an interest in your training."

I give it a minute, not saying anything. When I turn back to face him, Mark is glaring at me. "Look, man. It's not like that! Nothing happened."

"And nothing can," Mark says. He's looking at me now, his eyes dark. "I mean it."

"Mark," I say, fumbling for how to reply. "I'm—it's not—I mean, I would never..."

H"Yes, you would. You're not a bad guy, Andrus. I get that. But you're who you are, and my family, we're who we are, and I haven't known you very long, but I know you don't always think things through. My sister... I won't let her get hurt."

"I wouldn't hurt Lucy."

"You wouldn't mean to, but you would. You're not going to see her again. Promise me."

"I promise."

Mark stares at me a moment to make sure I'm serious, then looks out the window. The city is a blur.

I lean back and close my eyes, listening to the sound of the wheels. My fingers clench the stone. Mark's right, and I hate it. It makes me so mad. The stone grows warm, startling me. I open my fist. The stone is glowing. Just a little. I glance over at Mark, but he isn't paying attention. I slip the stone back into my pocket. The warmth fades.

I feel strange: exhilarated, exhausted. The next thing I know, I'm asleep.

WE GET TO GRIFFITH PARK at mid-afternoon, then catch the shuttle to Bronson Canyon. It's rugged, barren land. The shuttle drops us off and leaves. No one else is around. Far in the distance, the broken and stained HOLLYWOOD sign stands on a scrub-covered hill as a grim reminder of what our world used to be.

"Oh, hey! Wait a minute." I stop and rummage through my bag until I find the book on climbing. "Here," I say, handing it to him. "You should read this. It's got a lot of really good information."

"Thanks." Mark flips through it, pausing here and there to study the diagrams and illustrations. "This looks really useful. I was gonna ask if you had any books on climbing, but I wasn't sure you needed any."

"I'm good," I admit, "but not that good."

"That's a relief."

"Huh? Why's that?"

Mark shrugs. "Because if *you* needed a book to master climbing, then it makes me think maybe I'm not so hopeless after all."

I grin and punch him in the arm. "Don't get cocky. Hey, whatever happened with your research last night? You find out anything more about that weird cloud-girl?"

"I didn't find much. Just that it might not be a ghost or monster. It could be someone who knows magic or maybe found a magic item. That doesn't make me feel any better though."

"Why not?"

"Because magic is illegal! We should report it, but we can't—not without implicating me for breaking curfew. But if the Inquisition ever finds out that someone with magic helped us... Well, it wouldn't be good. We'd be fed to Cronus for sure!"

I get a sinking feeling. Because I'm magic. What if this cloud-girl is magic too? What if she's like me, but with different powers? What if...

Mark snaps his fingers in my face. "Andrus, you listening?"

"What? I mean, yeah. You were talking about magic."

"Sure I was, but that was two minutes ago! I'm talking about magic items now, and why that could be worse than if the girl was just a regular witch casting spells or whatever."

"Why is that worse?"

He rolls his eyes. "You really weren't listening, were you?"

"Maybe."

"Damn it! You better not have been daydreaming about my sister."

I laugh, then stop myself. "No, man. That's—just no. I swear I wasn't thinking about Lucy. I have a lot of stuff going on and..."

"You didn't look like you were thinking. You looked like you were spacing out. Why do you keep doing that? I mean, you got some kind of condition or what? You're not going to do that during the rematch are you? Or when we're caving today?"

"No, I'm fine. Go on. You were telling me about your research."

Mark grits his teeth, then sighs when he sees I won't budge on telling him more. "OK. I was saying most magic items were created by the Gods, not the Titans. The Titans didn't make many because they didn't need many. Whatever they touched became magic, but only while they needed it to be. That's how powerful they are. But the Gods were a different story. They needed magic items to help defeat the Titans."

"So what God would make a magic item that makes you look like a ghost and smell like death?" I ask the question, but we both already know the answer.

Hades, God of the Underworld.

"Of course, I could be wrong," Mark says. "That girl could just be a human witch."

"OK, but why is she helping us?"

There's no answer for that, so Mark and I keep walking. From everything I've read, witches don't help people out of the goodness of their heart. They're selfish and evil and they always want something, but what could a witch want from us?

No, I correct myself. *Not what does she want from Mark. What does she want from me?*

I LEAD MARK toward the cave I've explored before. It's a short hike past boulders and tumbleweeds. A short hike to find out it's closed. A gang of slaves are walling it off with stones while a pair of warriors and a bored-looking priest pass a wine bottle back and forth. As we get closer, I notice the stones are covered in magic symbols.

Mark tugs at my sleeve. "I don't like this. We should go."

I brush him off. I've come too far to turn back now, at least not until I know what's going on. I walk up to the priest and his escorts. The warriors step forward, hands on their sword hilts. One says, "This area's off limits, citizen. Move along."

I crane my neck around him, trying to get the priest's attention. "Excuse me," I call. "What happened? How long will the cave be closed?"

The priest waves me forward, and the warriors let me pass. He's maybe forty, a fat man with beady eyes and a wispy brown beard. His nose and cheeks are flushed red—maybe from sunburn, maybe from alcohol. "You're a bold one," he says, taking another swig. "Let me guess: rich parents?"

I nod.

He spits. "That's the problem with your kind, Rich-O. No manners. No respect! What gives you the right to inquire into Temple business?"

"Nothing," I say. "I'm sorry, I was just curious. I thought the caves were safe."

"Safe?" The priest laughs. "Of course they're safe—as long as you don't go in them."

"I meant this one in particular."

"So did I," he says. "See these stones?" He waves his free hand at the pile behind him. "They're good for keeping people out, but they're even better at keeping things in."

"What kind of things?"

The priest takes a long pull from the bottle, draining it. "Thirsty work," he says. "Thirsty day." He tosses the bottle at the slaves. "Work faster, damn you!"

I glance back at Mark and the two warriors. Mark looks worried. The warriors look bored. The priest continues to ignore me, but I know what he wants. I pull a bag of drachmas from my belt. The jingle of coins grabs his attention.

"A donation," I suggest.

He eyes the bag warily, then snakes out a hand to tuck it into a leather pouch at his side. It's illegal to bribe a priest, but it's not illegal to donate to the Temple—although I doubt my money will go towards anything but another bottle.

We eye each other for a moment, then the priest says, "There was an incident yesterday morning. Fissure opened up in this cave. Something got out. We're making sure nothing else does."

"What was it?"

The priest shrugs.

When he doesn't elaborate, I ask, "Did you see it?"

He shakes his head. "Not me, but I heard it was some kind of awful gray cloud."

My mouth goes dry. "Cloud?"

"Uh-huh. Wasn't a gas leak or anything like that. Just between you and me, I heard the cloud was shaped like a girl."

"So it's a ghost? Or a monster? Or..." I shut up, because I don't want to sound like I know too much.

The priest belches, then scratches himself through his tunic. "Can't say, except it's something the Temple isn't happy about, that's for sure. Why else would they have me out here working on a Saturday? And in this heat!" The priest spits again. "Ain't right."

"Thanks."

"No," he says, patting the leather pouch at his side. "Thank you, citizen. A thousand blessings upon you." He places his hands together, crossing his fingers and touching his thumbs while leaving a space between. He raises his hands to his forehead in the gesture of our faith. The Eye of Cronus. I return the gesture and walk away.

I don't make it ten feet before the priest's voice stops me. "Hey, kid!"

The warriors pause in their task, hands on their sword hilts, watching me for any sudden movements.

I freeze, wondering if I've somehow been caught, if this priest somehow knows I'm magic and his warriors will seize me and drag me to the Inquisition's dungeon. Can Mark can get away? I look over at him, see the panic in his eyes, the accusation.

What have I done?

Maybe I can cause a distraction to buy Mark time to get away, but he's no better at track then he is at climbing walls.

"Come here!" the priest calls.

When I turn and study the priest's face, he doesn't look angry. He waves me back to him.

"Yes?" I ask. "Is something wrong?"

I watch the warriors out of the corner of my eye. They haven't moved. The priest follows my gaze and snorts. He raises a dismissive hand to his men and they return to their duties.

"I wanted to warn you," the priest says, but there's no malice in his words. "Whatever that thing was that escaped from the cave... Well, it tore up a squad of warriors before it got out of the park. In broad daylight too! That sound like a monster to you"

"No," I say. "But that doesn't mean it isn't one."

"A new kind of monster," the priest muses. "I'll be sure to pray on that. You should take your friend and go. Me, I have to be here. But you? It's not safe."

"Thanks," I say. "We'll take your advice."

"I'm glad," the priest replies. "You know, I had a son like you once. He didn't listen for shit. Thought he knew better than me. Thought he was invincible."

"What happened?"

The priest's face darkens with anger. "What do you think happened? He's a damn zombie now!"

"I—I'm sorry. Was it a monster that got him?"

The priest looks down at his hands. "Yeah," he rasps. "A monster did it." He stares at his hands, clenching them into fists until the knuckles pop.

I don't know what to say, or even what to think. Does the priest mean a monster was to blame, or was it something else? Something worse? Did he turn his own son into a zombie?

The priest doesn't look up. When he speaks again, his voice is tight, quivering with violent emotion. "You should go," he says. "Now!"

I walk back to Mark. Behind us, the priest yells at his warriors to get the slaves working, to "put their backs into it." Soon, his shouts are followed by the angry crack of whips and screams of men.

"What were you thinking?" Mark whispers. "Why did you talk to that priest? What if he put us to work on the wall?"

"Don't exaggerate."

"I'm not. Maybe he couldn't put *you* to work, but I'm not rich, remember? Losers get enslaved on a whim. You want to take chances with your life, that's fine. Just don't take them with mine."

We make it another fifty feet, just out of sight of the priest, before Mark stops me. "Well?" he demands.

"Well, what?"

"Aren't you going to tell me what you found out?"

I hesitate. "You really want to know?"

"Yes, damn it!"

"That thing from last night... the cloud-girl."

"What about her?"

"That cave is where she came from."

16

THE OMEN

THE NEWS DOESN'T SIT with Mark any better than it does with me. I can't help but feel we're getting drawn closer and closer to whatever that thing from the cave is. *Whoever it is*, I correct myself.

"What if it's a God?" Mark asks. "That's a possibility we haven't considered."

"The Gods are dead."

"The Temple says they are," Mark agrees. "Except Hades. But what if some of the other Gods aren't dead? What if one or more Olympians survived?" This is not just radical statement coming from a guy who's training to become a priest. It's blasphemy.

"They're dead," I say. "All of them. Why would the Temple lie about that?"

"So no one worships them. Worship is power! Gods and Titans, they eat it up. Like spiritual candy."

I can't help but grin. "Spiritual candy?"

Mark shrugs. "I was trying to put it in terms you'd understand. I meant 'psychic energy.' Gods and Titans are energy beings. They have plenty of energy on their own, but are always hungry for more. They store it up and use it instead of having to use their own. You know to perform miracles, that sort of thing."

"And to take on physical form," I say.

"Exactly! That uses up a lot of energy, which is why we don't see them walking around everyday. Of course, that doesn't mean they're not lurking around in spirit form."

"Cronus is watching," I mutter.

Mark sighs. "You know, most people take that literally. They think the King of the Titans is omniscient, but I've been thinking..."

"Uh-oh."

"No, I'm serious. What if that means Cronus only sees whatever's in front of him? So he *could* be here watching us, or he could be somewhere else, but he couldn't be in both places at the same time?"

I gotta give Mark credit. That's a heavy thought for someone raised to believe the Titans are perfect, and that Cronus is the most perfect of all.

"Speaking of watching," Mark says, "don't look now, but there's a raven watching us."

I turn my head slowly and see the familiar black-feathered beast. It cocks its head, caws once, then takes off deeper into Bronson Canyon. Toward the forbidden caves.

"Ravens are the messengers of Hades," Mark says. "At least, that's what some people say. They're also known to be familiars for witches."

"Great! So do we follow it? Or would now be a good time to run?" I'm half-joking. I want to follow it, but I'm afraid of what we'll find. And what if it puts Mark in more danger? I'm responsible for him. I can't just go charging off after some mystery bird. I'm the one it's been following, not Mark. I can tell Mark is torn too, so I ask, "We don't have to do this. I remember what you said, about getting you in trouble."

"Thanks," Mark says. "But that bird is an omen. We can't ignore it."

"An omen, huh? They teach you about omens in priest class?"

"Yes," Mark says. "They do."

I can't argue with that, so we set off after the raven. We follow it for about a mile until it stops and begins circling overhead. Not over our heads, exactly. Over a cave. A cave that's been sealed shut the same way the last one was, with magic stones. Only it was sealed a long time ago. There's no one around. Just us and the bird.

There's something about this cave. Something important. Above us, the raven cries.

"Stay back," I warn Mark.

He shakes his head, then sees that isn't going to stop me. "Andrus! What are you going to do?"

I wave him off. Moving forward. Step by step, until I'm inches away from the sealed entrance. I reach out a hand to touch the wall... Sensing power, sensing magic.

The stones seem to pulse under my fingers. I wait, but nothing happens. The raven circles, scolding me. Daring me to do more.

I lay my hand on the wall.

"Well?" Mark shouts. "Anything?"

I look back over my shoulder. "No, nothing. I—"

I don't get to finish my sentence. An explosion throws me back. I lay on the ground, stunned. Dust and debris swirl through the air. Mark is at my side, helping me up. We cough and sputter as the earth moves beneath us, doing a crazy jig, then settles. Through the brown haze, I expect to see the wall shattered. But it's still there. Still intact.

"That doesn't make any sense," I say. "If it wasn't the wall, what blew up?"

Mark points. "Not the entrance, the side of the cave. See? A fissure opened up."

I go over to it as the dust settles. The rocks here are cracked, fractured wide open. Revealing a tunnel just big enough for us to fit through.

17

DEAL

THE INSIDE OF THE CAVE is dark and cool, at least ten degrees cooler than the temperature outside. We slide and scuff our way down the narrow fissure until we come out into the main cave. We flip on on our flashlights. The beams punch through the darkness, revealing a wide, dusty chamber. A tunnel leads deeper. We follow its gentle slope, our footsteps unnaturally loud in the enclosed space.

"It sure is spooky in here," Mark says.

I grunt something that sounds like agreement or sympathy, but that's not how I feel. I like it here. It's not spooky at all. It reminds me of home. Not just my rock collection, but of being surrounded by thick walls. *That's what it's like,* I think to myself. *It's like being inside my rock collection.* I reach out a hand to touch the wall, my fingertips trailing over stone.

Rough stone.

Welcoming stone.

There's a dull rumble, a tremor, and dust rains down from the ceiling. "Hold up," I warn. "Stay flat against the wall until it passes."

We wait, bodies pressed against soothing stone.

"Think it's safe?" Mark asks.

"This?" I say, playing my flashlight along a hairline crack in the ceiling. "Yeah, it's just an aftershock. Nothing to worry about."

"No, not that. I meant you don't think the priest will send those warriors in here, do you?"

"Nah. Why would he?" I resist the urge to shine my light back in the direction we came from. "They don't even know we're here. Come on, the tremor's passed. We should get moving."

Mark nods, but doesn't look convinced.

The way ahead gets steeper, until we must be a good hundred feet below ground. With each step, I feel more confident, more happy. At peace.

We emerge onto a long ledge overlooking a limestone chasm. Our flashlights can just make out the floor, fifty feet below. It's covered in stalagmites, like a bed of nails for giants. There are more tunnels at the bottom. Across the chasm, roughly opposite us, is another ledge with another tunnel. It must have connected to ours years ago. Looking up, the ceiling is covered in stalactites.

"Wow," Mark says. "They look like teeth."

"They're speleothems," I say, indicating the ceiling and floor formations. "Limestone deposits dissolved by water containing carbon dioxide. They form a calcium bicarbonate solution that drips into those formations. See the ones on the ceiling? Those are stalactites, and the bottom ones are stalagmites."

Mark stares at me.

"What?" I say. "I like rocks."

He chuckles. "I guess so. I just never thought of you as much of a student of... well, anything besides sports and stuff."

"Just because I'm a jock doesn't make me dumb. If I get interested in something, I learn everything I can about it."

"And you picked rocks?"

"What's wrong with rocks?"

"Nothing. It's just, I figured with your dad and all, you would have picked business."

I shrug. "They're not completely unrelated. Our oil business uses geology to know where to drill and how deep. But that's not really why I got into it—that just made it easier to convince my dad I wasn't wasting my time."

"Oh," Mark says. "I get it. You wanted to learn geology because of caving. So it is sports-related."

"Yes and no. I've just always had a thing for it. Haven't you ever studied something because you felt like you had to?"

"You mean like for my Academy scholarship?"

"No, not for any practical reason. Because you loved it, and you knew it loved you back. That you had a special connection. A talent, a gift."

"Not really," Mark says. "I never had that kind of luxury. Everything I studied, I did for my future. I don't want to be a priest because I love it. I'm doing it because I love what being a priest can do for my family." He falls silent for a moment. "But I understand what you're saying. And you know what? I'd do the same thing if I had your kind of time and money."

"I discovered the oil," I say. The words just pop out of me and hang there.

"What?"

"The oil," I explain. "On my parent's old property, the one we sold to buy the mansion. I discovered the oil."

"But your family's been rich at least a decade! You were only a little kid back then."

"I know. I was in the backyard, playing with my shovel, and something told me to dig. I dug, all right. I dug 'til my dad came home from work and caught me tearing up the backyard. He was mad at first, but then he saw the oil bubbling up, and... well, you know the rest."

"You were lucky," Mark says. "You couldn't have known."

"I couldn't?"

"No, that's crazy! I mean, isn't it?"

That's something I've often wondered myself. But now, after everything that's happened, I'm beginning to wonder. What if I'm more magic than I thought?

"We should get training," I say, breaking out the caving gear. It takes about ten minutes to show Mark how to use it. "OK, we're going to attach our nylon rope to the wall here—really pound those spikes in good—then rappel down the side of the chasm. It's fifty feet to the bottom, so we've got enough rope to make it."

"Just don't fall, right?" Mark jokes.

"Exactly. Don't freeze up, just keep moving. You want to push off from the wall a few feet, but not too far. You want a nice, safe, controlled descent."

"Got it."

"Great. OK, hook your flashlight to your belt and switch on your headlamp. After we get to the bottom, we're going to climb up the other side."

We pound our spikes in, secure our safety cables to our belts, then step to the edge. I give the rope a good, hard tug, and Mark does the same to his. They hold.

"Ready?" I ask.

Mark looks a bit queasy. "Hang on a second. I just thought of something."

"You mean how badass it's gonna be when we beat Blake and Brenda?"

Mark shakes his head. "No. What if... what if there are still ghosts and monsters in this cave? It was sealed, remember? What if they only sealed it up top, but not down where the tunnel to Tartarus is?"

"They wouldn't be that sloppy."

"Seriously? You saw how drunk that priest was outside!"

"That's because there was only one monster. Back when they sealed this cave, there were dozens, maybe even hundreds. The Temple would've been super-thorough. You're studying to be a priest. What did they tell you they did? That they half-assed it? Because I don't recall any monster prison breaks until yesterday. So they must have sealed up the Tartarus tunnel too, right? Otherwise, we would've seen some monsters by now. Great big ugly ones with sharp teeth."

Mark gulps. "I guess so. Look, I'm not trying to be a coward or get out of training, but I can't get hurt. My family's counting on me."

"Mine too. You think I'd bring you here if we had another choice? This is it. You want to be scared, or you want to be mad about it?"

"Mad?"

"No, man! Don't say it like a question. Say it like you mean it. Get mad, be mad! Mad at Blake for buying up that gym!"

"Mad at you for getting me into this mess?"

I laugh. "Sure, if that's what it takes. But we gotta work together. I'm not saying you can't be mad at me if you want, only now isn't a good time. I need you mad at Blake if we're gonna do this. Hate him. He's the one you have to beat."

Mark sighs, trying to psych himself up.

"Look, I'll make you a deal. If you're still pissed at me after we win Monday, then you can punch me."

"Punch you?" He looks at me suspiciously.

I point at my chin. "One free shot. Hey, it's not like I don't deserve it. I effed up. I admit that, and I'm sorry. I'm sorry about this, and I'm sorry about last night. So if you need to hit me to make it right, I'm all for it. Just try not to knock out any teeth, OK?"

Mark makes a fist and stares at it, then me. "Deal," he says, and steps off the ledge.

18

CONNECTED

I RUSH OVER to the side and look down. Mark is ten feet below, feet planted firmly against the chasm wall. His hands grip the nylon rope. He grins at me. "Guess the spikes will hold. You coming, or what?"

"Be right there." I join him, and soon we're keeping pace with each other. It feels good to be here, to be free among the stones. It almost feels good enough to forget why we came here. All that trouble and pain, the weirdness... Maybe it happened for a reason. Maybe we had to come here to get past our defenses and bond.

Mark whoops with joy as we hit the halfway mark and I can't help but join him. The sound of our voices echo, bouncing off the walls, the ceiling, and down the tunnels.

"Wait!" I caution. "Be quiet."

We hang there, listening.

"You hear something?" Mark whispers.

I cock my head, straining to hear something, anything, that might warn us we're not alone. But there's nothing. "Nah," I say. "Just being careful. I remembered that thing you said about not dying."

"Yeah," Mark says, "I remember, but you know what?"

"What?"

"Maybe I focus on not dying so much I forget how to live. Everything can't be about caution. Not if we're going to win." He swings away from the wall, another crazy whoop screaming out of him.

I follow, and soon we're at the bottom. I slap Mark on the back. "You did it! That was awesome."

"Thanks," Mark says. "You know what the difference is between this and the centaurs?"

"What?"

"Last night, we didn't have any control. Today, we faced danger on our terms. This was our choice. It was..."

"Exhilarating?"

"Empowering," Mark says. "This isn't like gym class, where Mr. Cross is always pressuring me. With you, I actually felt like I could do this. Thank you for that."

"That mean you don't want to hit me?"

Mark chuckles. "Ask me again after the rematch."

"Fair enough, but you do know that was the easy part, right? We still have to scale the opposite wall. It won't be nearly as easy going down."

He shrugs. "Then we better get it over with." He takes a step toward the opposite wall, then stops as his foot comes down on something hard and brittle. It crunches underfoot, and he jerks his leg back, grabbing for his flashlight. The beam shines on twisted shards of ivory. *The bones of a monster.* The skull is shattered from where Mark stepped on it, but not enough that we can't see the elongated snout, the ram's horns.

"Centaur," Mark says, then whips his flashlight around, playing the beam down the nearest tunnel. I add mine to it, but we don't see anything besides more monster bones sticking out of a dead end cave-in.

"They've been dead a long time," I say, kicking a ribcage out of my way. "That tunnel's sealed shut. Nothing to be afraid of."

"What about the other tunnels?" Mark asks. There are two more down here, not counting the one at the chasm's top.

"Wanna split up?" I ask.

"Not really."

"I thought you were feeling more like a hero now?"

"Half a hero," Mark says. "I can handle all this caving and climbing, but monsters freak me out."

"Me too. We don't want some hungry cyclops sneaking up on us."

"Cyclops? I meant centaurs! Next you'll be telling me to watch out for harpies and minotaurs."

"Not me."

"Why not?"

"Because you already warned yourself." I smile to let him know I'm joking. "Besides, a cyclops is too big for these tunnels. So you can rule them out along with any other kind of giants, not to mention hydras. Although a minotaur might fit..."

To my surprise, Mark walks away from me toward the next tunnel. "Clear," he says. "This one's caved-in too."

I walk over to him and shine my flashlight down it. This one's sealed closer to the front and I don't see any bones sticking out of the rubble. "Two down," I say, "one to go."

We head to the last tunnel. It slopes down and disappears around a corner. It could keep going ten feet or ten thousand and we'd never know. To make matters worse, there's a rancid, monster-y smell coming from it.

"You smell that?" Mark asks.

"Yeah. Could be monsters, but maybe not. Could be gas."

"Gas?"

"Methane, carbon monoxide, hydrogen sulfide," I explain. "You know, the toxic kind that knocks you out and kills you, or the kind that explodes. It's got that rotten eggs smell, but I can't be sure." There's another possibility, of course; one I don't mention: that cloud-girl from last night. She stank too, but from death and decay. This seems different, but I can't be a hundred percent sure her scent isn't mixed in with something else. Whatever it is, it's awful.

Mark sighs. "So what do you think? Gas or monsters?"

I motion him away from the tunnel. "If it was monsters, don't you think they'd have attacked by now?"

"Maybe," Mark says. "What if they're waiting?"

"For what?"

"For us to go in the tunnel, or to start climbing the wall."

"Only one way to find out." I lead us over to the wall we're going to climb, letting my flashlight pick out what looks like the easiest section. There are enough handholds and ridges here for me, but will they be enough for Mark?

"We can't use our gear," I explain, "since we won't have any in class, and we're going to have to clip our climbing belts together with the rope. That's how it'll be when we team up Monday. We're going to have to take it slow and trust each other."

Mark manages to crack a smile. "So far, so good. I just wish this cave was better lit, like gym will be."

"We should keep our flashlights on when they're hanging from our belts. That way, we can see if any monsters come sniffing around from that tunnel. Also, it will help us see where we're putting our feet."

Mark nods. "Good idea."

I tie us together with a ten foot line of nylon rope, double-checking to make sure the knots are tight, then tell him, "If something happens... if one of us passes out or falls and can't grab hold of the wall, use your knife to cut the rope." I point to the small knife we each have attached to our belts. "Cutting ourselves free isn't ideal, but it's better than both of us falling."

"Got it," Mark says. "OK, let's do this. Being half a hero is better than none."

The climb is hard. I have to constantly wait for Mark to adjust his grip, or reposition himself, or realize which handholds will be enough to hold onto or will support his weight. But he's doing all right. I offer as much encouragement as I can, but it's difficult keeping an eye on him while I'm trying to make my own progress.

Waiting for him to catch up slows me down, and I keep checking my watch to note the time. Clearly, we're not going to break any records today, but that's not what this is about. This is about getting Mark comfortable, getting him confident in his abilities. In a lot of ways, coming here was exactly what we both needed, though I hate to think Blake did us a favor throwing us out of that nice, safe gym.

I've never trained anyone before, but then, I'm sure Blake hasn't either. But he's popular, easygoing. He knows how to manipulate people. He's probably got Brenda so scared or in love with him that she'll be able to race up the rock wall in no time.

It's taken a lot for me to forge even this basic level of trust and teamwork with Mark, and it wouldn't take much to blow it. Like if Lucy and I saw each other again. I keep telling myself there's no way that will happen, so why do I keep thinking about her? Is it because she's the first girl I ever talked to about anything important? Or that she's so different from me? Or is it something more?

"Hey," Mark hisses, then says it again, louder when I don't respond. "Hey, Andrus!"

I snap out of my thoughts. "What?"

"There's something up on the ledge."

I look up. There's a shadow, but is it moving?

"See it?" Mark whispers.

"Yeah, but it might not be anything."

"That tunnel below," Mark asks, "could it be connected to the one up top? Could whatever was down there before be up here waiting for us?"

"Maybe," I whisper back. "But we don't know anything was down there! Not for sure. What do you wanna do?"

"Head back down?" Fear oozes into his voice, that same fear he's been fighting since I've known him.

"Are you kidding? We're halfway up! And you're half a hero, remember?"

"I know, but..." Mark stares past me to the ledge above. His eyes grow wide with shock. "It moved!" Mark gasps. "The shadow! I saw it! I—" He loses his grip and falls. I brace myself, digging my fingers and feet into the stone. Mark's frantic weight tries to tear me down. Beneath us, the rocky bed of stalagmites extend from the cavern floor.

Ready to impale.

"Grab on!" I yell. "Grab the wall!"

Mark flails. His hands claw for the stone, miss, then latch on. But it's awkward. He can't find a foothold, so he scrambles, trying to hug the wall with his knees. "I can't do it!" he shouts. "I'm gonna fall!"

"Hang on," I say. If Mark can just stay put, maybe I can get to him in time. I inch my way down, muscles straining. "Mark," I say, "can you move to your left? There's a better handhold there, and a foothold..."

Mark tries for it, fails, then tries again and loses his grip. He's deadweight and my muscles scream with it. There's no way I can hold us both, not like this. "Mark! Grab the wall!"

"I can't," Mark says. "I'm sorry." He reaches for something on his belt. *The knife.* He cuts the rope and plunges toward the cavern floor.

19

WHO WE ARE

As Mark falls, something bursts from the ledge above. In a wild fluttering of wings, something small and black flies at my face, orange claws uncurling. The raven!

I jerk away from it, flailing an arm out to protect my eyes. The claws graze my cheek, drawing blood, then the bird is gone, diving into the darkness below. My defense is just enough to unbalance me. I'm going to fall. I'm going to end up broken and crippled, speared on the stalagmites next to Mark, and we'll both suffer here until the flesh rots from our bones. Except the pain, the desperation, has set the rage burning in me, burning like never before. My fingers dig into the rock. *Literally.* I watch them sink inside the wall, and at the same time, there's something beyond anger—a kind of connection I feel with the stone. It spreads, rippling down the wall in a wave, and when it hits the bottom, I use its energy to flatten the stalagmites, to soften the chasm floor just as Mark's body hits.

A shadow looms from the ledge above. It's the girl. She leaps off the ledge, but doesn't fall. Instead, she turns into a familiar gray cloud, the one that saved us last night, and I swear I hear her laugh as she drifts by.

I hang from the wall for a moment, watching her descend, then have to work to pull my fingers from the wall. They come loose in a cracking of stone. I thread my way down the wall, and when I get to the bottom, I see the girl bending over Mark with that bird of hers flapping overhead. She's flesh now. The cloud is gone.

"Get away from him!" I yell.

The girl turns toward me, her expression unreadable. She's thin, black-haired, and pale, wearing a dark purple cloak and tunic. About my age. The smell of decay is gone. Her eyes are gray, not like stone, but fog. I can almost see the misty vapors moving behind her eyes, then they go as sharp and hard as ice. "Your friend," she says, making no move to leave his side, "he hit his head."

"But I softened the earth," I protest, realizing how foolish that sounds. "I mean, I know I did *something*."

"Yes, but just enough to keep him from splattering his brains. He's got a concussion. You weren't fast enough. I expected more from you."

"More? What are you talking about? I didn't even know I had any magic until this morning!"

"You knew," she says. "You've always known, but kept it buried. You wanted to be human so badly. How's that working out for you?"

"Fine!" I say. "And I *am* human." I stare at my hands, wondering at the power I feel there. "Well, human-ish."

"Ha!" she snorts. "Keep telling yourself that. Anyway, you want me to save your friend, or what?"

"What do you mean, save him? It's a concussion. He'll wake up in a few minutes."

"Hardly. There's bleeding on the brain."

"How do you know?"

She shrugs. "I can smell death on him—or what passes for it these days." As if to make me believe it, she puts her nose next to Mark's ear and inhales deeply. A strange look passes over her face, almost one of pleasure.

I don't know whether to be sick or fascinated. "What are you?"

She raises an eyebrow. "What are you?"

"I—I'm..." My words trail off. That was such an easy question yesterday. Now, I don't know how to answer. "Look, I don't know what I am, and Mark doesn't have time for us to play this guessing game. Can you fix him?"

"Fix him?"

"With your magic! You are magic, right? Like me?"

"Not like you," she says, "and I can't fix him, but I know someone who can."

"Great. And how is your friend supposed to find us here in this cave?"

She whistles to the raven. It lands on her shoulder. She presses her lips to its head, whispering a message I can't hear. The raven squawks once, then flies toward the tunnel we didn't explore.

"Are you sure that's safe? I thought I smelled poison gas."

"Shadow won't mind. Besides, he's taking a shortcut."

I watch as the raven evaporates into black smoke. Just like that, it's gone.

The girl stands and stretches her legs, which I can't help but notice are long and shapely. She catches me looking and smirks. "Really?" she teases. "Your entire life's turned upside-down and *that's* what you want to focus on?"

I feel myself blush and look away, guilty and embarrassed.

"I'm flattered," she says, "but I haven't been stalking you because I've got a crush. My name's Hannah, by the way. Hannah Stillwater."

"I'm Andrus Eaves—but I guess you already know that. And what do you mean you've been 'stalking' me?"

"My dad said I should find you."

"And your dad is... let me guess: Hades?"

"That's right," she says, leaning casually against a stalagmite. "The Unseen One, Lord of the Dead, God of the Underworld." She says it as if it's no big deal her father is one of the three most powerful Olympians, the older brother to Zeus and Poseidon.

I don't know what to make of that, but the look on her face says she's serious. "How is that even possible?" I ask.

She grins. "Well, my father took on mortal form and then he and my mother—"

I half-cough, half-laugh. "I don't mean that! I mean, isn't Hades imprisoned in Tartarus?"

Hannah nods. "He met my mom just before the end of the Gods War. You might say I'm his insurance policy."

"Insurance? You mean to bring him back?"

"Bingo! Plus the other Gods, of course—the ones that aren't dead. We're going to destroy Cronus and his Titans once and for all."

"So you're a Demigod and not a...?"

"A what?"

"Witch."

Hannah mock bows. "Can't a girl be both?"

I look at her in horror.

"Kidding! I'm not a witch. Well, actually I am, but that's really more of a hobby."

"A hobby?"

"Yeah, like your collection. The geodes and crystals? You use your knowledge of the earth to supplement your powers, the same way I use magic to supplement mine."

"Yeah," I say, not really understanding. "Of course. So is that cloud you turn into a spell or magic item?"

"Listen, we don't have a lot of time, so let's just keep this simple, all right? Here's what you really need to know about me: I've been on the run the past few years, doing damage to the Titans when I can, avoiding them when I can't, but mostly I've been training. Training and waiting."

"Waiting? For what?"

"For you, Rock Boy."

"OK, I get that I'm magic. I've got some kind of powers, but I'm no witch. And there's no way I'm a Demigod... am I?"

Hannah laughs like I've just told the best joke ever. "No, Andrus. You're not a Demigod. You're not even close."

Panic grips me. "Oh, shit! I'm not a monster, am I?"

"W-e-l-l," she says, drawing out the word, "that depends on who you ask. But no, you're not a monster. Not really. Think about it. Monsters can't go out in the daytime. Well, maybe a few of them can." She smiles strangely at me, and I can't tell if she's joking or not.

"So what am I?" I ask.

"You're something else," Hannah says. "*Something special.* I wasn't sure I believed it; that's why I had to test you. I had to make you emotional enough to get your powers out where I could see them and be sure Dad was right."

"But your dad's a God! Is he ever wrong?"

"He lost the war, didn't he?"

"Oh," I say. "Good point."

"Exactly!" Hannah begins pacing the chasm floor. "Look, you'll forgive me if I wanted to see for myself this mission wasn't some wild goose chase. We've got one shot at this, and I need to be sure of the people on my team."

"Wait, what? You want me on your team? To overthrow Cronus? I can't do that! I've got gym class Monday." She glares at me like I'm a complete idiot. And right now, I feel like one. "No, seriously! I know how dumb that sounds, but it's important. Mark and I have to win this climbing contest. If we don't, our whole future is ruined."

Hannah shakes her head. "That's your old life."

"Maybe, but it's not Mark's! I can't leave him hanging. I—I've kind of screwed up his life a lot already, you know? I can't do that to him again."

She sighs. "Loyal and stubborn, just like Dad said to expect. Fine, Rock Boy, have it your way. You win your stupid competition, then you come with me." She sticks out her hand. "Deal?"

I reach out, then hesitate. How can I leave everyone and everything behind? How can I even consider overthrowing the Titans? "You still haven't told me what I am."

"Yeah," Hannah says. "Why do you think that is?"

"I don't know! You seem more interested in telling me what I'm not."

She runs a hand over her forehead in exasperation. "Has it ever occurred to you that I'm not the only one looking for you?"

"You mean there are other Demigods looking for me?"

"No, genius. Not Demigods. *Titans.* And unlike me, they don't want to be your friend. They don't want you to help them change the world. They want to kill you—which they can't, until my father is freed—so in the mean time, they'll settle for the next best thing."

"Like what?" An image of the zombie girl, head bashed in, doomed to wander forever, fills my mind. Or being fed to Cronus and slowly digested over a thousand years. "You mean torture?"

"That's just for a start! They'll find the deepest, darkest pit in Tartarus and put you in it. Just like they did to my dad. You've only got one defense, and that's secrecy. The Titans don't know who you are yet. But believe me, every priest has been briefed to be on the lookout for someone with your powers."

I think of the Inquisitor Anton, and how interested he seemed in my activities. How suspicious. But if he thought I was some kind of mythic being, he wouldn't have come to my house alone, and he certainly wouldn't have left without trying to arrest me. Unless he was waiting to see me use my powers, just like Hannah.

"I'm not going to tell you what you are because that way you can't tell anyone else," Hannah says. "What you don't know can't hurt you—or me. But what I am going to tell you is, *do not use your powers in public.* Not again. They're still raw, undeveloped and unpredictable, so keep a lid on your emotions. Don't get too mad, too excited, too anything! Your powers respond to heightened emotions, especially anger. That's how you'll give yourself away."

There's a loud *pafft!* Her raven, Shadow, reappears in a blast of black smoke. Wings flapping, it makes its way over to us. The bird looks slightly singed.

"What happened?" I ask. "Is your raven all right?"

"He's fine," Hannah says. "One of the hazards of inter-dimensional travel."

"Inter-dimensional?" I choke on the word, barely comprehending the enormity of something this girl takes for granted. "OK, but where did you send him? And who was he supposed to bring back?"

"I sent him to Tartarus," Hannah says, "to find a ghost."

"A ghost?" I'm not sure this day can get any weirder, but then the raven caws, coughing up a thick gray cloud that takes on the shape of a man.

Hannah says, "Andrus, meet Herophilos. He's a doctor."

20

PSYCHIC SURGERY

THE GHOST BOWS, its once-vague features sharpen to resemble a wise man in his fifties.

"OK, so he's a doctor, but, um, are you sure he's—you know—qualified? How long has he been dead?"

"I'll let him answer that," Hannah says.

Herophilos gives a vaporous shrug. "I have been beyond this mortal life since 280 B.C." His words are formal, stilted by an ancient Greek accent, "but, I assure you, death is no obstacle to education. I have continued to practice medicine with men and spirits, even among the Gods themselves! My most recent position was Court Physician to my lord, Hades, until the Gods War necessitated a change of scenery..."

Herophilos stops to look at Hannah a moment. Something passes between them, but I can't tell what.

"You can skip that part," she prompts him. "Just tell Andrus your qualifications."

The ghost sniffs disdainfully before continuing. "As to my earthly qualifications, beyond writing the preeminent text on blood flow, I was the world's first anatomist—the first to dissect cadavers to gain knowledge of human anatomy. My earthly advances in medicine were unequalled for 1,600 years after my death, but,"—and here he pauses to give a self-satisfied smile—"when you take into account I've never stopped practicing, I am sure you will, by necessity, come to the correct conclusion that I am more than qualified."

"So you're a genius," I reply, not sure I believe him.

"I prefer the word 'visionary,' but yes, I am a genius." His smile broadens into a grin that threatens to grow wider than his ghostly face will allow. The effect is disconcerting, like watching clouds drift in different directions.

Hannah coughs politely. "Your face," she reminds him.

"My face? Oh, yes. Pardon me." The ghostly features of Herophilos become pure roiling mist, then reform minus the smile. "Better?" he asks.

"Much," Hannah says.

"Excellent. As I was saying, Andrus, the mind goes where the body cannot. We never stop learning... even in death. I know you must think me pompous, but trust me: Modesty is for the living; the dead have no time for it. In death, our achievements are all we have."

I look at Mark, then the ghost. "You really think you can fix him?"

Herophilos nods. "It is a simple matter of psychic surgery. I will go inside the patient's head to ease the swelling... with your permission, of course."

"Fine," I say. "If you're sure."

Once more, the ghost loses its sharp features. It becomes a gray funnel, whirling its way into Mark's skull through his mouth, nose, and ears. I can see it moving under the skin, Mark's face stretching and shrinking as the ghost goes about its strange business.

"So," I ask, "as Hades's daughter, you get to hang with a lot of ghosts?"

"Some. Imagine having access to train with the best minds, the brightest talents the centuries have to offer. As a Demigod, I was born with certain powers, and Hades gave me magic items, but those weren't the greatest gift he gave me—it was the ghosts."

"I get it; the ghosts meant you were never alone. It must be nice, always knowing who you are, what you have to do. All I have is money, but you—you have ghosts and Gods!"

"*A God,*" Hannah says. "And in the past tense, at least until we rescue him."

"But you still had advantages I can only dream of."

"Yes, but it's not as amazing as it sounds. Hades is... well, you'll know when you meet him."

"I'm sorry. I don't want to be jealous. Maybe if you told me what I am, I might not be."

"Andrus, I want to, believe me..." Hannah chews her lower lip, and I can tell she's wrestling with the idea, but Shadow croaks a warning and she grows cold and distant again. "I'll tell you, Andrus. I promise. Monday, after your competition."

I take a step forward. "Tell me now, Hannah. Please! How am I supposed to go on not knowing? How am I supposed to—"

Mark's entire body jerks, muscles spasming. Froth appears on his lips.

I kneel next to Mark and restrain him, try to keep him from hurting himself. "What's going on?" I demand. "What is that crazy ghost doing to him?"

"It's nothing," Hannah says. "I've seen this before. He zigged when he should have zagged. Herophilos will fix it. He always does."

I wait, holding Mark until the tremors pass. His head tilts to one side, mouth gaping open as the ghost pours out in a wet, hissing mist then fades away.

"Is that it?" I ask. "Where's Herophilos going?"

"He only has enough energy to materialize for so long," Hannah says. "Healing Mark used it all up. Give it a minute. You'll see."

"You better be right."

"I am. Oh, and don't bother going back the way you came; that priest is resealing it. Use the tunnel I came from instead, then come back to this cave Monday after your rematch—or sooner, if anything goes wrong. I'll be waiting."

"And then you'll tell me what I am?"

"Among other things." Hannah looks down at Mark, then back at me. "I wish we had more time to talk, but I have to go. Your friend will be waking up soon. Don't tell him about me." She turns into a gray cloud and floats up and away, leaving the smell of death in her wake.

I'm glad she doesn't smell like that when she's in human form. Actually, now that I think about it, she smelled pretty good. Not like flowers or perfume, not like any girl I've ever known before. But like what exactly?

Magic.

Hannah smells like how I feel when I do my magic. I don't know how else to explain it. I know it doesn't make a lot of sense. How can feelings have a smell?

Almost as if the raven can read my mind, Shadow flaps his wings and scolds me, then disappears in a puff of smoke.

Mark groans. His eyes open, but they're rolled up inside his head with only the whites showing. It takes about thirty seconds for the pupils to come down, then another half-minute to focus. His mouth works, jaw clicking from side to side to form one slow, painful word: *"Ouch."*

"Mark! You OK? Hey, don't get up too fast."

"I'm fine," Mark insists. "Bit of a headache, that's all. What happened?"

"Not much... You thought you saw a monster, panicked, and fell. Lucky for me you landed on your head."

"The toughest part of me," Mark jokes, but his laughter turns into a cough. "Gah! Got an awful taste in my mouth..." He spits. "So we're safe? No monsters?"

"No monsters," I reassure him, but in my head, I'm thinking just Demigods, ghosts, and magic birds. "So you feel good enough to climb? We can rest if you want."

"Nah, I feel all right." He looks a little dizzy for a moment, then reaches out a hand to steady himself against the chasm wall. "OK, maybe not. Gimme five minutes. *Then* we scale that mother."

I slap him on the back. "Let's make it ten. I'm a little tired myself."

After the rest, we scale the wall. To my relief, Mark doesn't have many problems. I'm impressed with his progress—and his recovery.

Whatever Herophilos did, Mark sure isn't acting like a guy with a head injury.

When we get to the top, we high five and whoop it up. I tell him I've got a good feeling about the tunnel in front of us, explaining that the priest would have sealed up the way we came in by now.

We follow the tunnel to a dead end, only it isn't that dead. It's sealed, but not all the way. One of the stones is cracked, breaking the warding symbol, and some of the stones are loose enough we can pull them out. It's not fast or easy, but twenty minutes later, we're back in Bronson Canyon. The sun is low on the horizon. We have just enough time to catch the last shuttle back to Griffith Park. My dad's limo is waiting.

"Thanks," Mark says. "That was quite an adventure."

"No problem. Half a hero, remember?"

"Yeah. Maybe I'll upgrade to a full one Monday."

On the ride to his house, Mark looks like he wants to ask me something—maybe a million somethings—but I'm glad he doesn't. They must be the kind of questions he doesn't want to ask in front of the limo driver. Instead, all we do is make plans to meet up at the Temple tomorrow after Sunday services. Maybe we'll go back to the cave to practice, maybe we won't.

We drop him off at his house, and I see Lucy wave to me from the window. I wave back on instinct.

21

ISN'T IT PERFECT?

HOME FEELS DIFFERENT. Or maybe it's exactly the same and I'm the one that's different. James is there to greet me, asking about my day, and I tell him everything's fine because what else can I tell him?

James says, "Your parents were worried when they got the message you'd be at the park instead of the gym."

"I figured as much. I knew they wouldn't like it, but I didn't have a choice. I explained all that in the message."

James nods. "Your parents appreciated that. Your message was rather more detailed than usual."

"Yeah, with everything that's happened, I didn't want Mom and Dad to freak out... well, no more than usual."

James allows himself the tiniest of smiles. "Very good, sir. I'll let them know you've arrived safely. That is..."

"What?" I stare at him.

"There wasn't any more trouble, was there?"

"No, James. No trouble."

"And the raven you were worried about?"

I force a laugh. "Just nerves. Forget about it."

James sighs in relief. "I'm relieved to hear it. Perhaps you'd care to rest before dinner?"

"Thanks, I'll do that." I head upstairs to my room and shut the door. I wish I could have confided in James, but these new secrets I have, they aren't teenage mischief. They're big and terrible and totally illegal.

I take the rock from my pocket and put it in my collection. I run my hands over the different stones and crystals. I close my eyes and feel them, not as separate objects, but as part of a larger whole. Part of me. There's a sense of peace, a low-pitched, tingly hum that spreads over my body.

What am I?

I open my eyes and see my collection circling around me. It's beautiful, like looking at Lucy, like riding earthquakes, like bathing in hot, bubbling lava... Suddenly I can see myself in the center of the earth, rising from the magma, carried by gentle hands. Warm, nurturing hands. Where are they taking me? Everything becomes dark, cold. A giant eye opens, glowing red, and I want to scream, want to wake up. I must wake up!

I'm back in my room. The rock collection drops the floor. Some of the crystals shatter. I curse, kneel down, and pick up the shards. They're sharp. That gives me an idea.

I take the largest shards to my desk, pull out my rockhounding tools, and begin shaping them: smoothing the sides, sharpening the tips. When James calls me to dinner, I have three long, thin, crystal daggers. White, like icicles, only these won't melt. If I run into danger again, I'll be ready.

I TELL MY PARENTS the safe, boring version of my day: Mark and I went to Bronson Canyon but never inside the caves. We climbed the outside. Mom and Dad don't know the outsides are crumbling and unsuitable, so they swallow the story.

"We have some news," Mom says, giving Dad a meaningful look.

He takes a sip of wine before elaborating. "After I received your note, I had a long talk with Mr. Harryhausen, the owner of the gym. I explained to him what a mistake he was making closing his facility to our son."

"Get to the good part," Mom says.

"You got him to change his mind? So Mark and I can train there tomorrow?"

"Better," Dad gloats. "I convinced him to sell me the gym. Blake's rental for tomorrow has been canceled and refunded."

"It's all yours," Mom says. "Isn't it perfect, Andrus?"

"It is. Thank you! But I never expected..."

Dad flashes one of his rare smiles. "Nonsense. It was the least we could do." He raises his glass and Mom and I join him in the toast. "To our family," Dad says, "and to our son, who will bring us honor and glory."

"Honor and glory!" Mom and I echo.

I don't get why they're being so nice. Normally, I work hard and stay out of trouble—well, serious trouble—and they act like I can't do anything right. Now, today, after screwing up in the worst way possible and bringing the Inquisition down on our heads, they're acting like I can do no wrong. I notice they both seem to be drinking more than usual and wonder if that's it. Maybe they're drunk out of relief things aren't worse. Or maybe it's because they're hiding something...

The problem is, I've never been very good at talking to my parents, so I don't know how to find out which it is, or if it's something I haven't even thought of. What if they're being nice because things are getting so messed up they might never get another chance? Didn't I already see some cracks in their armor earlier today? That weird look that passed between them when I asked if humans could be magic... They said no. But Hannah is half-human, half-God. So what does that make me?

After dinner, I excuse myself and go to my room. All that small talk with my parents has made me tired. I put my rock collection back in order, then hide the crystal daggers under my pillow. Just in case.

I drift into a deep but troubled sleep. I'm climbing Mount

Olympus again— climbing up, out of the earth. Lightning crashes. Thunder booms. Cold wind burns my face.

I am the mountain.

I am one with it.

I am one with the earth.

My fingers dig into stone. I climb, and with each passing second, the mountain becomes more me, and I, it. I can feel the stone in me. It's mine. Stone like flesh, stone like blood. Above me, Zeus is waiting. Below me, Darkness—the darkness of the ages, endless centuries spent locked in tragic Nothing.

This mountain is mine. This world is mine!

Below me, red light flares. A giant eye is opening.

My eyes are opening...

I wake in a blinding sweat. Hot. Baking. I sit up, throwing off the sheet, letting cool night air bathe me. I swing my legs over the bed and sit there a moment, trying to hold onto the dream, to the sense of power I felt.

It's gone.

I switch on the lamp and that's when I notice the blood.

PART II

THE RIVER OF HATE AND PROMISES

22

THE UNBLINKING EYE

RED STAIN. White sheets.

I stare at the bloody smear in disbelief. It starts under my pillow, then stretches down to where my right hand is. My hand is covered in blood, but it's dry, clotted, crusty. It has to be my new daggers; I must have cut myself on them while I was sleeping.

I flip back the pillow.

The daggers are gone.

Which makes no sense. Neither does the fact that despite all the blood, I can't find a wound. Not a cut, not a slice. Not even a scrape. My hand throbs a little when I make a fist, but that's it.

My window is shut and locked, so nothing could have come in from outside except maybe a ghost, and ghosts don't bleed.

I tear my bed apart, searching under and around, but the daggers aren't there. I make another fist. I get a mental flash of the red eye, or maybe it's just fire. I tighten my fist, holding it with my other hand. The throbbing intensifies, then recedes. A moment later, it's gone. More than that, I feel great. *Powerful.* I'm almost manic with it. Like I want to break things.

Smashing up my room in the middle of the night seems like a bad idea, but I have to do something to work off this nameless energy that's coursing through me. First, I hide my bloodstained sheets and pillow, then I throw on sweatpants and head downstairs to our home gym. I workout for an hour, and what's weird is, I'm lifting and benching way more than normal. I keep adding weight, but don't have a spotter, so I stop when I hit double my usual amount. It feels incredible, and I barely break a sweat.

After that, I manage to get a few hours' sleep, then am woken by the two male slaves who attend me in the morning. They dress and groom me, and I put up with it as usual. I'd much rather do it myself, but the few times I've tried in the past never met with my parents' approval. Worse, I got the slaves in trouble. So I sigh, and let one oil and shape my hair while the other drapes my whitest tunic just so, then straps golden sandals to my feet. Today is Sunday, the day we go to Temple, so I'm expected to look my best. I wonder if Inquisitor Anton will be there, but already know the answer. Of course he will.

"Master Andrus," one of the slaves asks, "what happened to your sheets and pillow?"

"Um, I spilled some wine on them and threw them out. I need you to tell the maids to bring new ones."

The two slaves look at each other, then me.

I see the questions forming in their minds, but the words never reach their lips. Slaves can think whatever they want, but they can't say it. Not without consequences.

"Don't get in trouble with James or my parents on my account," I tell them. "If it's a problem, blame me."

I know they won't, of course. And maybe thats part of the problem. It's their job to make me look perfect, but it's an unwinnable task. A whole legion of slaves couldn't even pull that off. And yet the charade goes on.

I leave the slaves to join my parents downstairs for breakfast. There's the usual small talk, asking if I slept all right, what lovely weather we're having, that sort of thing, but no one says what we're really thinking: that we wish we didn't have to go to Temple today. It's going to be awkward, but I don't need my parents to explain how much more awkward it will get if we don't go. The Inquisition would love to use that against us in their investigation.

Sometimes, you have to do the thing you hate because not doing it is worse.

———————

THE TEMPLE OF THE UNBLINKING EYE is a huge white building in downtown Othrys. The heart of our city. It rises up in the ancient Greek style, supported by ornate columns. But it's not just a place of worship. The Temple is a sprawling administrative complex, home to the high priest, Archieréas Vola, and his officials, the Great Library, and the training college for priests. The Inquisition is based here, as is the Night Patrol. Some say the Titans themselves live behind these walls, and maybe they do from time to time, but there is also a portal to their world and to Tartarus.

We file up the broad stone steps with the rest of the worshippers. The wealthy and elite stride through the golden front, the Losers and less fortunate are funneled to the less impressive side entrance. Normally, the classes have as little to do with each other as possible, but today, as every Sunday, all must bow before the might of the Titans.

My parents and I make our way to our seats near the dais where the High Priest speaks from his golden *bema*, which is Greek for pulpit. In ancient Greece, as now, the bema is not just a place for giving religious sermons, but also for passing judgment.

Dad once told me that before the NGT, the authority of church and state were separate. Growing up in a theocracy, that concept is confusing. I guess it must have worked something like how the Day Patrol and Night Patrol are different, but the same.

I never much cared for history, and that's just as well because taking an interest in the past is discouraged. Only that's not entirely true, since the priests talk about the past all the time, but only about the glorious birth of the Titans, their original rule, and return. Everything else is painted in negative terms if it is discussed at all. So it's not that all interest in history is discouraged, only the *wrong* interest.

I crane my neck up to look at the balcony above and behind us where the Losers are forced to sit. I've heard these seats referred to as the "nosebleed section" since they are so high up. I strain my eyes, hoping to pick Mark and Lucy out of the crowd, but it's impossible.

"Looking for someone?" Anton asks. The inquisitor is standing in the aisle next to me. One hand rests on the hilt of his gold mace.

"No," I answer quickly. "Just people watching."

Anton smirks. "An admirable skill, but one best reserved for an inquisitor—at least I get paid for it." His thin attempt at humor can't cover the menace behind his words.

The skin of my right hand itches. I scratch it, shifting uncomfortably in my seat. In the most respectful tone I can muster, I say, "That's great. What do you want?"

"Oh, I want many things," Anton replies, "those wants that can be met by religion shall be met here today, by the grace of our great and terrible lord! As for my other wants... well, I hope to meet them soon, Andrus. Very soon." The inquisitor gives my parents a mocking bow. "Mr. Eaves, Mrs. Eaves, please enjoy the sermon. I'm sure you will find it... inspiring." Anton moves away, giving us one long, last look before disappearing behind a rich blue curtain to the left of the bema.

My parents look like they want to say something, but they know better than to do it in Temple, where the wrong word can go in the right ear faster than anywhere in Othrys.

It isn't long before the Archieréas appears; his name is Enoch Vola, and he is the high priest of the Temple. He is also Cronus's Chosen, chief theocrat and administrator of the New Greece Theocracy. Unless directly contradicted by a Titan, his word is law. And the Titans don't trouble themselves with the day to day administration of their earthly realm. They leave that to the priests, and I imagine that's the way they like it. Archieréas Vola most of all.

A hush falls over the assembled worshippers as the Archieréas takes the bema. Enoch Vola is an elderly, craggy-faced man with a long white beard, two sides split in braids, the center shot through with a long strip of black. His bushy eyebrows are waxed to points, as is his mustache. He wears regal robes of azure blue trimmed with gold, and a twelve-horned crown with a central ruby eye. The twelve horns represent the original twelve Titans. The ruby represents the Unblinking Eye of Cronus.

When Archieréas Vola speaks, his voice is tinged with power. "Brothers! Sisters! We come together this day under the banner of our most holy king and savior, Cronus!"

The crowd stands, echoing the name, then kneels on the hard stone floor, where we must remain for the duration of the sermon. Anyone who fails to kneel to the end will be declared a blasphemer and dragged away by armed guards that prowl through the crowd.

"We all know the story of the Titans, firstborn children of Earth and Sky, who once ruled and now rule again! But did you know their story is the story of man? And not just mankind, but each and every one of us? In the years before the Gods, man was happy under the rule of the Titans. Then the Gods came, imprisoned the Titans, and enslaved mankind, robbing us of our true potential, our true destiny as the servants of Cronus! And the world wept tears of blood, and the stars looked down with sadness, until the combined weight of their despair released the Titans from Tartarus and swept the cruel Gods away. And more than that, they swept the old world away! Now there are no more countries at each other's throats, no threat of guns or nuclear weapons. We have peace," Vola says reverently. "We have order."

The crowd murmurs in assent.

Vola raises his hands over his head. "The NGT is all there is! The NGT is all we need! In it, we are bonded together, bonded by one common heritage, one common language. We are lifted up from doubt and made certain of our lives. There is no other way to think, to be, and we need do nothing but that which we were created for: to serve the Titans with honor and glory. All praise Cronus! All praise His Watchful Eye!"

The crowd repeats Vola's last two lines: "ALL PRAISE CRONUS! ALL PRAISE HIS WATCHFUL EYE!"

Vola smiles beneath his beard, his piercing blue eyes bright with faith. "Yes, we are truly blessed! Death is gone! Doubt is gone! We are people without fear! There are no hostile foreign powers, no more Gods in the sky. Our borders are secure because our enemies are defeated. So shall it be, now and forever!"

In a throaty yell, the crowd repeats, "NOW AND FOREVER!"

There's a scream of protest from the balcony as two warriors grab an old man who must have come out of the kneeling position. The old Loser is frail, matchstick thin, but in his panic he manages to get away from the warriors, only to be grabbed up by the crowd and pitched over the railing to the aisle below. He falls with a shrill, hopeless cry, and the sound of his legs breaking against the marble floor echo through the Temple. But of course he doesn't die. He can't.

Another pair of warriors approach and grab the Loser by his broken legs. They drag him down the aisle toward one of the side doors, but the Archieréas has a better idea. "Wait!" Vola calls to the warriors, and they immediately stop and turn to face the high priest. "Bring the vile blasphemer to me!"

They drag the old man toward the bema.

"Lift him up!" Vola commands. "Lift him high, so the faithful may look upon this loathsome wretch, this baseborn scum that dares to stand against our lord's truth!"

The warriors hold the man up by his arms as he screams and babbles for mercy. Sensing a spectacle, the mood of the crowd changes, becoming louder, wilder. They know what's coming and they love it.

"Humans," Vola addresses the crowd, "were meant to worship on our knees! So said Cronus, when he chose to spare us after the Gods War. Even after millennia serving false Gods, false prophets, and our own pitiful egos, Cronus saw fit to show us mercy! And all he asks in return is one day a week in his Temple, a few moments on our knees, so that we might honor him and remember our place. Is that too much to ask?"

"NO!" the crowd roars.

Vola nods. "It is not our place to question the will of Cronus. To show mercy is to show weakness. Perhaps this scum is a true blasphemer with hate in his heart, or perhaps his body betrayed him. But I say to you, it does not matter! For is not the body the temple of the soul? If a soul is pious and true to the Titans, it will prevent the body from moving in disobedience. But if a soul is poisoned by thoughts of blasphemy, it will cause the body to move, to act out and against our great and terrible lord! So I say unto you, whether this man knew it or not, he was corrupt! It is only by the grace of Cronus that he revealed his lack of faith before us today. And what about you?" he asks us all. "Are your souls pure in their devotion? Do you believe in the power of Cronus?"

Without hesitation, the crowd shouts, "WE BELIEVE!"

Vola points at the broken man. "And what happens to blasphemers?"

"PUNISHMENT!"

"That's right," Vola says. "Punishment! And what is the punishment for those who refuse to kneel before our lord?"

"THE WORM!"

An unseen operator lowers a long chain with a meathook from the Temple ceiling. It is one of twelve such chains, each ending in a hook, each operated by a pulley system.

Almost as if on cue, Anton appears from behind the curtain he exited through earlier. The inquisitor bows to Vola, but he's looking at me. Smiling. He produces a gold-plated hacksaw from beneath his robe and holds it up to the crowd.

"Behold!" Vola shouts. "The Worm-Maker! A blade blessed by Cronus himself."

Anton walks from one end of the bema to the other, letting the crowd get a good look at the gleaming tool.

The prisoner screams and struggles, but is held fast in the

warrior's grip. Anton approaches the front row, showing the hacksaw, inviting them to touch it. He stops in front of me.

Waiting.

I reach out and touch it, expecting that will be enough. But it's not. "Your lips or your legs," he sneers.

I hesitate, looking from Anton to my parents. My parents plead with me to kiss it, so I do. Anton grins in triumph. "Another day, then." He steps back and holds up the Worm-Maker to the crowd once more.

They yell, "WORM! WORM! WORM!" I mouth the words as I've mouthed so many others, and wish for this day to be over.

Vola announces, "Let the punishment begin!"

One of the warriors grabs the meathook on the chain and jams it into the prisoner's back. The chain is raised, hauling the thrashing man off the floor. When his knees are level with the warrior's chests, the chain stops. The warriors each grab hold of one of the man's legs, preventing him from swaying or fighting back.

Anton looks to Vola, who nods grimly. The inquisitor saws off the man's left leg, just under the knee. Blood sprays everywhere. Anton holds up the severed leg, then tosses it into the crowd. He saws off the other leg.

I can hear the flesh tear, the bones snap, and smell the sharp tang of copper as the blood flows.

Anton holds up the second severed leg, then throws it directly at me. Hoping I'll move. Hoping I'll come off my knees and be revealed as a blasphemer so he can make a worm of me too.

The bloody limb bounces off my chest. I flinch, but don't dare move my body out of position. The leg hits the floor, still gushing blood. Soaking me.

Anton laughs, then motions to the warriors to let the prisoner down.

Arms lifted high, Vola sways back and forth in some kind of trance, a look of ecstasy on his bearded face.

Anton kicks the prisoner, forcing him onto his belly. The hook is still in his back, but now he has the slack to move.

The crowd is relentless: "WORM! WORM! WORM!"

"Crawl, worm!" Anton tells the prisoner. "Crawl before your betters! If you can make one complete pass around the Temple and get back to me in twelve minutes, you will be spared the rest."

The dismembered man crawls, trailing blood from his stumps. He has twelve minutes, one for each of the twelve Titans he has blasphemed against. The warriors follow him, one kicking him to motivate him to go in the right direction, the other ensuring the chain doesn't get stuck or tangled in the crowd.

"WORM! WORM! WORM!"

In all my years, I've only seen one man succeed. He was a big man, a well-muscled athlete. His reward was getting his brains bashed in and forced to crawl forever as a zombie. As for those who didn't make it...

"Time's up!" Anton says.

Vola snaps out of his trance. "You've all seen it! The blasphemer fails to repent! He is not even fit to be a worm; there is no place left for him in our world, so we must show him into another."

Two things happen: The hook is hoisted up, dragging the legless man over the crowd. Blood falls like rain as he is relentlessly maneuvered toward the bema. At the same time, the bema begins to slide back into the wall, revealing a giant circular pit. It's slow enough that Vola, Anton, and the warriors have plenty of time to ceremoniously step off and away from the bema, taking up positions in the aisle next to us.

Vola says, "Let this miserable worm feed Cronus's hunger! Let him suffer untold centuries of torment digesting in our lord's stomach like the traitor Gods and blasphemers before him! So say we all. So says our lord, Cronus!"

The pit is pitch black at first. Gradually, there is a dull orange glow that turns to fiery yellow. The prisoner on the chain dangles over the pit. Screaming. Crying. The chain lowers, sending him down, down into impossible hunger. Into eternal agony and beyond.

"Take this offering!" Vola shouts. "Take it, King Cronus, so your

Unblinking Eye may see us and separate the faithful from the unworthy!"

"SEE US!" the crowd chants. "SEE THE FAITHFUL!"

There is a long, wailing scream from the pit, then nothing. The crowd falls silent. The chain comes up, still smoking. The hook is scorched black.

The worm is gone.

23

SOME STAINS

AFTER WE FINISH SINGING our praises to Cronus, the sermon ends. We're given an opportunity to clean up in the Temple bathrooms which have long washing troughs opposite the urinals just for this purpose. I scrub my tunic as best I can, but can't get the blood out. I know it's the least of my problems, but it's the one I can do something about.

"You'll do better with soap." A nondescript middle-aged man hands me a fresh bar. "Quite a sermon," he says.

I don't reply.

"I always feel so alive afterward," the man continues. "So *blessed*. Don't you?"

I look up from soaping my tunic. "Yeah," I say, because to say anything different would be blasphemy.

The man has dull brown hair and dead brown eyes. Not thin, not fat. In fact, he's the most boring, average man I've ever seen, but there's something I hate about him. Maybe that he's OK with what just happened. Or maybe what I hate isn't him so much as it is what he represents. It's like he's asleep, and I've just woken up.

People empty out of the bathroom until it's only me and the Soap

Man. "A little soap fixes everything," he says. "You just wash your problems away."

I can feel his eyes on me as I continue to scrub. The soap helps, but only at turning my tunic pink. I scrub harder. "The stain's not coming out."

"Some stains never do," the man says. "Others... well, others can be gone just like that—if you know where to scrub." He walks to the bathroom door, and I think he's going to leave, but he doesn't. He locks the door instead. "They're testing you, you know," the man says, confident we won't be interrupted. "The Inquisition. They tested me once. You know how I beat it?"

I eye him warily. "No."

"I redoubled my faith. They don't turn the faithful into worms. Not if you believe hard enough and loud enough."

"Thanks, I'll remember that. Um, you can go now."

"You know," he continues, "this test could actually be an opportunity. For you, I mean."

"Oh? How's that?"

"There's always a way... The Inquisition hunts traitors and blasphemers. That's their job, right?"

"Right." "So give them a target! Take the Eye off you and put it on someone else. That's what I did, and life's been sweet ever since."

"Hold on. I thought you said you did it by redoubling your faith?"

"Exactly!" he says. "That's how I redoubled it. Look, once the Eye is on you, you gotta pass it on to make it go away. I gave it to my parents. It wasn't my fault I'd been led astray. *It was theirs.* They told me things against the priesthood, against the NGT. Hell, even against the Titans themselves. They were false things. Nasty things that got me in trouble when I repeated them. Did your parents ever tell you anything like that?"

"No."

He shrugs, then gives me a sly wink. "Doesn't matter. You could always say they did. The Inquisition takes the side of the accuser, not the accused. That's why it's important to accuse others before they accuse you."

When I don't respond, the Soap Man explains, "My parents weren't good people. They were hard. Cold. They never loved me, never brought me anything but pain. You know what the best part of turning them in was? Not the worm part, but afterward?"

I grit my teeth. "No."

"The Inquisition let me keep the house and my parents' business! You're Andrus Eaves, right? I'm just saying, you could be the new head of Eaves Oil, starting tomorrow. All it takes is you pointing a finger in the right direction and..." He makes a slit throat gesture and winks. "Goodbye parents, hello fortune!"

I want to hurt this man, but that won't solve anything. He's probably working for Anton. The Inquisition use plain clothes spies to root out enemies all the time. So instead I say, "Thanks for the advice. I'll keep it in mind."

"Great, then we're done here." He unlocks the door, opens it, and gives me another sly wink. "Can I give you another piece of advice?"

"Sure."

"Don't drop the soap." He laughs at his joke, but never takes his eyes off me as I brush past him. I slam the bar of soap into his chest with my left hand because my right's itching to lash out, to punch him right in the guts, to kill that laugh as dead as I can make anything in this messed-up world.

I get nervous when I notice the man follow me out of the bathroom into the Temple, but then he loses himself in the crowd.

I meet up with Mom and Dad and tell them I'm going to find Mark. "You'll need these," Dad says. He hands me a set of keys. "For your new gym," he adds.

I hug him, then Mom, and say my goodbyes. Outside the Temple, I see Mark sitting on the steps with his sister, Lucy. He's got his nose buried in that climbing book I loaned him.

Lucy stands, quickly running her hands along her dress to smooth out the wrinkles. "Andrus! Hi." A blush appears on her cheeks. "We were waiting for you."

"Sorry, I had to clean up a little."

"Oh," she gasps. "Right! Of course. I'm so sorry." She hugs me tight. "Are you OK?"

"Yeah, I guess. It was nothing we haven't seen before."

"That's true, only to be so close to it! It must have been so..." She lets the sentence trail off, gives me another squeeze, then steps back with a coy look. "Well, enough about that. Why didn't you stop in the house yesterday?"

Before I can answer, Mark coughs to interrupt us. "Lucy wants to watch us practice," he says. "She won't take no for an answer."

Lucy puts her hands on her hips. "So? Can you blame me? It's not like I don't have a stake in how your training turns out. Somebody's got to make sure you two are ready for Monday."

She's right, and despite my promise to Mark, part of me is glad Lucy's coming. That's the part that worries me.

24

FEMALE DIPLOMACY

WHEN WE GET to the Harryhausen gym, there's a CLOSED sign on the door. A sign in the window says, UNDER NEW MANAGEMENT. Blake and Brenda are standing around outside. They look clueless. Blake has a split lip from where I punched him yesterday.

"Hey Blake," I say. "What's the problem? Didn't you rent the place again?"

"I did," Blake growls back. "Only the jerk refunded my money. Says he sold the place, and if I wanna rent it again, I gotta talk to the new owner. Only he ain't here."

"You and Brenda planning to wait around all day?" I ask.

"Yeah," Blake says, "and don't get any funny ideas about cutting in front of us. We were here first. Made an appointment and everything."

I pull out the set of keys Dad gave me, give them a spiteful twirl, then unlock the front door. I usher Mark and Lucy in, then block Blake and Brenda.

"Hey! What gives?" Blake demands. "Where'd you get those keys?"

"Yeah," Brenda echoes. "What are you, like, the new owner or something?"

"Exactly," I say. "Consider this your appointment. The gym's all booked up. Private party."

Brenda looks stunned, almost like she might cry, and Blake takes a menacing step forward. "So keep your damn gym! I still owe you a punch in the face."

My right hand curls into a fist. "Bring it," I snarl.

"Andrus, wait!" Mark says. "You don't need to fight him. He's trespassing and threatening assault. Let's just call for the Day Patrol. They'll arrest him, and then we can get on with our training."

Blake puffs out his chest. "Call them, coward! You and your pink tunic will have to get by me first."

Brenda tugs at his arm. "Blake, maybe we should go. This isn't worth it. If we're in jail, how are we supposed to train?"

Blake scowls. "Our parents are rich! They'll bail us out in no time. Besides, I can't wait to teach this punk a lesson..."

"You're all being stupid," Lucy says. She pulls me out of the doorway. "I get that you don't want to help them, but don't you think letting them practice can help you?"

"I'd rather kick his ass," I grumble.

"You and what army?" Blake snaps. "Who do you think you are, Hercules?"

"Enough!" Lucy shouts. "If you boys would just chill on the testosterone, I'm trying to give us all a win/win."

"We're listening," Brenda says.

"Fine," Blake agrees. "But only for a minute, then I'm gonna stomp this fool so bad he'll look like a centaur tap-danced on his head."

Lucy steps between us. "Look, both teams need to practice, so competing against each other here will be more effective than training separately. If Andrus and Mark train here, and Blake and Brenda somewhere else, you won't know what you're up against Monday. You really want to have that kind of surprise when the stakes are this high?"

There are more nods and murmurs of agreement.

"I never would have believed it," Blake says, "but your Loser girl-friend makes sense."

"She's not my girlfriend," I say, then look at Lucy, part of me wishing she was. "OK, let's set some ground rules. If I let you two in to train with us, you gotta behave. No wrecking things or fooling around. And if you piss me off, you leave when I say so. Deal?"

"Deal," Brenda says.

"Not good enough. I wanna hear it from Blake."

"Deal," he says, then surprises me by sticking out his hand. I shake it reluctantly, feeling the hate in his grip. "I'm still gonna kick your ass," he promises, then grins and lets go. "On the wall, I mean."

I go to lock the door, but there's a man standing in the way. "Got room for one more?" he asks.

25

UP TO SOMETHING

"MR. CROSS!" I back up to let our gym teacher in. "What are you doing here?"

"I came to warn you the rematch has drawn the attention of the Temple. There will be a priest, a representative from Archieréas Vola there. The principal tells me he's a kind of talent scout."

"Is his name Anton?" I ask.

"The principal didn't say. He just made it clear that both teams were going to be brought to the Temple: the winners to receive some special reward, the losers... well, I can't imagine it will be good. I'm sorry."

"Why is the Temple so concerned with a high school gym contest?" Lucy asks.

"Sometimes, they just are," Mr. Cross says. "But there could be another reason. Have any of you been up to something? Something that would draw the attention of the Temple?"

Mark and I exchange glances. "No," I say before the silence grows too long. "But maybe Blake has."

Blake sneers. "Up yours, weirdo! Do I look like the kind of guy that would get in trouble with the Temple?"

I open my mouth to answer, then think better of it. "It doesn't matter who brought the heat down. What matters is we can't mess around. We need to train hard. Now."

"I'd like to watch." Mr. Cross says, and no one argues with him. He takes a seat near the rock climbing wall. He pulls out a metal flask and holds it to his lips. Lucy sits next to him, white-faced. He offers her the flask and she takes a long gulp from it. I can't help but wonder what's wrong. She was so strong a few minutes ago. She made this all happen, now she's a nervous wreck.

"How's your head?" I ask Mark when we go to get the climbing gear. "No dizziness or anything?"

"I'm OK," he says. "I mean, maybe not a hundred, but ninety, ninety-five percent. I can do this. It's not like I have a choice."

"Yeah," I say. I take the opportunity to change out of my blood-stained clothes into a clean workout tunic. "Hey, what's up with your sister?"

Mark sighs. "I don't know. She gets like that sometimes. Fierce one minute, frail the next. It's probably a girl thing. I wouldn't worry about it. What about you?"

"What do you mean?"

"I saw what happened to you at the Temple. The worm... That must have been hard to—"

"Scrub out?" I grab a handful of my stained tunic for emphasis.

"No, I meant to process."

"I'm fine."

"Sure," Mark says. "I'm just saying that, well, if you need to talk or—"

"I said I'm fine." My words come out harsher than I intend, but there's no other way I can say them.

Mark doesn't take the hint. "If—I mean when I become a priest, I want you to know I wouldn't be like that. I'd work in the records or administrative division, someplace non-violent."

"Don't," I say. "Don't talk to me about the Temple or being a priest right now. I can't, OK? I just can't. Besides, I know you're not like that."

Mark nods.

We gather up enough climbing gear for both teams, then head back to hand it out. We hook ourselves together into two teams. I get a brief flashback of the hook going into the old man, swinging him up, over the pit, then that long, final scream.

26

ANYTHING YOU WANT

AFTER TRAINING ENDS and Blake and Brenda are gone, I thank Lucy for letting the rival team practice with us. "It really helped having them here," I tell her. "I mean, it probably helped them too, but now we have a much better feel for what tomorrow will be like."

Lucy nods. "I know you wanted to throw Blake out, and I don't blame you, but what's one brief moment of satisfaction worth versus long-term gain?"

"It might not be that long-term," Mark says. "Those guys were good. They beat us to the top as many times as we beat them."

"And now you know you need to be better," Lucy says. "What's more you know *how* to do it. You know how the other team moves, how they work together, some of the tricks they'll try to pull."

"What do you think, Mr. Cross?" Mark asks. "You think Andrus and I can beat them?"

Our teacher takes another sip from his flask. "From what I saw here today, I think you've got a chance. Andrus and Blake are my top students, Mark, but you've really improved."

"I had a good teacher," Mark says, then grins sheepishly. "Um, I mean you too, Mr. Cross."

Our teacher laughs. "This isn't the Academy; you can speak freely. Of course, a little more respect wouldn't hurt."

"Sorry, sir. I didn't mean that in a bad way, but—"

"You think I'm a hard-ass?"

Mark squirms. "Well..."

"It's OK," Mr. Cross says. "A lot of kids feel that way. And if I was teaching you skills you'd never need, you'd be right."

"Begging your pardon, sir," Mark asks, "but if you hadn't put me in this rematch, I don't think I would have needed to learn how to scale a wall."

"Maybe, but it's not muscles or climbing skill you needed, Mark. *It's courage.* Confidence. I didn't put you in this contest to punish you. I put you in because I see your true potential. It was the fastest way I knew how to help you grow into a—"

"Hero?" Mark suggests.

"*Man,*" Mr. Cross says. "But hero works. Is that how you see yourself?"

"No, but I'm getting there. At least I think I am."

"Know how to tell when you become one?"

"Not really."

"When you survive tomorrow."

Mark pales, but I don't think Mr. Cross meant it in a threatening way, more like an inspiring one, so I jump into the conversation. "You think we will? You think what you saw today was enough?"

"Maybe," Mr. Cross says. "There's one thing I know, and that's even with your skills, you won't win just by relying on each other. Teamwork's important, but there's one thing you can't train for..." He suddenly throws his flask at Mark's chest as hard as he can.

I don't know how, but my right hand reaches out and catches it. "Expect the unexpected?" I answer, then hand the flask back to him.

"Exactly," Mr. Cross says. "Good, Andrus. Those are some... unusual reflexes you have there." He's smiling, but I sense something besides amusement in him. Something I can't quite place. It's not the cold, creepy feeling I got from Anton, but it feels like Mr. Cross is testing me in the same kind of way.

"Thanks. I've been practicing."

"I can see that," Mr. Cross says. He holds my gaze a moment longer, then drains his flask. "Well, I should be going. All of you remember what I said: *Expect the unexpected.*"

I escort him to the front door and unlock it. Mr. Cross opens it, then pauses in the doorway. The late afternoon sun makes a golden halo around him. He places a friendly hand on my shoulder; as he does, the sun seems hotter, brighter, and his outline shimmers in the heat. He leans in, his words low and urgent: "Good luck. If there's anything you want, anything you might regret not doing, don't put it off."

"Why? Because you think we're going to lose?"

"No," Mr. Cross says. "Because I think you're going to win. But either way, your life's about to change." He lets go of me. The shimmer is gone. He heads out to the street and hails a taxi. I watch my teacher drive off, not sure what just happened, only that something did. I touch the spot on my shoulder where his hand was. It feels strange. Warm, maybe. I'm not sure. I grab it, wondering if maybe there's a weird pulse or some trace of magic, but there isn't.

I look back to Mark and Lucy to ask them if they noticed anything weird, but they're talking to each other and not even looking this way.

"Hey," I call to them. "You guys wanna spend the night at my house?"

27

CONFESSIONS

As the limousine pulls up to my house, Lucy sucks in her breath. "Nice castle! Where'd you hide the princesses?"

"I buried them in the garden out back."

She laughs. "That was morbid. Should I be worried?"

"Nah. Your brother would kill me if anything happened to you."

"You really live here?" Mark says, ignoring our banter. "It's... I mean, it's so..."

"Big?"

He nods. "Thanks for paying that messenger to tell our mom we'd be staying over. The last thing we need is another repeat of Friday with her worrying."

"Yeah," I say. "No problem. Hey, before we go in, I want you guys to know I can't promise you a good time. My parents are... well, let's just say they aren't as open as I am to strangers."

"You mean Losers," Lucy says. "Like Mark and me."

"I have a confession to make: I wasn't supposed to invite you guys over. I was supposed to forget all about you after tomorrow, but there might not be an 'after tomorrow' for Mark and me if we lose. Even if we win, I have a feeling life is going to change for us in ways we can't even begin to imagine. I don't know what's going to happen, but I want you both to know we'll always be friends. No matter what. Hanging out together these past few days has meant a lot to me."

"Thanks, man!" Mark says. "I appreciate that."

Lucy smiles, but it seems sort of sad, and I wonder if she's still upset about whatever bugged her at the gym or if it's something I said—or didn't say.

I tell them to just ignore my parents if they're rude and enjoy the rest of it. When we get inside, James looks puzzled by my guests, but warms when I introduce them as my friends. He escorts them to my room, but I stay behind to talk to my parents in the living room. They don't seem happy at first, but when I explain about the Temple's interest in the rematch and how bad things can get, they agree that giving Mark and Lucy one night of luxury isn't really too much to ask. Mom leaves, but I hear her outside the door telling James to "lock up the good silver." I roll my eyes and turn to leave, but Dad stops me.

"This is my fault," he says.

"What? No, Dad! It's not. It's because of me—what I did the other night. Breaking curfew."

"I've been frustrated dealing with the Temple's red tape. I may have said and done some things that could have been interpreted unfavorably by the priesthood."

"You mean the Inquisition?"

Dad sighs and pours himself a glass of whiskey. "Being a businessman isn't easy. This house, Eaves Oil, everything I've built, there's been a price to pay. Maybe I just got sick of paying it. Maybe I thought I had the power to change things, to make things better. I wish I did, but the priests always find a way to stop me... Only sometimes, it's not even them. Sometimes, it's me. I built all this, and I'm afraid of losing it." He drains his glass and pours another. "When you have everything, you tend to be cautious. You can't be bold enough when you're afraid for your family, for your business, when you see what can happen and how far you can fall."

"That's not true, Dad. You've been plenty bold."

"Not really. All I did was talk about change and pull a few shady deals. It felt like I was doing more. I thought I was doing it for you, for your mother, for the company, hell—even for the world—but really, I was doing it for my own ego so I wouldn't feel powerless. I'm sorry. I haven't been the best father. I've been cold, distant, but it never meant I didn't love you or wasn't proud of you."

I hug him. "It's not your fault, Dad."

"It is," he says, and pulls away. He goes to the bar and tops off his glass.

I follow. "Look, even if it is your fault, it's not *all yours*. I still lost in gym. I still broke curfew. I screwed up."

"There's no room for error in this world," Dad says. "Sooner or later, the Eye of Cronus always spots it."

"Yeah, but nobody's perfect."

"That's the problem," Dad says. "Everyone's trying to be, and everyone's failing, only no one wants to admit it. The world wants me to be the perfect man, the perfect husband, the perfect father... How can I be those things when I can't even be myself? I really screwed up."

"Don't say that."

"Why not, son? It's true. You know what the worst part is? I covered my tracks too good. The Inquisition can't get me, so they're after you instead. They want to use you to break me. It won't stop at the rematch tomorrow. Even if you win, they'll find a way to make our family lose. I swear, it's all some kind of sick game to them."

"Everything's going to be all right." I say the words because I want to believe them and want my dad to believe them. He seems to need them even more than I do. I've never seen him this sad, this vulnerable.

"There's more," Dad says.

"What do you mean?"

"Not now. I shouldn't have said anything. It's just that if anything happens to your mother and me, check the safe."

"The one in your home office?"

"No. I had another one installed. In the basement, hidden under the floor, beneath that pile of boxes in the corner opposite the furnace. The combination is the date you discovered oil on our old property. You remember?"

"Hard to forget. I guess I'm surprised you do."

"I remember," Dad says. "You're the whole reason Eaves Oil even exists. I'm sorry I haven't always acted like it. Your mother and I, well... you'll never know how grateful we are you came into our lives. You're more special than you know."

Does Dad know I'm magic? Does he know what I am? Before I can ask, he says, "The safe in the basement—don't open it unless something happens to your mother and me."

"Why? What's in it?"

"Nothing that will help you now. But if anything happens..." He coughs and looks out the bay window. Outside, the sun is setting, a blood-red smear behind the treeline.

"Dad..."

"No." He finishes his whiskey and sets the glass on the bar top. "I shouldn't have brought it up; I don't mean to add to your worries. You need to focus on winning that rematch. Promise me you won't open the safe before it's time."

"I promise."

"And don't tell your mother I mentioned it." Dad tries on a smile that doesn't quite touch his eyes; there's still too much sadness in it. "Go see your friends. Have fun. Dinner is in half an hour."

I turn to leave, then hesitate in the doorway. "Dad, you and Mom will be at the rematch tomorrow, right?"

"Yes, son. We wouldn't miss it for the world."

28

DINNER IS AWKWARD, but my parents do their best to make Mark and Lucy feel welcome. Afterward, I give my friends a tour of the house and grounds, then we hang out in my room. I can't believe how long it's been since I've had anyone over. That feels weird enough, but what's even weirder is this may be the last time I'll even sleep here. Mark and Lucy chatter about how amazing my place is, and I know it must be to them, but to me, it's just home.

I never really appreciated Mom and Dad as much as I should have. And now that things are finally getting better, now that we're beginning to understand each other, is it too little, too late?

I pick up the rock I snatched out of the air yesterday morning. It's still flat, still smooth gray, perfect for throwing. My palm closes over it. Feeling its warmth, feeling...

"Hey!" Lucy says. "You weren't kidding. You really do love rocks." She picks up a geode to study the crystals inside. "It's quite a collection."

"Huh?" When I open my hand, the rock is gone. I look on the floor to see where I must have dropped it, but it's not there. "Um, did you guys see a rock? I think I lost one."

"What kind of rock?" Lucy asks.

"Just an ordinary gray one."

Mark and Lucy help me look, but it's no use. The rock is gone. My right hand feels itchy. I scratch it, wondering what's going on.

James knocks, then tells us that the guest bedrooms are ready. I guess I must have looked guilty or scared because James asks if anything's wrong. I tell him no, but mention that one of the rocks from my collection is missing.

"I can help you look," James offers.

"No, it's not important. It probably rolled under the furniture. I'll find it in a minute."

"Very good, sir," James says. "Your parents were quite insistent regarding you and your friends getting to bed at a decent hour. They want you well-rested for the competition."

I yawn and stretch. "Mark, Lucy, I'll see you guys in the morning, OK? Oh, and it's great having you over. Hopefully, we can do it again."

"If we win, you can bet on it," Mark says. "Hey, we should have a party here. You know, really celebrate!"

I grin. "Yeah, I'd like that." Then I remember I'm supposed to meet Hannah at the cave tomorrow, and my grin falters. Mark doesn't notice, but his sister does.

"Andrus?" Lucy asks, "you all right?"

I force the grin to come back, wider this time. "Totally. I was just thinking about the rematch, that's all."

Lucy comes up and hugs me. "You can do it," she says, then smiles at her brother. "You both can!"

That's how we end it—on a high, happy note. Minutes after she's gone, I can still feel Lucy pressed against me, still smell the delicate fragrance of her hair.

James appears in the doorway, coughing politely to get my attention. "I thought I'd come back and help you look for that missing piece of your collection."

We search my room for the missing rock one more time, even moving the furniture, but still can't find it.

"Was it very valuable, sir?" James asks. "I can make inquiries of the household staff, particularly the maids..."

"That won't be necessary. It's not anything expensive. It was just some rock I found when I was coming home from Mark and Lucy's, but I don't know, it's got..."

"Sentimental value?" James fills in the blank. "Well, I can certainly see why. That Miss Lucy is quite attractive. Are you sure it was wise to bring her here? You do remember what we talked about? That your loving her won't leave her worse off than before she knew you?"

I feel the blood rush to my cheeks. "I—it's not like that," I stammer. "I mean, we're friends, James. Nothing happened. I already told you that."

James raises an eyebrow. "You mean nothing happened *yet*. And here she is, in a bed a few rooms away, and tomorrow is the day that will decide your fate. Don't let it decide hers too."

"OK," I say. "I get it. Did my mom put you up to this?"

James nods. "Your mother wanted me to remind you there was to be no 'funny business,' but the context I chose to put it in was mine. I think that while she and I both agree there is to be no fooling around, our motivations differ. Hers are for the family honor, while mine are for yours—and the girl's."

"Thanks, James. It makes a lot more sense coming from you."

He smiles. "I try to be of use. And if you'll pardon a change of subject, I want you to know that I wish I could there for you tomorrow at the rematch. Do you feel confident you can win?"

"Yeah," I say. "I think so. It's what happens after that I'm worried about."

"After? How do you mean, sir?"

"I wish I knew. But thanks for everything, James. You know I love you, right? You've been like a father to me." We hug, and when we pull away, the old man's eyes are brimming with tears. "I'm going to free you," I say. "Just as soon as I inherit."

"I wouldn't even know what to do with my freedom," James says. "The world outside these walls is a dangerous place. Where would I go? What would I do?"

I hadn't thought about that, only that it seemed like the right thing to do—but for him or me? There's real fear on his face.

"You wouldn't have to go anywhere," I say. "Not if you don't want to. I'll pay you to stay here and do whatever you want. All I ask in return is a little of your famous advice now and then."

"That's very kind, sir," James says, but still seems uncomfortable with the idea. "But I've worked my whole life. I'd like to keep managing the house, if it's all the same to you. An estate this size doesn't run itself. I'd hate to see you taken advantage of by some scheming replacement."

We leave it at that, but I'm determined I'll send James on a vacation some day. A surprise. Give him a chance to put his feet up for a few days at some quiet beachfront resort. It's the least I can do.

I shut the door and strip to my shorts. It's a hot night. I go to bed, but sleep won't come. I toss and turn, my thoughts alternating between Lucy, Hannah, the rematch, and what happens after. Finally, I drift off, but then I'm dreaming Lucy is in bed with me, snuggling up beside me in her night gown, her breath soft in my ear.

"Andrus," the dream girl says. "Wake up."

There's no way I want to, not with her lying next to me, but then I open my eyes and see she's no dream.

"Lucy," I whisper. "What are you doing—"

She covers my lips with hers, and I try to resist, but she's so beautiful, so forbidden! It's crazy to resist, crazy not to take her in my arms... So I let it happen until it seems like it's going to go right to the edge, to that irreversible, screaming moment of desire when neither of us will be able to stop even if we wanted to.

I tear my mouth from hers. "No, Lucy! We can't."

"Oh," she says, pulling away. "I get it. I'm not good enough." She goes cold, all the fire of seconds before extinguished in an instant.

I sit up, taking her hands in mine. "That's not it," I say. "You're plenty good enough! Only my parents, your brother..."

"They don't have to know."

"But we will," I say. "And they'll find out somehow. I don't want them to think any less of you. You're too important."

"I am?" she says. "You really think so?"

We kiss again, and it's electric, and even harder to stop. She's all soft skin and warm breath and I know she'll do anything for me, which is why I can't do anything to her. Not now, not like this.

"After tomorrow," I say.

She places a slim hand on my chest and kisses me playfully. "After tomorrow, what, Andrus?"

"After tomorrow, we'll figure out a way to do this. To do *us* in a way that won't hurt anyone, especially not you."

Lucy stops, and it's not the reaction I expect. She's gone cold again. Distant.

"What is it? What's wrong? I thought you'd be happy."

"I am." She sniffles. "I just never thought... no one's ever... I mean, I don't know. It's complicated."

"Tell me about it."

She smiles in the darkness, reaches down and pulls my hand to her face. She plants a kiss on my palm, then presses my hand to her cheek. "I wanted to be with you tonight, because tomorrow... well, we don't know what's going to happen. I don't want to have any regrets."

"Yeah," I say. "I don't want any either. That's what makes this so hard."

"I could make a joke about that," she says, "but I better not."

"Probably for the best," I agree. I like being with her here, the intimacy, the vulnerability.

"Andrus, I need to tell you something. About me." She lets go of my hand, then pauses to adjust the straps of her night gown. "Today, at the gym..."

"What about it? I mean, I noticed you acting sort of weird, and how you kept drinking Mr. Cross's whiskey. What is it? Was it something I did?"

"No," Lucy says, "it was nothing you did. It was something you said. A question you asked Mr. Cross."

"About what?"

"About the priest—the one who's coming to watch tomorrow. You asked if his name was Anton."

"Anton's with the Inquisition. He was at my house yesterday, and the Temple today."

"I know. I saw him."

"And you were afraid because he'll be at the rematch? Look, what happened at the Temple was horrible, but just because he turned that man into a worm doesn't mean he's going to do the same to Mark and me."

Lucy hunches her shoulders and begins to cry. Her whole body shivers. "You don't get it!" she sobs. "You just don't!"

I put my arm around her. "I guess not. Why don't you tell me?"

There's a long pause and more tears before she can get the words out. "Andrus, Anton is the priest who raped me."

29

ANOTHER REASON

"I'LL KILL HIM!" My hands knot into killing fists. The fists I'll use to break Anton, to smash him into helpless pulp.

"No," Lucy says. "That's not why I told you. Besides, you can't kill him. No one dies anymore, remember?"

"I don't care! I can still hurt him. I can make Anton wish he was dead."

Lucy grabs my face with both hands. Looking deep into my eyes, she says, "No! It's too dangerous, Andrus, and even if you do hurt him, you'll have the rest of the Inquisition to deal with. I only mentioned it because... Anton cost me my future. I don't want him to take yours from you, and not from Mark—not after everything I sacrificed. You understand, right?"

"Yeah, but I can't let Anton get away with it. Somebody has to do something!"

"No," she says, "not you. And certainly not now. Tomorrow is too important, and this isn't about Anton. This is about you, me, and Mark. What's best for us. Revenge..." she pauses, and I can see her wrestling with her emotions, "revenge, justice—whatever you want to call it—will have to wait. We may never get the chance, but if we do, we have to be smart about it. Promise me you won't do anything stupid. Promise me you won't do anything without telling me first."

"But—"

She kisses me hard, as if the pressure of her lips can drive the promise home.

It can.

"OK," I say when the kiss is over. "I'll wait. I won't do anything stupid."

She sighs in relief. "Good. I need you to promise me one more thing: that you won't tell Mark about Anton. It would destroy him. My brother would throw everything away to get revenge: your future and his. He needs to stay focused on the competition, and—damn it!"

"What?"

"I shouldn't have told you it was Anton. I don't know why I did; it was selfish. It's not going to help you focus tomorrow. You'll see Anton in the crowd and—"

"Hey," I tell her. "No, it's OK. You just gave me another reason to win when I look at him, that's all."

"Are you sure? I mean, knowing he was the one, that isn't too much? I don't want to be one more thing for you to worry about."

I pull her close. "You aren't." Our lips meet, and then she's nuzzling my shoulder. "I'm going to help you get justice," I whisper. "Whenever you want."

She nods, snuggling into me. We fit together so easily, so naturally, it isn't long before our breathing slows and we're asleep.

30

ALL I FEEL

LUCY'S GONE when I wake. I wonder if it was all a dream, but no, I can still smell her, still feel the warmth of her body in the empty space next to me. I don't want to get up. I just want to lay here and remember the look, the feel, the smell of her. So beautiful. Then I remember what she told me about Anton and I know that promise or no promise, I'm going to make the inquisitor suffer. Maybe not today, maybe not tomorrow, but someday.

The hours before school are surreal. It's like I woke up in someone else's life. I do my morning workout and eat a light breakfast, going through the motions of smiling and nodding because it's the only thing I can do to keep from freaking out. I look at the faces of my parents, at Mark and Lucy, and wonder if they're going through the motions too.

Everything changes today.

I look out the dining room window and see Shadow in the tree. The raven cocks its head, caws once, then flaps its wings. I take it as a sign of encouragement, but I know it has another meaning: *Be ready to leave this world behind.*

I look away, then back. The raven is gone.

Can I really do this? Can I leave Mom and Dad? Mark and Lucy?

It's all so crazy! These kinds of things don't happen to kids, not even kids like me. Hell, they don't happen to adults either.

They happen to heroes.

I wish I knew what I was. I wish Hannah had told me. Then I'd know what to do. How can you know what to do if you don't know who you are?

Dad makes a joke—one of his rare ones—and everyone laughs like it's a normal day. The kind of day I've wished for but never had.

I force myself to smile, saying, "Good one, Dad."

He beams at me, and I wonder why it's only at the end of things that we truly become ourselves. If only we could reach this point sooner, what a world we would live in...

"A toast," Dad says. "To you, son, and your success. I know you'll make us proud."

"No, to us," I say. "To all of us." I raise my glass to my family and friends, then give a last lift to James, who stands in the doorway. He smiles, waiting the appropriate number of seconds for us to finish toasting before announcing the limo is ready to take us to school.

But it's not just to school. It's to everything.

I look around the table, trying to hold on to this moment, to press it so deeply into my mind that it will never go away. If this is the last time I'll ever be here, with them, I want it to be a good memory. The best memory: hopeful, kind, loving. So I push back against the fear, the doubt, the anger. I push down hard until all I feel is love.

31

SOME DREAMS

EVERYONE STARES and whispers when we arrive at Axios. The Academy is where this all began and where it must end. Kids I know and kids I don't are rooting for me or rooting for Blake, but it in the end, they're rooting for blood, for glory.

Glory to Axios.

Glory to Cronus.

And a thrill for themselves.

Outside the locker room, Mark and I say goodbye to my parents and Lucy. There are proud hugs, tearful kisses, then we leave them behind. Inside, the locker room is empty except for Mr. Cross. He nods at us, grim-faced. We nod back.

"Renovations done?" I ask.

"Yes, boys. It's all been done..." Mr. Cross turns away, then stops. "Remember what I told you at the gym yesterday?"

"Expect the unexpected?"

He smiles. "Exactly, Andrus. You've both come a long way, but the road is long and never ends. Especially for heroes. Especially when..." He pauses, as if considering whether to say more.

"Mr. Cross?" I ask. "On Friday, after class, you warned me that 'dreams will destroy you in this world.'"

"I did."

"Well, I've been thinking about that. A lot, actually, and you're right. This world isn't fair. It's a harsh place, and it's easy to give in and stop dreaming of something better. Or worse, to dream the wrong dreams. The kind that make the world better for you but worse for everyone else. Only..."

"Only what?" Mr. Cross asks.

"I think some dreams are worth destroying yourself over. And destruction doesn't have to mean the end, but the beginning."

Mr. Cross nods. "I was wondering when you were going to figure that out."

"Really? It's not like I had a choice."

"No," Mr. Cross says, "but the timing was important. For you to possess this wisdom now, before the rematch, makes everything that is to come easier. Easier, but not without cost."

"Wait," I say. "What do you mean, 'what is to come' and 'not without cost'?"

Mark looks from me to the teacher. "Um, guys? Am I missing something? Don't keep me in the dark here..."

The locker room door slams. Blake Masters struts in, cocky as ever. "Morning, ladies!" he says, "Who's ready to get their ass whupped?"

Mr. Cross steps out from behind the row of lockers that's obscuring him from the door. Blake gulps. "Sorry, Mr. Cross. I, uh, didn't see you standing there."

"Where I stand shouldn't matter, Blake. This is my locker room. You know I don't allow that kind of talk."

"Sorry," Blake mumbles. "I was just trying to psych them out is all."

"And trying to psych yourself up," Mr. Cross adds.

"Yeah," Blake admits, "that too. You got me." He comes over to us, holding out his hand. "Good luck today, guys."

I shake reluctantly, wincing as he tries to crush my hand in his. Our eyes meet and Blake grins. "You'll need it."

"We all will," Mark mutters. And he's right.

32

THE CURTAIN FALLS

WHEN I ENTER THE GYM, the first thing I notice is the sound. The crowd is bigger than I thought. The bleachers are packed. I thought this was supposed to be a rematch for our class, but it looks like the whole school's here. Could this be a mandatory assembly? It must be—there's the principal, Mrs. Ploddin, and all the teachers. I scan the crowd and see my parents and Lucy in the front row. I also see Anton lurking nearby, flanked by two warriors and looking as venomous as ever. His gold mace is looped to his belt. He smirks as we lock eyes, and to my surprise, he stalks toward me, the warriors keeping pace behind him, then fanning out to push Mark and Blake back out of earshot.

Anton gestures at the crowd. "I hope you don't mind an audience. Do you think it will effect your performance?"

"No. Your trick won't work."

"My trick?" Anton rolls his eyes. "The assembly wasn't my idea. I would have preferred to keep this private, but it seems your family is not without influence... for now."

"You mean my parents arranged this?"

"You mean they didn't tell you? Well, no doubt they wanted to keep it a surprise. Get the whole school to cheer you on and witness your victory."

"But not you," I say. "You want me to fail."

Anton laughs. "Not at all! On the contrary, I want to see you win more than you know. Good luck, and remember—"

"Cronus is watching," I finish for him.

"Yes!" Anton cackles. "Yes, indeed! Cronus *is* watching. Isn't it funny how intuitive we can be about some things, yet so desperately clueless about others?" He grins at me, near wide enough to split his evil face, and it makes me wonder about what he's not telling me.

What don't I know?

"The crowd isn't the only surprise," Anton adds, pointing at the rock climbing wall—or rather, where it used to be. There's a large blue and white curtain hanging from floor to ceiling. Two slaves stand by, one on each end, each holding a gold rope that ties the curtain in place.

Why the mystery? What have they done to renovate the wall? I turn to ask Anton, but the inquisitor is already moving away, taking his warriors with him. Mark comes up and demands to know what he said.

"He says he wants us to win."

"He does? Really? That's great!"

"No," I say. "I don't think it is."

Mark gives me a puzzled look. "But why? I mean, I guess it doesn't matter because we have to win or else."

"Yeah, I know. We don't have a choice. We're gonna win, no doubt. I'm just not sure what's going to happen when we do."

"Are you kidding?" Mark says. "They'll probably throw us a party! I tell you, Andrus, our luck is changing. Don't be so paranoid. Enjoy the moment."

I glance at Blake and Brenda, who are giving us the evil eye. No doubt they're jealous Anton didn't come over to wish them well. They should be glad he didn't.

Mark follows my gaze. "Hey, don't let them psych you out. We got this, right?"

"Definitely." I know not to say anything more. Whatever my fears, whatever my doubts, I need to keep them to myself. Whatever happens, I need Mark to stay confident.

"So what do you think's under the curtain?" Mark asks.

"Nothing to worry about," I lie. "We got this."

The principal comes out and says a few words to introduce the event, then Anton as our special guest. He doesn't mention our guest is an inquisitor. That would only make people nervous. Beaming, the principal hands the mic to Mr. Cross and takes his seat next to Anton.

Mr. Cross addresses the crowd, explaining the rematch as a contest of champions from which only one team will emerge victorious. "Tied to Andrus and Blake are the two lowest ranking students in my class..."

This gets boos from the audience. Mark and Brenda squirm. Mr. Cross holds up his free hand for silence. "Quiet, please! That is not to say that Mark and Brenda are not excellent students in their other classes. They are. And normally, we would not expect perfection in every area of their education; after all, that is why there are priests and warriors."

Cheers erupt, the response clearly divided between the jocks and brains, each thinking their side is superior.

Mr. Cross continues, "As you know, each of us is called to serve the Titans in our own way, and we, the faculty at Axios, are here to help guide our students to the appropriate choice. However..." He pauses to glance at me. "We want our graduates to be as well-rounded as possible. To be last in anything is not acceptable. So I say that the best owe it to those who are struggling the most to help them rise up. And by their rising, they raise us all in the eyes of the Titans! That is why Andrus and Blake are here. To help Mark and Brenda reach their full potential."

More cheers.

"As many of you know, Andrus and Blake have battled before. They have won much glory, but now let us see who is the stronger! Who has done the most to help train their partner? Which team will stand atop the new wall and serve as a shining example of strength and courage? Let us find out now together, for Axios!"

"FOR AXIOS!" the crowd shouts.

"And for the Titans!" Mr. Cross adds, pausing to give me a long, curious look.

"FOR THE TITANS!" the crowd screams.

Mr. Cross turns back to the audience. "May the Titans watch over and bless us all. Reveal the new wall!" He nods to the pair of slaves by the curtain. They yank the gold ropes.

The curtain falls.

And everything changes.

33

FACE THE WALL

THE NEW ROCK climbing wall is like the mountain in my dreams: *Olympus*. The same stone, the same color. I can't believe it. This isn't a remodel, this is a reimagining of what a rock climbing wall can be. There's even a snow-topped summit. It's fake, of course—the snow, all of it—but how did they get it to match the Mount Olympus in my dream?

Or did my dream match their design? Could I have known through some psychic sense, some precognition? Or was it an omen? Sent by who? The Gods? The Titans? Cronus himself? What if everything has been leading up to this moment? That it's not just a competition, but...

"It's just a wall," Mark says.

"What?" I shake my head to snap out of the weird state I'm in.

Mark frowns. "I said, it's just a wall. Don't look so freaked out. I admit it looks tough, but I didn't think I'd be the one telling you not to be worried."

I crack a grin. "Sorry. It's not the wall. Not exactly. It's hard to explain, but don't worry. I'm OK. We've got this."

"You sure?" Mark asks.

I nod. "Just follow my lead."

We stretch to warm-up before the climb. I keep stealing glances at the wall. Sizing it up. The artificial handholds aren't there; instead, there are natural grips—cracks and crevices, ledges and even a few fake scrubs. It's designed to work like the real thing.

"You see what I see?" I ask Mark.

"Yeah. It's more like Bronson Canyon than the one at the gym. Good thing we went caving—despite the concussion. I'll try not to screw up this time." He makes a joke out of it, and I realize how hard he's trying to hold it together. How brave he's being despite the fact he isn't ready for a climb like this. I'm not sure I am either.

"You get anything out of that book I loaned you?"

"A little," Mark says.

I raise an eyebrow.

"OK, a lot," he adds with a smile. "Enough, I think. I only read it twice."

That makes me feel better. The book's full of good techniques and practical advice, covering far more situations than we've had time to go over together. Mark starts to tell me some of the most important things he's learned. I nod, relieved to hear him speaking with such confidence, but find my attention wandering to our opponents.

Blake and Brenda don't look happy. He's giving her a pep talk, trying to reign in her fear. I can't help thinking it's funny how enemies think they're cheating us, holding us back, when they're really forcing us to think outside the box. To get better, stronger. *Smarter.*

When Blake blocked us from using the downtown gym, he had no way of knowing what a bad decision he'd made. He forced us to practice on a real wall. By screwing us over, he may have lost the rematch. I'm glad I let Brenda and him use the gym yesterday. Glad I listened to Lucy and didn't take the low road, the same road Blake took. I wanted to. I really did. But Blake's not my real enemy, and I'm better than that—at least, I try to be.

We finish warming up. I look over at Anton, feeling the rage, the frustration it's so hard to keep in check. I can't give in to it; I can't let it control me. I have to control it to win this and everything that comes after. And I have to do it without losing myself in the process.

My right hand itches. I scratch idly at it, hoping it won't bother me during the climb. My palm feels warmer than it should. But there's no more time to worry about this or anything else because Mr. Cross asks if the teams are ready.

"Always," Blake answers smoothly. He seems to have Brenda's fear under control—and his own. But that's just for now. Once we get on the wall, anything can happen. I know he'll do anything to win, including pulling dirty tricks.

Expect the unexpected.

But I don't think Blake is what Mr. Cross meant.

"Andrus, Mark?" Mr. Cross asks. "Is your team ready?"

"We're ready," I reply.

I take one last look at my parents and Lucy, watching in the front row. I give them a big smile and thumbs-up, then turn and face the wall.

34

MY MOUNTAIN

OUR TEAMS START on opposite sides of the wall. Mark and I take the left, Blake and Brenda the right. A nylon rope clipped to our climbing belts binds us to our teammate. Mr. Cross says, "First team to the top wins. On your marks..."

I dig my heels into the gym floor, feeling my muscles tense.

"Ready..."

I glance over at Blake and Brenda. They glance back. Determined. Daring me to beat them.

"Set..."

This won't be easy. I have to gain focus. Get control.

"Go!" Mr. Cross clicks his stop watch.

We begin to climb. I'm surprised how real the wall feels, even more surprised when I realize the stone's not fake. Somehow, they've shaved off the side of a mountain, broken it down, and reassembled it in our gym. What bothers me most isn't how they did it, but *why*.

The first third of the climb goes well. No surprises. I almost lose myself in the simple joy of hands on rock, feet on stone, every part of me thrusting toward truth, toward destiny.

I take a moment to check on Blake and Brenda; they aren't far behind. They're edging closer to our position, and I remember how

Blake tried to yank me off the wall the last time we competed here. Blake sees me and shouts, "We're coming for you, Andrus!"

I dare a quick glance at the upturned faces of the crowd, picking out the people that matter: My parents. Lucy. Mr. Cross.

Anton pulls a black box from his tunic, no longer looking at the contest. Is he that unconcerned? What could he be doing that's more important than—

I hear a click and a whirr. Something shifts under my feet. My footholds vanish, retracting into the wall!

I call a warning to Mark as I swing my legs awkwardly to the next highest foothold. Across from us, Brenda yelps in terror as her handholds retract. Whatever Anton's doing, at least it's to both teams.

"The wall's not all real," I tell Mark. "Some of it's fake, blended to hide traps. I think we should—"

Another click. A metal pipe sticks out from the crevice between two rocks. It's pointed at my face.

"Look out!" Mark warns.

I swing sideways as far as I can go, one hand flailing for a handhold as a jet of steam shoots from the pipe, scalding the air where my face was seconds before. A shrill scream from below tells me Brenda isn't so lucky.

The crowd gasps. They're beginning to understand this isn't an ordinary competition. This is something far more dangerous.

The steam fizzles to curling mist. I adjust my position to get a better grip. I need to get away from this pipe, need to make sure it can't hit Mark in case it decides to spray again. I climb above it and to the side.

Below me, Mark is trying to get up, but I warn him to wait. I don't trust that pipe. Sure enough, it blows again, right where Mark would be if I hadn't stopped him. There's no other way up for Mark then the way I've gone. "It's on a timer," I tell him. "Go now, but be ready to move fast."

Mark swings to safety right before the steam jet fires again. "That was close," he says, visibly shaken. "We better take it nice and easy, watch where we're putting our hands."

"Not to mention the rest of us," I say. "Did you see Brenda's leg? It's boiled, man! Beet red."

Her injury is slowing her team, not stopping them. Of course not. Nothing stops Blake except his own ego.

"You all right?" I call to Brenda.

"Fine," she grunts through gritted teeth. Her leg is burned so bad I see blisters forming, bubbling her flesh ghost-white. She must be operating on pure adrenaline. I have to give her credit for not giving up. As big a bastard as Blake is, at least he taught her that much—or maybe she had it in her the whole time and Blake is just as surprised as I am.

"Andrus!" Mark says. "What are you doing? Waiting for them to catch up? We have to move!"

I take the hint. We're climbing again, angling up and away from Blake and Brenda as sudden thunder booms from hidden speakers. The gym lights snap off. A bright flash strobes across my vision. Lightning. I'm hanging off the side of Mount Olympus. Mark, the gym, everything and everyone is gone, except the mountain—the mountain and what waits for me above.

No, not what. *Who.* Someone I hate, and someone who hates me. But it's not just hate, there's love mixed in too, like poison, like acid burning in my veins. If I can just get to the top, I can see who it is. Face them. End this, the way it should have ended...

I AM THE MOUNTAIN.
   I am one with it.
   I am one with the earth.

"ANDRUS!" Mark shouts. "Look out!"

I snap out of my dream to find the gym lights back on. Barbed spikes emerge from the wall, punching into my right hand. I feel them pushing, pressing, but strangely, there's no pain. The machinery behind the spikes strains. Smoke pours from the trap hole in a grinding screech.

I pull my hand away. The spikes should have skewered my flesh, left it a ruined, worthless mess and ended this contest. Instead, the spikes are bent, broken. There are angry pink spots on my palm from where the points tried to dig in, but no blood. As I stare in disbelief, the spots fade. Something moves inside my palm, shifting under the surface. It doesn't hurt. It feels weird, but good. Like it's part of me.

My lost rock! Could I have absorbed it and used it to block the spikes? I flex my hand, mystified. What kind of magic is this? What the hell am I?

"You OK?" Mark asks, and I realize from his vantage point he can't tell what happened. "How's your hand?"

"Great," I say. "I'm not hurt. The trap must have malfunctioned. Let's keep climbing."

We're halfway up the mountain—I mean, the wall—and it's surreal. I'm here and not here. I have to fight back the visions of Olympus, keep myself anchored in a world that feels increasingly less real, less important.

Try telling that to the people who are counting on me.

The thought rips through the dream, but does nothing to diminish the hate it puts in me, the anger. Anton, Vola, Nessus, Blake. All of them trying to cheat me. Trying to usurp me. They're taking what should be mine, forcing me to waste my time, my resources, when I should be... what, exactly?

At the top of the mountain. I must tear my enemies down, crush the traitors in the molten belly of the earth...

I shake my head, clearing it. Something's wrong. These thoughts aren't mine, are they? How could they be? I force them out. I've got to focus.

As I strain for the next handhold, my boot breaks through a fake stone, sends me scrambling to find a hold that suddenly isn't there. Then I'm falling, trying to relax for the shock of the rope that binds me to Mark. There's a heavy jolt on the line. I slam into the wall, the impact snapping the breath from my lungs. I spin on the rope, looking wildly up at Mark death-gripping the wall, then at the snowy summit looming overhead.

"Tough break," Blake sneers as he and Brenda climb past me. "See you at the top, asshole!"

Brenda offers me a sympathetic look, but nothing more.

I take a shuddering breath, then climb.

35

FIVE FINGERS FROM DEATH

"COME ON," Mark says. "Hurry!" He takes his eyes off Blake to say it, and that proves to be a mistake. Blake avoided me when he passed by, staying just out of range of my flailing hands, but he's angled closer to Mark as he climbed.

"So long, Loser!" He sends a savage kick at Mark's ribs, catching him off guard. The blow knocks Mark off the wall.

I press myself tightly to the rock, bracing myself.

Mark sails by, eyes wide, too scared to scream.

My fingers dig into the wall, waiting for the jolt of his weight when he runs out of rope. It happens fast: the shock, the pain. My left hand loses its grip. With a mechanical whir, all my handholds and footholds begin to retract into the wall. It's a matter of seconds, but it's time enough to imagine Anton laughing, pushing buttons on his black box. Which doesn't make sense. He said he wanted me to win...

Instead, I'm falling. A low growl rips from my throat. Something cracks—not in me, but in the wall. The fingers of my right hand claw through stone, slowing our descent. Slowing, slowing, then stopping.

The crowd roars with excitement.

We hang there, five fingers from death. There's no time to think, only to do. My left arm swings up, fingers punching through the rocky surface. Ignoring the pain of bruised muscles and the frantic weight of Mark, I pull myself up, legs scrambling for a perch. Finding none, I kick out, imagining Blake's face on the other end of my boot. It punches through the rock. I do it again, imagining Anton. Now the wall's design doesn't matter. I can make my own custom handholds and footholds wherever I need them.

I peer at Mark's anxious face. "Don't panic. I'm gonna pull us up, all right? Use the hand holds I'm making; they won't be trapped."

Mark fires off some questions, like how the hell am I making holds, but I ignore them. I focus on the climb, trusting Mark will do what I tell him. Trusting I have the strength—*and the magic*—to win.

As we catch up to the rival team, I call Blake's name. He looks down and I see surprise written in his eyes. Surprise that turns to fear, then hate. The two of us have been here before, many times in many contests, but the stakes have never been this high.

Hand over hand, I claw my way toward him and Brenda. It's getting easier; my fingers practically drill themselves into the stone now. I'm drawing strength from it, and why shouldn't I?

It's my mountain.

"What the hell is he doing?" Brenda asks Blake. There's a rising note of hysteria in her voice. All she gets back is a string of curse words and his demand to climb faster. Blake doesn't need to tell her twice.

As they climb frantically up the wall, Blake says, "You're a freak, Andrus! A damn freak! I always suspected you were cheating. Even if you beat me, I'll still win! You hear me? I'll turn you over to the Inquisition; I'll make sure you—"

Brenda's burned leg suddenly gives out, and the panicked motion cuts off Blake's threat in mid-sentence. Brenda scrabbles back toward the foothold she missed, digs her foot into it with a grimace of pain. Her entire body goes tense with effort. The effort to hold on, to hang in there, despite the pain. Despite the fear. Her eyes are screwed shut, her lips moving in silent prayer.

Blake growls at her. "What are you doing? *They're gaining.* Move it, you stupid bitch!"

Brenda moves, but we're right behind her. I'm just pulling myself level with her legs when a brutal buzzing fills the air—a buzzing attached to a spinning saw blade. It slides from its concealed partition between the rocks, a flash of silver ready to cut through Brenda's legs and my face.

Brenda screams.

Pink mist blinds me. I blink away the blood, watching Brenda's legs fall away at the knees. She slumps, unconscious, the rope tying her to Blake the only thing keeping her from tumbling to the gym floor.

The blade slashes toward me. I throw out my right hand. The buzzing grows higher and higher-pitched, then stops. I pull my hand away. Not even a scratch. I can't say the same for the blade; its teeth have dulled to nubs.

"I don't believe it," Mark says. "What are you? How are you doing that?"

"I don't know. Just be glad I am."

Above us, Blake struggles to hang on. There's nothing any of us can do for Brenda. The summit is close now—the summit and victory.

With Blake struggling not to fall, Mark and I make good time. Soon, I'm right next to him.

"I don't need... to bring... all of Brenda to the top," Blake says through gritted teeth, "just enough to beat you!"

I don't say anything.

"You were never better than me," Blake snarls. "How could you be? You're not even human! You're nothing but a monster." He kicks me. It hurts, but I take it. He kicks me again. Harder.

Something snaps free.

Something beyond my control.

Thunder booms, and this time, it's not just a sound effect, it's a low rumbling from above. Part of the mountaintop crumbles, forming an avalanche.

Black stone.

Blinding snow.

"Hug the wall!" I warn Mark.

I will the avalanche to pass over me, over us. It plows into Blake instead. He has time to scream before the first boulder hits, then he's falling, taking Brenda with him, and it's a long way down, long enough there's time for me to look away.

I hear the distant crunch, the pop of two red balloons bursting on the gym floor. The crowd goes wild, as crowds always do. This is the blood they've been waiting for.

36

IT DOESN'T CHANGE ANYTHING

I CHIN MYSELF UP and over the snow-dusted summit, then reach down to help Mark up. We've won. But at what cost? Below us, the slaves clear away the bent, broken bodies of Blake and Brenda, leaving a sticky red smear on the gym floor. I'm not sure if the crowd is cheering for us or howling for more blood. There's no time to feel remorse, no time to feel anything but empty.

"I can't believe they're gone," Mark says. "Was that avalanche another trap or did you..."

"It was me."

Mark nods, looking at me out of the corner of his eyes. I know he's got a million questions, but I don't have anywhere near that number of answers.

"What are you?" he asks.

"I don't know, but we'd both be screwed if I wasn't what I am. You know that, right? You know I'm on your side?"

"Yeah, man. I know. But it's not me you should be worried about."

"You think anybody noticed what I did? We're pretty high up."

"They may not have noticed the small stuff, but I'm sure they saw the avalanche."

"I'm so screwed! That priest down there is with the inquisition."

Mark frowns. "OK, I say we play dumb, that we thought it was another trap. When the inquisitor says it wasn't, I'll pin it on the pipes."

"The steam pipes? What do you mean?"

"Steam requires pressure to vent, so the boiler must have malfunctioned. The steam got trapped and that's what caused the wall to explode."

"Seriously? That's awesome. You're a genius!"

"I have my moments," Mark agrees. "So what should we do now?"

"Only one thing to do: Act like they expect."

We raise our hands in victory. The crowd breaks into a riot of applause. We did it. We won.

There's a flutter of black from the pipes in the ceiling above us. Hannah's raven, Shadow, croaks at me, telling me it's time to go, to leave Axios behind. What's weird is I feel ready, more ready than I thought I would. After all, I did what I set out to do and more. *I won.* I saved Mark. I made up with my parents. And maybe, just maybe, I fell in love with Lucy...

Mr. Cross has left a pair of nylon ropes attached to the pipe. We can use them to rappel down the back of the wall, away from the traps. We clip our belts to the ropes and get ready to descend.

"I might have to take off for a while after this," I tell Mark. "I need to figure out what I am and what I can do. I can't do that here. But once I figure it out, I'll be back."

"What am I supposed to tell people?" Mark asks.

"Tell them the truth: You don't know what I am or where I've gone. I'd tell you more if I could, but it's better you don't know. I'm only giving you this much because I don't want you or anyone else to worry."

"Anyone else?"

"You know, like my parents."

"Or my sister."

"Yeah," I say. "Her too."

"Do you love her?"

"Yeah, man. I do."

He nods. "I know she spent the night with you."

"She did, but we didn't—I mean, it wasn't like that."

"I don't need details," Mark says. "I just need your promise: Don't hurt her."

"I won't." That seems to settle the matter, and we both break into stupid grins.

"By the way," Mark says. "Thanks! You really saved my ass back there."

"You saved mine too. I fell first, remember?"

"Yeah, you did. Guess I got my upgrade; I'm a full hero now." He laughs and kicks off the ledge toward the gym below.

When we reach the floor, there's a small group waiting for us. Mr. Cross is there, my parents, and Lucy. They don't look as happy as they should. That's because Anton is with them; his gold mace is in his hand and now he doesn't just have his two bodyguards, but a squad of ten warriors. They form a circle around the group, cutting off any chance of escape.

"Congratulations," Mr. Cross says sadly. "You won."

Anton barks laughter. "Yes, congratulations! Your victory was more spectacular than I could have hoped for."

I frown. "If you're so happy, why all the guards?"

"Why to arrest you, of course!"

"On what charge?" my dad demands.

"Blasphemy, for a start."

"Blasphemy?" Dad shakes his head. "That's impossible! My son has never said a single word against the Temple or the Titans."

"Perhaps, but it's not by his words that I bring the charges; it's on his vile, blasphemous nature. Andrus is not human. You saw him use magic. He's an abomination! One the Eye of Cronus has been seeking for a long time." His mouth twists into a smirk. "Oh, I had my suspicions the moment we met, boy, but Archieréas Vola said I had to be sure, so I took advantage of the renovations to the wall... and made a few improvements of my own. A rather clever way for you to reveal your true nature in a manner that cannot be denied. It's amazing what fear can bring out in people... and hate." He gives a short swing of his mace to emphasize the last word.

"The boiler exploded," Mark says, putting himself between the inquisitor and me. "It wasn't magic! Did you hear me? I said it wasn't magic!" But no one's listening to him. Dimly, I hear Mark trying to convince Anton, telling him about steam pressure and boiler failure, but none of that matters now. All my focus is on my parents.

"Mom? Dad? What's Anton talking about?"

My parents faces crease with worry. They're wrestling with something, something they know will hurt me. Could it be the secret Dad hid in the safe?

Lucy steps forward, more beautiful than ever. "Whatever Andrus is, it doesn't change anything with me. I love you, Andrus. And I always will." She stands in front of Anton as the inquisitor sneers in disgust.

"How touching!" he mocks. "A Loser in love with an abomination. You saved your brother once, my dear, but do you really think you can save this... this creature?"

"Yes," she says. "I do." A thin blade slips out of Lucy's robe and into her hand. No one notices but me. We exchange a look, so much emotion passing between us that there's nothing I can do, nothing I can say except, *"I love you."*

It's enough.

Lucy smiles, and in one fluid motion, she plunges the knife into Anton.

37

A LITTLE BLOOD

ANTON REELS FROM THE BLOW, the violent motion tearing the slim knife from Lucy's hand. The blade sticks out from his chest like an accusing finger. Blood stains his tunic. He lashes out with his mace, crashing it into Lucy's head. She goes down.

The closest warriors rush forward to form a defensive circle around the injured Inquisitor, swords and shields at the ready.

From behind the front rank, Anton shrieks, "Arrest them! Arrest them all!"

Five of the warriors advance. Two grab my parents. Three come for Mark and me. On instinct, I raise my right hand, pull it back, make a fist. The three missing crystals from my room tunnel out from between my knuckles. *I must have absorbed them like I did the rock.* There's no pain and only a little blood. I launch myself at the three nearest warriors, swinging my newly weaponized hand to take one man in the throat. He staggers back, a crimson fountain spurting from his pierced neck.

I swing at the next man. He blocks and my crystal claws ring off his shield. The other warrior slashes at me. I duck. A narrow miss.

I have to save my parents. I have to save Lucy, but she's lying face-down in a pool of red. I dodge another sword blow, but when I try to get past the warriors, they batter me back. I curse and come at them, claws striking sparks off their shields. There's no time to think, only to act.

"Mom! Dad! I'm coming!"

"Don't worry about us," Dad says, "Run!"

Anton orders four of the five men guarding him into the fray, keeping one to help bind his wound. The knife is out of his chest. I want to finish what Lucy started. I want my claws buried in his stinking guts, want to make him feel the pain he's caused her, the pain he's caused everyone...

"Andrus, we need to go!" Mark tugs at my arm.

I resist, feeling my claws connect with a second warrior, ripping through his tunic, sinking past flesh, past bone. He falls to his knees then topples over, dead before he hits the ground.

The reinforcements are coming. I parry a vicious cut, wishing I could get to Anton. If I could only reach him, I could end this. I could avenge Lucy...

And with just that simple thought, one of the crystal claws streaks from my hand. It flies like an arrow between the rushing warriors toward Anton, whose eyes grow wide with terror. His remaining bodyguard raises his shield, but it's not enough. The crystal punches through the metal, close enough to graze Anton's cheek before stopping. A snarl of satisfaction dies on my lips. So close!

And then Mark's voice is desperate in my ear: "Andrus, come on!"

I shake my head. "No! I have to finish this. I have to—" But I see it's impossible. There are too many of them and I don't even know what I'm doing or how I'm doing it. I let Mark drag me toward the exit. The warriors, who had held back when they saw I could shoot crystals through their shields, now come after us as Anton howls for my blood. There are five in pursuit, and that's five too many. We're not going to get far unless...

I point my fist at the hardwood floor and fire a claw directly in front of the enemy. It shatters because I want it to shatter. I want it to tear through them. It does, exploding like a grenade. Two of the men go down clutching at shrapnel in their legs. A third staggers sideways, limping from a gashed thigh. The remaining two—the ones farthest from the center of the blast—sport superficial cuts. They keep coming, followed distantly by their limping companion.

Mark and I hit the exit running. We burst into the parking lot, eyes stinging from the too-bright sun. Behind us come pounding feet and angry swords.

We head for the woods, hoping to lose them. I don't have much of a plan after that. Part of me wants to go home to see what my father's left for me in the safe, but that's too obvious. Anton will look for me there first if he doesn't have men there already. That only leaves one course of action: Get to the cave. Get to Hannah.

But Mark has another idea: "We have to save my mom."

"They'll expect that," I say as we leave the parking lot behind. "That'd be as dumb as me going home."

"Still," Mark says. "I have to."

A raven swoops by us. Shadow. He flies toward the warriors, croaking and cawing. When I dare to glance back, I see one of the warriors with a bloody hand clasped over his eyes. He's blinded. Screaming. The other warrior crashes into the bushes after us.

"Monster!" he shouts. "Abomination! Face me!"

I stop and point my remaining crystal at him. "Face this!" The crystal streaks from my fist, skewering his chest. He pitches into the dirt and doesn't get up. I run to him and pull the crystal free, messily jamming it back into my hand just as the last limping warrior appears in the treeline.

I raise my fist and fire.

38

NO OPTIONS

IT TAKES FOREVER to get to Mark's house. We may not have made it all if we hadn't stolen hooded cloaks from a clothesline. Our disguises aren't perfect, but by playing the part of crippled beggars, we manage to blend into Loserville and avoid the attention of the Day Patrol.

Despite the hours it's been since we fled the Academy, there hasn't been much time to talk, let alone process what happened. We're wanted fugitives. Our old lives forever gone. My parents arrested. Lucy hurt, maybe a zombie now... But no, I can't believe that. Lucy's all right. She has to be. I'm going to save her. I'm going to fix this. Fix all of it! I try to make Mark understand, but he doesn't want to talk about it.

"It's not because I don't want to," he explains. "It's because I can't. I can't focus on Lucy now. I gotta focus on my mom."

"But don't you care?"

"Yeah, man. Of course I care! *She's my sister.* I love her, but we can't help her now. So we have to do the one thing she'd want us to do: rescue her mom."

"Sorry. I didn't mean it. I'm just so pissed off! I can't believe this happened. We had everything, then it all fell apart. I'm sorry about your sister. I'm sorry I dragged you into this mess."

"It's all right. You couldn't help it. And it means a lot you want to do something for her—so do this. Help me, OK?"

"Of course."

We ease into a garbage-strewn alley near Mark's shabby house. The threadbare curtains are drawn over the windows. We don't see any sign the place is under guard or being watched, but we decide to wait a few minutes just in case. The last thing we need is to go barging into a trap.

"It looks clear," Mark whispers. "Maybe they didn't bother to arrest my mom."

"Maybe," I reply, but I'm not convinced. Anton is too thorough, too spiteful, not to have sent men here. "Let's give it a few more minutes, OK?"

"They might not have come yet," Mark objects. "Or if they already left, they might come back. Either way, we should get inside now."

"Hang on." I keep an eye on the windows. I thought I saw movement behind the curtains, but can't be sure. Even if I did, it might be Mark's mom... or it might not. I hate all this creeping around, feeling powerless. But it's the right thing to do—well, the only smart thing. We should be heading to Bronson Canyon to meet up with Hannah.

I fidget with the sole remaining crystal sticking out of my fist, wishing I hadn't lost the others at the gym. I experiment with popping the crystal in and out of my flesh until I notice it's freaking Mark out.

"Seriously?" He shifts away and draws his cloak tighter around his body. "Can you please stop doing that?"

I retract the crystal back into my body. "Sorry. It's gross, huh?"

"It's, um... going to take some getting used to. Are you sure you don't know what you are? You don't have a craving to eat brains or anything, do you?"

"No. I'm pretty sure I'm not part-centaur, if that's what you're worried about."

That gets a laugh, then we both go back to watching the house. Nothing moves. It's quiet. Maybe too quiet.

Mark breaks the silence: "Hey, I got a question. Did you see what happened to Mr. Cross? Did he get arrested?"

"Why would he? He didn't do anything."

Mark sighs. "Good point. I didn't see the guards go for him. Maybe he slipped out when everything went to shit. That's what I would've done."

"You'd sneak out? I thought you were a full hero now?"

"I am, Andrus, but I'm not stupid. I can't shoot spikes out of my fists. I'm not a warrior; I have to outthink my enemies."

I don't argue that trying to save his mom is the opposite of outthinking Anton. It's playing right into the inquisitor's hands. But it's not like we can wait for dark. The Night Patrol will be out and looking for us. Part of me says bring them on; I can't wait to fight Captain Nessus with my new powers. The other part of me says we need to get to Bronson Canyon before dark. Judging by how many hours of daylight we've burned, there's no time to waste.

"All right," I whisper. "Let's do this. I'll go first. You wait here; I'll signal when it's safe." Acting every part the lame beggar, I hobble out of the alley into the street. There's no alarm, no running feet. I pretend-cough to explain why I'm just standing there if anyone's watching, then limp over to the house. I press my ear to the door and listen. Nothing. I knock. No one answers.

I hope I'm not being an idiot. I knock again and wait, each second an eternity. Still no answer. I try the door. It's locked. I look around and don't notice anyone watching, so I use my crystal as the ultimate lock pick. Well, more like *lock punch*. When I try the door again, it creaks open. I peer in. The house is dark. No sign of any disturbance. I wave Mark over. He drunkenly stumbles across the street and it's the worst case of overacting I've seen.

"Never mind that," I hiss. "Get in here!"

He hurries the last few steps and then we're inside. I shut the door, then cross to the window. I peer out from behind the curtain. A real beggar is weaving down the street, singing a merry tune. He stops in front of the house to belch and scratch himself in all the wrong places. That's when I realize what we should have done. We should have hired him—or a guy like him—to knock on the door for us. That way, if it was a trap, we'd be safe. Not a very heroic plan, maybe, but better than us getting caught...

"Mom?" Mark calls. "Mom, you here?"

I drop the curtain and turn toward Mark. "I don't think she's home or she would have answered the door."

He points at the empty wine bottle on the table. "She might not have heard."

His mom's a drunk, so he has a point. That would also explain why she wasn't at the rematch today. Either she was drunk or couldn't get past school security. Probably both.

Mark says, "I'm gonna check her bedroom. Keep an eye on the street." He vanishes through the door.

When I turn back to the window, the beggar's gone. The sun is going down. We need to get out of here now, while we still can.

"Mark!" I shout. "Mark! Did you find her?"

He doesn't answer.

A pair of red patrol vans pull up and block the street at both ends. The doors slide back. A squad of warriors pour out of each van. They move to surround the house.

Twenty men. Twenty swords. Too many to fight.

I run to the bedroom and push the door open. I find Mark with a knife to his throat. He's being held by a man it takes me a moment to recognize: a man with dull brown hair and dead brown eyes. The Soap Man from the Temple.

Hanging from the rafters is Mark's mom. She's not dead, because without Hades no one can die, but she's beyond saving. Face blue. Tongue out. She's brain dead, still writhing against the rope in her ragged, wine-stained dress.

"Hello, Andrus," the Soap Man says. "Anton sends his regards. He would have been here himself, but alas, he's in the hospital. I understand he might not make it."

"Good. I hope he suffers!"

The Soap Man shrugs. "So do I! Confidentially, I never liked the fellow. It was shameful the way he treated those poor, innocent girls... like this one's sister."

"What are you talking about?" Mark gasps.

"You mean you don't know the sacrifice she made to ensure you got your scholarship? How she let Anton have his way with her?"

"No! That's a lie!" Mark says.

"Unfortunately, it's true," the Soap Man replies. "She should have given it up the first time he asked, but she said no, tried to make a deal for you. She should have known there's no option to compromise, not with men like that. And you know what happened? Anton had her anyway, and she lost her scholarship in the bargain. Such a sad story. Your sister could have had a bright future. So bright! But it's a harsh world; you either bend or you break. I'm always telling people that. It's a shame so few listen. So how about it, Andrus?"

"How about what?"

"How about you listen to my advice and surrender?"

"I can't do that."

"Really?" He presses the knife against Mark's skin 'til it bleeds. "I can't say I'm surprised. I find that most people express a certain unwillingness to face unpleasant situations at first. They want options."

"And mine are?"

"That's the thing, isn't it? Yesterday, you had so many. Today, you have none. Not even escape. That is, unless you want me to slit this Loser's throat?"

I hesitate. "Let Mark go and I'll surrender. None of this is his fault."

The Soap Man chuckles. "There you go, demanding options. Fault doesn't matter. The truth is what the Temple says it is. Don't you know that by now? You can't win. You can only obey."

"Fine." I raise my hands slowly. "I surrender. Just don't hurt him."

The Soap Man sighs. "There you go again. You just don't listen. No options, remember? No compromise..." He takes his cold, dead eyes off me for a second, just long enough I can see the tension build in his arm, to see the knife move. He's going to slit Mark's throat no matter what I do.

I swing my right fist up, send the last crystal hurtling through the space between us. It sinks into the Soap Man's eye. He staggers sideways, knife hand slashing empty air, the other holding his gore-slimed face. He backs into Mark's hanging mom. Her zombified body jerks and thrashes wildly, knocking him to the floor.

I grab Mark and we run. I have no idea how we're going to get past the warriors outside, no idea why they haven't come in to fight us. I throw open the front door, ready for anything, but not what I find.

Outside, it's a massacre. The twenty warriors lie scattered on the ground, broken like a child's toys. They groan and gag on their own blood, twitching in the road. Only one man is standing: Mr. Cross. He smiles and flicks the blood from his twin swords. The blades are gold, smoking, and engraved with magic symbols.

"Hello, boys," Mr. Cross says. "I thought you could use a little help."

39

SEE ME

THERE'S NO TIME for questions. Mr. Cross arms us with swords and shields from the defeated warriors, then piles us into one of the patrol vans. He climbs behind the wheel and backs the van up, running over a few fallen men in the process. We roll to an unblocked cross street. Mr. Cross hits the sirens, then we're tearing through Loserville.

The rutted streets make for a bone-jarring ride, but I'm glad to be moving. Glad to be away from that house, from Axios, from everything.

I lean over to Mr. Cross. "We need to go to—"

He holds up a hand to cut me off. "Bronson Canyon, right?"

"Yeah, but how did you know?"

Mr. Cross shrugs. "I'm a teacher; I know everything. You should check on your friend."

Mark seems dazed and I don't blame him. I put my hand on his shoulder. There's nothing to say. Nothing I can think of, anyway. We lock eyes for a moment, and I hope he sees how much I care, how he's not just my friend, he's my brother. Were bonded now. Bonded by blood, by tragedy, and revenge. Mark nods sadly, then looks at the floor.

I let Mark grieve, joining Mr. Cross in front of the van. As I slide into the passenger seat, my teacher lays into the horn, causing the anxious pre-curfew traffic to scatter. We barrel through an intersection and narrowly miss a rusty orange pickup truck, then the street is ours again.

I have to raise my voice to be heard over the sirens. "Thanks! You saved us."

Mr. Cross glances over at me. "It was nothing."

"It wasn't nothing," I insist.

"It was to me."

I frown, not sure what to make of that.

"Oh, I don't mean saving you was nothing—I mean slaughtering them was."

"But you took down twenty armed men in a few minutes!"

"Minutes?" Mr. Cross says. "No, Andrus. Give me some credit! I defeated those fools in a matter of seconds."

"Seconds? But how—"

"I'm not who you think I am."

"You mean you're not a gym teacher?"

He grins. "No—well, yes. It's complicated." He hits the horn again. A green sedan pulls over to let us pass.

"Complicated? Complicated how?"

"I'm not entirely human."

"You mean you're like me?"

Mr. Cross laughs. "No, not like you, Andrus. No one is like you. I'm an avatar."

"An avatar? What's that?"

"They don't teach you about us at Axios. Gods are energy beings, and an avatar is when a God takes on physical form by possessing an animal or human."

"But the Gods are dead!"

"Not all of us, though the Titans would have you believe otherwise. It's in their best interest to look all-powerful. Keeps the people kneeling at the altar."

"So which God are you?"

"Which one do you think?"

I know he's not Hades, so I'm hoping for Zeus or Poseidon, the other two strongest Gods. But no, that can't be right. He's got to be one of the other ones...

I'm not sure, so I try a joke instead: "Well, the way you were drinking yesterday, I'd guess you were Dionysus, God of Partying."

"I don't want you to guess," Mr. Cross says. "I want you to *see*. Focus, Andrus. Concentrate! *See me as I really am.*"

I wrinkle my brow in concentration. Mr. Cross's outline shimmers, his form blurs. It reminds me of the glow I saw around him at the gym downtown, when he stood in the doorway and told me my life was about to change. Suddenly, he's not my gym teacher anymore. He's a heavily muscled giant of a man in blood-red armor, face hidden behind a Corinthian helmet. Only his eyes are visible through the slits. They glow, smoking orange embers in the blackness, and reflected in them I see all the war and death that has ever been, and that ever will be. Centuries of it, millennia—from the first thrown rock to the last fired nuke.

"You're Ares, God of War."

His eyes flare, then the armored giant is gone, and it's my teacher behind the wheel. "Yes, I'm Ares, but I'm also Mr. Cross. My energy is inside him. It's a disguise, a cloak of flesh, but it can only house so much of my energy. It's what allowed me to escape the Eye of Cronus."

"Is that why you couldn't save us back at the gym?"

He snaps the siren off with an irritated gesture. "I am a God, Andrus! I do not exist for mortals. Mortals exist for me! Yes, I could have intervened. I could have easily destroyed everyone and everything in that gym, but that was not my mission. Some think chaos is all I bring, chaos and suffering, but that is not true. I rage, but it is a controlled rage. Do you understand?"

"Not really."

"Undirected anger burns its owner from within. Directed anger breeds power! This is what your suffering must teach you. If you would save your friends and family, you must control your anger to grow your power!"

"Is that what I did when I grew those claws?"

Mr. Cross—I mean Ares—smirks and changes lanes. "It was the beginning. When you lost everything today, you had to feel that anger, channel it. There is no growth without pain. That is what allowed you to change, to win!"

I stare at my hands. "It wasn't enough. And I didn't win anything. Not yet."

"You won your freedom from this world. You won your trans-formation."

"Yeah, but into what?"

"Look under your seat."

I bend down and pull out a black case. It's heavy. "What's in it?"

"Open it."

I place my thumbs on the clasps. The briefcase opens. It's my rock collection, plus three new crystals and a pair of flashlights.

"I took the liberty of stopping by your house before the Inquisi-tion did."

"And the extras?"

"I picked those up on the way to Mark's. You need replacement claws, don't you?"

I need a lot more than that, but I thank him anyway. We blast out of Loserville into downtown Othrys. The buildings loom over us like tombstones, gray against the fading sun.

"You're going to want to absorb as many of those rocks and geodes as you can before we get to Bronson Canyon."

"How do you know about that?"

"I'm a God." When I scowl at him, he sighs. "Very well. Hannah told me."

"Who's Hannah?" Mark asks from the back of the van.

I turn to Mark and say, "I'll tell you later," then look at Ares. "You and Hannah are friends?"

"Not exactly, but we are family. I know all about you going to Tartarus to rescue my uncle."

"You mean Hades."

He nods. "Things move quickly once you step outside your world. Be ready. What you have seen and suffered so far is nothing compared to what awaits you in the Underworld."

Mark speaks up. "What we suffered is *not* nothing! My mother, my sister... You may be a God, but you don't get to dismiss them like that. You don't get to dismiss what I feel!"

Ares's knuckles whiten where they grip the wheel. He's not used to being spoken to this way.

"Mark, you might not want to piss Ares off. He did save our lives."

"Yeah, but he didn't save Lucy! He didn't save my mom. Why? Because he wanted you to suffer enough that your powers would come out?"

I open my mouth to say something, but there's no point denying it. That's exactly why he didn't help. And part of me hates him for it, but part of me knows he's right. That it had to be this way, or I'd never be ready to rescue Hades.

"Look at him," Mark snorts. "He's like one of your rocks! Doesn't he feel anything?"

Ares shrugs. "Gods do not feel as mortals do, despite the myths. What we feel—or do not feel—you cannot hope to understand. I say this not to be cruel, but to prepare you. Where you are going is not the mortal realm. Your grief will not help you there... Hear me when I say that to carry grief into the Underworld is to carry a vulture that gnaws at your heart. It is both the drug and weapon of choice for ghosts, for demons, and far worse things. Better to turn your grief to anger, to channel that energy to propel you toward your goal, not tear you from it."

Mark glares at Ares, then me. "Andrus, is this guy for real?"

"Yeah, man. He is. Show him, Ares. Show him what you really look like."

"I cannot. Mortals lack the ability to see things for what they truly are. That is why they must have faith. That is why they suffer and kneel—" He jerks the wheel hard to the left, knocking Mark to the floor as we sail up the freeway onramp. "Almost missed our turn," he explains with grim satisfaction. "We should arrive at Bronson Canyon in ten minutes. I would appreciate silence until then. Andrus, start absorbing those rocks. Begin with the geodes."

"I don't know how."

"Feel the rock. *Will* the rock to become part of you, and you, part of it. It is the same process you used before... the only difference is now you are aware of it. Oh, and you might want to hurry."

"Why?"

"We're being followed." He steps on the gas, forcing the speedometer into the red.

I look in the rearview mirror. No cars. Just the last rays of a dying sun as it slips over the horizon. "I don't see anything."

"Look again," Ares says. "Roll down the window."

I stick my head out the window and squint toward the sky. Clouds. Clouds and darkness. But that's not all—not for long. Winged shadows climb the horizon.

Harpies.

40

I LIVE FOR WAR

THERE'S A WELCOMING COMMITTEE waiting at Griffith Park. Captain Nessus and his centaurs block the road to Bronson Canyon. Their yellow eyes blaze in the glow of our headlights. Behind us, the harpies are only a minute away.

Ares hits the brakes.

"It's the Night Patrol," Mark whispers. "What are we gonna do?"

Ares tightens his grip on the wheel. "Fight."

"Yeah, but how?"

"With everything we've got." I shove the last of the crystals between my knuckles, willing them to become part of me.

The centaurs stamp the asphalt with their hooves, anxious for battle.

The God of War revs the engine. "I'm going to ram those Titan-born bastards and punch our way through. I'll get you as close to the caves as I can, then I want you both to run."

"We can't just leave you," I protest.

"You can, and you will! Get to the cave, Andrus. Get to Hannah. Rescue Hades and free your world. Don't worry about me. I live for war; I'm a God, remember?"

"An avatar," I remind him. "You're not at full strength."

He grins. "That's why this fight will be a challenge."

I stare into the empty case. I've absorbed the rocks, the geodes, everything. "I'm ready. Let's do it."

The centaurs raise their spears and bray with goat-like rage. The van plows forward, scattering centaurs to either side. Barbed spears scrape the paint job, which seems kind of pathetic until I see one actually punch through the wall, narrowly missing Mark. I'd forgotten how strong centaurs are.

The rearview mirror shows them galloping after us, Captain Nessus in the lead. His brothers, Democ and Ruvo, are right behind him. Then something even more hideous dives in front of them, and it's much closer. The mirror fills with the wrinkled, ravenous face of a shrieking vulture-woman. The harpy is all feathers and fury with an evil beaked face and the body of a beautiful woman. Where her arms should be are wings, and where her legs should be are long, bird-like talons.

Something hard hits the roof. Then something else.

"What's that?" Mark asks.

I don't need to tell him. The beaks punching through the roof tell Mark everything. His worst childhood memory is back. The harpies use their claws to tear holes in the roof, hoping to widen them enough to fit through. Mark thrusts his sword through one of the holes, provoking an angry squawk from one of the monsters.

"Get them off!" Mark shouts. "Get them off!" There's a note of panic in his voice.

"Hang on!" Ares swerves the van. Through the rearview mirror, I see one of the vulture-women thrown from the roof, but it doesn't stop her long. She flaps relentlessly back toward us.

I join Mark in the rear of the van. The harpy we didn't shake free has succeeded in curling back a section of the vehicle's roof. Her grotesque face swings inside the cabin on its long, bird-like neck. Mark flails with his sword and the harpy catches the blade in her beak, nearly ripping the weapon from his hand. She makes a gloating, guttural sound. This is just a game to her. Playing with her food. Playing with our lives.

I bring my sword down on her neck, feeling tendons tear and feathered flesh give. The harpy's head drops to the floor in a foul splash of gore. Black, tar-like blood pumps from her mangled neck. Mark pulls his sword from her beak and I kick the severed head away.

"One down," I mutter.

"Thanks," Mark says. "That was kind of a flashback for me, you know?"

I nod, remembering what Mark said the harpy had told him as a child: 'You can't eat dreams.' *But dreams can eat you.* Almost to prove it, the harpy's still-living head emits an awful cackling gurgle. Her cruel, black eyes glare hate—hate and hunger.

"We're coming up on the canyon," Ares warns. "Be ready to run!"

Mark and I exchange a look. Are we really heroes? Can we do this? The answer comes in a squeal of tires. We throw the van doors open and plunge into the night.

41

FIGHT TO THE END

ADRENALINE TAKES OVER. My heart wants to stand with Ares and fight, but my gut tells me to run. A backward glance shows Ares draw his golden swords and wade into the oncoming horde of monsters. The God of War is smiling his terrible smile, a butcher's grin as his blades sing and the screams chorus.

He'll be all right. This is what Ares does. I'm just glad he's doing it for us. "We have to get off the road," I tell Mark. "Follow me!"

We cut through the park, the sound of wings and hooves growing more distant. I want to put trees between us and the monsters. Trees to hide us from harpies, low-hanging branches to slow the centaurs.

Use the earth. Be the earth.

The thought pops into my head, and with it, some wild gulf opens. A sense of freedom. Safety. Protection. I can't explain it. I should be terrified, but I'm not. I'm willing to fight to the end, but not here, not if I can help it. I have to get to the cave. I have to get to Hannah.

We break from the trees into Bronson Canyon, stumbling over uneven ground. So many trails! Which one leads to the cave? Everywhere I turn, the canyon looks the same in the moonlight: rocks and dust and scrub. It's a barren and desolate place, and it will be our end unless we find the right path.

Shadow appears from the trail to the right. He flaps and caws, then takes off back the way he came. We follow, but the extra weight of our swords and shields slow us and I'm tempted to cast them aside. After all, I'm a living weapon now, but Mark isn't. I can't speed up only to leave him behind. He's panting, breath loud, brain panicked.

The night brings another sound: the shrill cry of harpies. The centaurs can't be far behind.

"Come on," I urge Mark. "We're almost there!"

The cave where I talked to the drunk priest is just ahead. The priest and his slaves are gone, but I can see the sealed entrance they left behind. Seeing the landmark lets us know we're close. Unfortunately, the Night Patrol is close too. In a rush of wings, a harpy swoops down.

"Shields!" I shout, raising mine. Mark gets his up just in time. The harpy's talons scrape off the embossed metal, throwing sparks. As she wings past, I nearly choke on the smell of decay that accompanies her. She smells like bad meat and broken dreams.

"Found you!" the harpy croaks, then cackles madly and comes in for another pass. She flexes her talons, chanting, "Give me your eyes! Your eyes!" And then I see why—she's wearing a necklace of human eyes strung together like a popcorn garland.

"Swords!" I yell, and in a clatter of steel, they leap from our scabbards. Remembering my warrior training, I add, "Shields up!"

Seeing our defense, the harpy breaks off her dive in a shriek of anger. Flapping wildly, she heads back the way she came calling, "Sisters! Sisters, come quick! The humans are escaping!"

We run.

Shadow leads the way, his scolding squawks urging us to get to the cave. Over the constant sound of our pounding feet comes the sound of inhuman pursuit: hungry hooves, wicked wings.

"Surrender!" booms the voice of Captain Nessus. It doesn't come from behind us. It comes from straight ahead. Somehow the captain has led a squad of five centaurs to outflank us as five more, led by

Democ and Ruvo, gallop in from behind. Their lathered skin glows in the moonlight.

Overhead, three harpies circle like the fiendish vultures they are.

Mark and I have no choice but to stop. We're trapped. The canyon walls rise up on either side. I could climb them, but there's no way Mark can—not without equipment. The only good thing is the walls limit how many monsters can attack us at the same time.

"I've been looking forward to this." The captain's voice is gruff and gloating. "There is no escape for you now."

"The eyes!" the harpy with the necklace calls. "Save us the eyes!"

"You'll get what we leave and like it," Nessus growls.

The harpies screech menacingly. "We found them first! They are ours by right."

"You may have found them," Nessus agrees, "but you did not finish them! Therefore, the flesh is ours." The other centaurs raise their spears and stamp their hooves in approval.

It's then I remember even though the monsters are on the same side, they don't like each other. They only work together because Cronus commands it. Which means they work together badly, and avoid joint missions when they can. But not this one. Too much is at stake, and the Temple and Titans know it.

"Wait!" I say loud enough for both sides to hear. "The harpies found us first. If they want our eyes so bad, why not let them have a chance to take them?"

"The boy speaks true!" the harpy with the necklace says.

"Once they take our eyes, you can have our brains," I say to Nessus.

"Brains! The brains!" the harpies chant. "We get the eyes, you get the brains."

"Take them then," Captain Nessus says. "If you can." He motions his squad to back up and give the bird-women room.

Cackling, the harpies dive.

I raise my right hand, curl it into a fist, and fire crystal daggers. Two of the harpies plummet to the earth, each sprouting a dagger between her ribs. The she-beasts land with a sickening thud.

The one with the necklace rips the shield from my arm. I pump a spike into her, but she's too fast. It damages her wing instead of sinking into her heart. She screams and drops the shield, flapping desperately to gain altitude before she plows into the centaurs watching behind us.

At the last second, she lifts her feathered body up and over the sea of horns and spears, climbing high above the canyon wall. She flies away, screeching curses. And just like that, I've removed the centaurs's aerial support.

"Give her a minute," I boast. "Maybe she'll be back."

"Harpies,"Nessus snorts. "Stupid creatures... but they have their uses. We were warned about your tricks, boy. So tell me, do you have any those crystal daggers left?"

"Come find out," I taunt.

Nessus tosses his shaggy, horned head and brays laughter. "Your boldness shall be your undoing." He motions to his squad. "Company, present arms!" The centaurs lower their spears, ready to run us through. The barbed points glitter silver—promising pain, promising horror.

"It's me Cronus wants," I say. "Leave Mark out of it."

Nessus clops forward a few steps. "Ever the noble hero! Yes, by all means, surrender, and we will let the Loser go." He looks at Mark and licks his lips. "He is of limited use, but you... you are the prize our master wants."

"What the hell are you doing?" Mark says. *"I won't let you surrender."*

"I'm not talking about surrender," I tell Mark, then say to the centaurs, "I challenge the captain to single combat!"

"Oh-ho!" Nessus roars with mirth. "A challenge!" His squad growls in anticipation. "And if you win?"

"I surrender, but Mark goes free."

The captain's yellow eyes narrow, considering my offer. "Very well. And if I win?"

"You can do with both of us as you please."

"Great," Mark grumbles. "Guess my brains are on the menu... again."

Nessus trots forward to address us all. "A challenge has been made, brothers, and a challenge accepted! I fight for the glory of Cronus!"

"FOR GLORY!" the centaurs shout, and step back to make room for us.

Nessus points at Mark with his spear. "Well, boy? Will you stand there, or will you step aside?"

Mark looks from the captain to me, unsure what to do.

"It's OK," I tell him. "They won't hurt you."

"I don't trust them," Mark says.

"I'm not asking you to. I'm asking you to trust me." I lean in close and lower my voice. "If I'm wrong... if I fail, I need you to run the direction Shadow flew. If you can get to Hannah, you might have a chance. She's waiting at the cave we explored."

Mark nods, sheathes his sword and hurries over to the captain's line. The four centaurs there leave him be, though they don't take their eyes off him either.

"We fight to the end," I tell Nessus.

"The bitter end," the captain agrees. "I shall enjoy watching you suffer!" He backs up, giving himself room to charge.

I hope I'm not making a mistake, but this is better than fighting all ten of them. I dig my heels into the dirt, not just to brace myself, but to feel that elemental connection again:

Use the earth. Be the earth.

Nessus charges, the earth vibrating, telling me where to step, where to be. I'm ready for him, side-stepping the thrust of his barbed spear. I lash out with my sword, hitting the captain in the flank. It's a shallow cut, dripping black blood. If it hurts him, he doesn't react, just continues on his path. Nessus slows as he approaches the half of his squad blocking the way we came.

"First blood," I taunt, flicking the beads of gore from my blade the same way Ares did.

"Your first," Nessus says. "And your last!" He charges again, faster than I expect, and this time he's ready for my parry. His spear strikes my chest, only it doesn't sink in. It shatters instead. I look down in wonder, seeing a patch of geode crystal through my ripped tunic. It covers my flesh where my wound should be.

"More tricks!" Nessus howls. "You cheat, but you shall not rob me of my victory." He grabs a spear from one of his brothers. "I will taste your brains!" The captain thunders toward me.

I ready my defense, only this time, he throws the spear and draws his sword. The blade isn't his; it's one of the golden swords of Ares.

I manage to dodge the spear, but not the sword. It crunches into my left shoulder. When I touch the smoking wound, I see my crystal armor is broken there. I pull my hand away and it's stained with blood and bits of crystal. It hurts, but I can still use my arm. I'm more concerned about how Nessus got the sword—what happened to Ares?

"You're not the only one with tricks," the captain says as he wheels around to come at me again. "This blade is cyclops-forged steel! It can cut through anything—even you!"

I half-dodge, half-dive away from him. His sword slices air as I hit the dirt and roll to my feet. Breathing hard. Bleeding. I wasn't expecting this. For a second, I thought I was invincible. Now I'm just mad. The anger bubbles up in me like lava. There's no way this brain-eating monster is going to stop me, magic sword or not.

"For glory!" Nessus rears up on his hind legs, sword raised high. "For Cronus!"

"FOR CRONUS!" his brothers yell as one. Their yellow eyes gleam with excitement.

The captain charges. "Now we end this! Now you are mine!"

In a clash of steel, our swords meet; my human-forged blade is no match against his. It breaks in a shower of sparks. Nessus rears, smashing his hooves against my chest. The blows don't get past my crystal armor, but that doesn't mean I don't feel them, and they hurt.

They hurt a lot!

I twist past the hooves to launch myself at his back. All my old pankration skills come surging in as I get the captain into a headlock.

Nessus grunts and rears up, bucking wildly to throw me off. He nearly does, but I wrap my legs around his torso. Holding on.

Applying more pressure to his throat. The centaur's foul breath hisses and foam flecks his bestial black lips. His blade jabs at me over his shoulder. I have to duck to avoid it and that's all the edge he needs. With a massive buck, Nessus knocks me to the canyon floor. Then his stolen sword is cleaving down, and there's no time to dodge, no way to defend.

I've lost.

There's a shrill bird call, and for a second, I think the harpy has returned, but it's too close. Too small. In a flash of feathers, Shadow swoops in to savagely claw the captain's snarling face. It's not much, but it's enough for his attack to miss.

A ghostly blur flashes into view, surrounding me in a gray cloud before I can react. I sense more than see motion, and then I'm some-where down the trail. Past the centaurs. Just outside the cave.

The cloud turns from a girl-shaped outline to a real flesh and blood girl. Hannah. "Hello, Rock Boy." She pauses to stretch out her arm for Shadow to perch on. She pets the bird, then turns to me. "Sorry to crash the party, and not to put down your macho moves or anything, but you were taking forever. We can't keep Hades waiting."

I hear the distant cries and clatter of hooves, then look around wildly. "Where's Mark?"

"Right here," he says, stepping out from behind a boulder. "She rescued me first—not that anyone noticed."

I hug him. "I'm glad you're all right! I would have gone back for you. You know that, right?"

"*I* knew," Hannah says. "That's why I rescued him first. Well, that, and I'm not a total bitch. Didn't I tell you not to bring him?"

"Yeah, I know. It's complicated."

"It sure is," she says. "Speaking of complicated, that jackass priest sealed the cave entrance you made. It's our ticket to Tartarus, so if you don't mind..."

"Tartarus," Mark says. "Of course! We're going to save Hades." He shakes his head. "Why not?" Then he grows serious, and I can tell he's thinking of his mom and Lucy. Justice and revenge. "Whatever happens, you can count on me. The Titans have to pay for what they've done."

"First, we rescue Hades," Hannah says. "Then we'll worry about settling up with Cronus and his kind." She gives me a weird look when she says it. When I stare back, curious, she shrugs impatiently. "The seal, Andrus! It's warded against Gods and Demigods, not just ghosts and monsters. I can't break it. Only you can."

I try to summon my energy to break the seal. But no matter how hard I try, nothing happens.

"What are you doing?" Hannah demands. "What's taking so long?"

"I don't know, I—"

Hannah slaps me. Hard across the face.

"Ow! Hey, what was that for?" I ask.

She slaps me again. "You lost your anger! Now focus. Concentrate your rage."

I scowl. "No need to worry. It's concentrated, all right."

"Um, guys," Mark says. "You hear those hooves? The centaurs are coming!"

I turn toward the cave and summon my power. It comes easily this time. The ground ripples. A crack forms at my feet, then zig-zags toward the sealed entrance. The magic symbols in the bricks glow with arcane power, then shatter.

Captain Nessus and his centaurs round the bend. Seeing us, they howl their hate and charge.

"We need to go," Hannah says. "Now!" We rush into the cave and once we're inside, Hannah commands me to seal the entrance.

I focus, feeling myself become one with the cave. And just as the first of the centaurs enter, I collapse the entrance. Their screams end in thudding stone and crushing doom. My only regret is Captain Nessus wasn't among them. The bastard knew better, and he'll know better next time. I saw it in his hateful yellow eyes.

42

EVERYTHING I NEED

WE HEAD DEEPER into the cave. Mark and I use the flashlights Ares gave me to pick our way through. When we get to the chasm, we stop. It's fifty feet straight down with no rope or climbing gear. "No problem," Hannah says. "I can float down, and I know what you can do, Andrus. Your friend here can ride on your back."

"My name's Mark."

She sighs. "Fine. *Mark* can ride down on your back. Not a very dignified way to travel, but when you're human, you don't get a lot of options."

"Wait," Mark asks her. "You mean you're not human either?"

"Demigod," Hannah explains. "Daughter of Hades. My name's Hannah Stillwater." The raven on her shoulder croaks a greeting. "And this little fellow is my familiar, Shadow."

"Nice to meet you," Mark says. "I'm confused. How do you know Andrus and Mr. Cross?"

"You mean Ares, son of Zeus. He's my cousin."

"Yeah, Ares. It's kind of weird to find out my gym teacher is a God."

"An avatar."

Mark runs his fingers through his hair. "Right... So can you just answer my questions without correcting me every five seconds?"

Hannah opens her mouth to say something—something I assume will be sarcastic—so I step in and answer for her. "I met Hannah here in the cave while you were knocked out. She saved your life."

She grins. "See? I'm not so bad after all."

"Well, it wasn't her so much as the ghost of Herophilos that saved you. He's a surgeon—at least he was before he died."

Hannah coughs politely.

"But she summoned him," I add hastily. The raven scolds me, forcing me to say, "Shadow helped." It caws and bobs its head up and down.

"So Hannah is the 'cloud-girl' we saw the other night. OK, things are beginning to make sense. But why didn't you tell me, Andrus?"

"Because I was freaking out, and I didn't want you freaking out too. You had to stay focused on the rematch. I couldn't burden you with... with all this. I thought about it, of course, but there was never a good time."

He raises an eyebrow. "And now is?"

There's a far-off rumbling from the front of the cave.

"Now is the only time," Hannah says. "So are you coming with us, or staying here?"

Mark doesn't even think about it. "Are you serious? Of course I'm coming with you!"

We descend the wall, each of us in our own way. It feels good to sink my fingers into the the rock wall. It feels nourishing. When we get to the bottom, Hannah leads us to the tunnel Mark and I left unexplored the last time we were here. There's still a rancid, monster-y smell coming from it.

"Ugh!" Mark scowls. "What's that stink?"

"Sulfur, methane, some other toxic gasses. Perfectly harmless to Andrus and I, but not so much to you."

"Hannah, we can't just leave him," I say.

"We won't." She reaches into her strange dark cloak and

rummages through an inner pocket. She pulls out a wispy ball made of mist and tosses it at Mark. It flows over his head, conforming to the shape of his face but giving him a decidedly skull-like, undead appearance. "It's a ghost-mask," she explains. "It won't hurt you. It filters the gasses into breathable air. You'll need to keep it on while you're in the Underworld."

Mark fidgets with it. "How do I get it off?"

"You don't," Hannah replies. "Not unless you want to choke to death and become a zombie."

Mark pales beneath the translucent mask and I know he must be seeing his mother hanging from the rafters.

"Probably best not to mention zombies right now. Is there anything else he should know about the ghost-mask?"

Hannah shrugs. "Just that mortals aren't generally welcome in Tartarus. Few who enter ever leave. That mask will let you blend in with the local spirit population."

"You mean ghosts," Mark says. "Great. What about you and Andrus?"

"Oh, we'll fit right in. Not just with the ghosts, but with everything else that's down there."

"Everything else? Like what?"

"Only one way to find out." Hannah winks and walks into the tunnel. "Come on, Rock Boy. We've got work to do."

Following her into the tunnel feels weird, and not just because we're marching into Tartarus. My lungs begin to sting, then burn. "H-Hannah!" I choke on her name. "Something's not right!"

She pauses ahead of me. "Sorry, I forgot. It takes a minute to adjust if you've never used your lungs this way before."

Mark comes up and puts his hand on my shoulder. "You OK?"

I try to answer, but double over in a coughing fit. It feels worse than ever, until suddenly, it doesn't. I stand up, surprised by how fine I am. "I'm all right. You?"

Mark nods. "The mask works. What does it look like?"

"You don't want to know."

He smiles, making himself look even more ghoulish. "So how do we get to Tartarus, Hannah? We just go down this tunnel?"

"Not that simple. We take the tunnel to the River Styx, then hitch a ride with Charon, the Ferryman of the Dead. From there, well, Tartarus is a big place... but don't worry. I know where to get off and exactly where we need to go."

I have to wonder what she's not telling us about the trip or the dangers we'll face. "Do you think Ares is all right? He stayed behind to hold the monsters off. The centaur captain took one of his swords."

Hannah looks alarmed. "Really? That's not good."

"Yeah, I know! He could be hurt or captured or—"

"That's not what I meant. Ares can take care of himself. But with one of his magic swords, the monsters could be chopping their way through the cave-in."

I let that sink in. "Even so, they're half-horse. They can't climb the chasm wall."

"They don't need to," Hannah says. "That's what the harpies are for."

"But I got rid of them!"

"You got rid of the first wave, dumb ass! There are always more."

As if on cue, the familiar shrieking cry of the vulture-women echoes down the tunnel. They're in the cave. "Give us your eyes!" the harpies shriek. "Your eyes! Your eyes!"

I hesitate, shuddering at the memory of the eyeball necklace the one harpy wore and how she wanted to add mine to it. Hannah tries to slap me, but I grab her wrist. "No," I say. "I'm OK. I think I'm getting the hang of this." She smiles and steps back.

I touch the wall, channeling my anger into the power of the earth, directing the energy into another cave-in. It's a spectacular collapse that blocks the way back to Othrys. A wave of dust billows from the blast, covering us.

Hannah coughs and brushes her tunic free of the worst of it. "Way to go, Rock Boy. You saved the day again."

"Yeah," Mark says. "Say, what are you, Andrus?"

"I'd like to know too. Hannah promised she'd tell me."

"Did I?" She walks away, forcing us to hurry after her. "You mean you haven't figured it out on your own?"

"I've figured out what I'm not. I'm not a God, Demigod, or monster, and I'm certainly not a ghost. I couldn't have broken through the cave seals if I was any of those things."

"That's right. So what's left?"

"I don't know."

"Yes, you do."

"No, I don't! Quit playing games and tell me!"

"Holy shit," Mark gasps. "I think I can guess: You're a Titan."

I laugh and feel sick at the same time. "What? But that's crazy! Look, man, I get that you're supposed to be smart and all, but you're way off-base."

"Why not?" Hannah asks. "It's no crazier than me being a Demigod, and you didn't question that."

"But we're *fighting* the Titans. I can't be one of them!"

"Of course you can," Hannah says, "that's what makes you an ideal ally. Remember how some of the Titans sided with the Gods back in Ancient Greece?"

"You mean like Prometheus? That didn't work out so well for him. After they won the war, Zeus chained him to a rock and had an eagle rip out his guts over and over again!"

Hannah smirks. "They let him go eventually. Anyway, aren't you curious who your parents are?"

"I know who my parents are," I say stubbornly. "George and Carol Eaves."

She rolls her eyes. "Not your adopted parents; your biological ones. Especially your father. Who is he?"

I think of the original twelve Titans, and pick the worst possible one just to spite her. "Cronus?"

"Yes, you're the son of Cronus."

"That can't be. You're lying!" I punch the tunnel wall and don't even feel it. "Cronus is pure evil. Everything that's happened is his fault."

"And everything that happens next can be yours," Hannah says. "But nothing is pure evil, Andrus, just like nothing is pure good. You'd do well to remember that."

All my dreams make sense now... climbing Mount Olympus in anger, in hatred. Somehow, I was reliving Cronus scaling Mount Olympus during the Gods War. I was trying to kill Zeus and the other Gods.

I was trying to kill my own children to hold on to the past, to my own power. Just like I'd killed my father, Ouranos, to seize it. I flash back to a lifetime ago in Mrs. Ploddin's history class. Everything I need to know was in her lecture. Everything I need to know and nothing I want to hear.

Mark lays a hand on my shoulder. "Hey, it's gonna be all right. Titan or not, you're still my friend."

"Thanks," I grumble. "Just give me a minute, OK?"

"Sure." He jogs to catch up to Hannah, then they disappear around a bend in the tunnel. Leaving me alone. Alone with my darkness. Alone with my hate.

I stay there for I don't know how long. Trying to process, to accept what I am. *A Titan.* But no matter how hard I try to put it together, something's still missing. Something I have to know.

I come out of the tunnel and join Mark and Hannah in a narrow cavern. A river cuts through it. The water is still and black. It reeks of sulfur and death, a stench that gets in my nose and makes me wince.

"Don't mind the smell," Hannah explains. "This is the Styx, the River of Hate and Promises. I get my last name from it, you know: Stillwater."

Looking into its shadowy depths, I sense a disturbing movement under the surface... but what's down there, I can't exactly say. All I know is I don't want to find out.

"Don't look too closely," Hannah warns, "and whatever you do, don't fall in." She pulls off her cloak and carefully dips it into the black water.

"What are you doing?" I ask.

"Recharging my cloak's power. It taps into the river's magical properties."

"And its stink," I add.

"Not all magic items can be as glamorous as Ares's swords," Hannah says curtly. "My cloak might not be pretty, but it gets the job done."

"Just as I suspected," Mark says. "Did Hades make it?"

"Of course." Hannah pulls the cloak from the river, mutters a spell, and the fabric is instantly dry again. She whips it around her shoulders and fastens it. "Got any more questions, you two? Charon will be here any minute."

Mark starts to ask her about being a witch and if she can teach him any magic spells, but I cut him off. "Hang on," I say. "I've got a question! A big one: If my father is Cronus, then who's my mother? Rhea? She's Cronus's wife."

"Your mother's not Rhea; you don't have a mother. Well, not technically. Not in any normal kind of way."

"I don't understand." I'm getting a very bad feeling, the kind that makes me want to punch stuff.

"Hmm... No mother, you say?" Mark paces back and forth, that priestly brain of his working overtime. And instead of adding to the conversation, he only adds to the mystery. Not saying a word.

There's a slight smirk on Hannah's face. She's enjoying stretching this out, making us work for it. When she catches me watching her, she pretends to be interested in looking for the ferryman.

"How do you know Charon's coming?" I ask.

"He knows everything that happens along the river. The minute we stepped onto the bank, he knew. That's why he's so good at his job."

"And he won't report us to Cronus or the monsters?"

"Not a chance. Charon's a workaholic. He gets his kicks ferrying the dead to Tartarus. Not much call for that since there's no more death—at least not until we free my father."

"So he's on our side?"

"We're the only ones who can give him what he wants, so yeah, we can trust him."

Mark finishes pacing. "I think I've figured out who your mother is, Andrus." He looks at me, and he must be hoping I got it too, but I just stare at him.

"OK, so we all know Cronus devoured his children so they couldn't usurp him. All of them except Zeus. Am I getting warm?" Mark asks Hannah.

"You're warm," she admits.

"And Rhea was—pardon the pun—fed up with her children being devoured. So after she gave birth to Zeus, she hid him and substituted a rock disguised to look like a child in his place, and Cronus ate the rock. Am I hot yet?"

Hannah nods. "Scalding."

"Wait," I say, "where the hell is this going?"

Mark holds up a hand to stop me. "Hang on, I'm getting to it. So Cronus ate the rock and it joined the children in his stomach who were still alive. Cronus absorbed their power and added it to his own—but of course, he couldn't do that with the rock."

I remember how Mrs. Ploddin sighed when Mark had mentioned that. How the whole class had laughed. They thought he was being pedantic, a stupid nerd obsessed with pointless details. But what if he was also being prophetic?

Mark and Hannah look at me expectantly. An angry, embarrassed heat flushes my cheeks. "What? So I'm the rock? Is that what you're telling me?"

"Hey," Hannah says, "you said it, not us! But yeah. Congratulations, Rock Boy. You figured it out."

Now it's my turn to pace. "That doesn't make any sense! How can I be a rock?"

"Not just any rock," Mark says. "*A magic rock.*"

"Great! Even better."

"What you don't understand is that while you were in Cronus's stomach, while he was absorbing the Gods' powers, you were absorbing his—including those he stole from the Gods."

"But that was over a thousand years ago! I haven't been alive that long."

"You only think you're a teenager," Hannah says. "Your mother, who had given you to Rhea, took you back and hid you in her womb until she knew it was time to bring you into the world."

I stop pacing and turn on her. "I thought you said I didn't have a mom?"

"Not in the normal sense. You're a rock, Andrus! Think about it. What kind of woman gives birth to a rock?"

"Gaia," Mark says. "Goddess of the Earth, Mother of the Titans. She must have created Andrus to serve as a balance between Gods and Titans in case things ever got this bad."

"Balance? Let's worry about that after we free Hades and kill Cronus. The rest of the Titans won't exactly be begging for peace until their king is dead."

"I'm not a goddamn rock!" I shout. But deep down, I know it's true. *I can feel it.* It's crazy and it hurts. It's also strangely liberating. It explains everything about me, from discovering oil in my parents' backyard to my fascination with rockhounding, caving, climbing. The dreams, the magic. All of it.

"Hey, man," Mark says. "It's OK. We're all *something*. I'm human, Hannah's a Demigod, and you—you're a rock. A very important rock that can change the world. But we're all heroes. We're all in this fight together. And that means accepting ourselves as much as it means accepting each other. That's the only way we win."

Hannah gives him a respectful nod. "Well, well. I take it back, Andrus. I'm glad you brought him."

"Maybe my wisdom is my magic," Mark suggests.

"Don't get your hopes up." She turns away from us and points to an approaching boat. "At last! Charon's here."

The wooden craft is long and narrow, like a gondola, and decorated with the bones and skulls of the dead. A hooded, dark-robed figure stands at the rear clutching a rafting pole. It's Charon, and when the ferryman lifts his head toward us, I see his bleached and bearded skeletal face. He peers at us through empty sockets, yet I sense he can see us. The boat skims to a halt. Charon keeps one bony hand on the pole while the other reaches toward me with a dry, clacking sound.

"He's asking to get paid," Hannah says. "Charon may break some rules—like helping us—but getting paid is the one rule he never breaks. Did either of you bring any drachmas?"

Mark checks his pockets and comes up empty. "I'm out. Andrus? What about you?"

I don't have any either, but I do have something in my hand that wasn't there a second ago: the first rock I absorbed.

"I don't think he accepts rocks," Hannah says. "What else you got?"

Without thinking, I squeeze my fingers around the rock and wish. There's a grinding pressure, and when I open my hand, the rock is now a diamond. I hand it to Charon; his long-dead hand clacks shut around the gem and whisks it into his robe.

"Interesting," Hannah says as she steps into the boat. "Your powers are evolving."

I join her. "Not just my powers, Ghost Girl. *Me.*"

"We're all evolving," Mark says as he steps in beside us.

And he's right—our old lives are dust. Our new lives await, fraught with new challenges, new horrors. New everything. It's a fight I'm not sure we can win, but we have to try.

For my parents, for Lucy, for the world.

So the three of us sit. Facing forward, facing destiny as the ferryman pushes off from the shore, and then there are no more words, no more thoughts, just the soft shush of black, still water.

Tartarus awaits.

Did you enjoy this book?

If you did, please take a moment to **leave an online review**. Even just a single short sentence will help this book reach new fans!

Our heroes return in *The Gods War, Book II*
— KINGDOM OF THE DEAD —
Be ready, citizen. Cronus is watching...

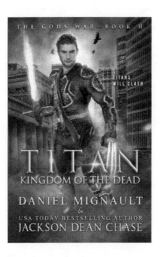

Book II: *Kingdom of the Dead* releases July 20, 2018

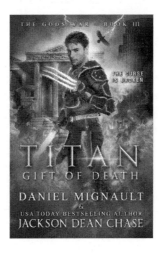

Book III: *Gift of Death* releases July 27, 2018

SPECIAL FREE BOOK OFFER

GLOSSARY

- **Archieréas:** The high priest of Cronus who serves as administrator, pope, and president of the New Greece Theocracy. The current office holder is Enoch Vola. Pronounced Ar-CUH-ray-us.
- **Cronus:** King of the Titans, father of the Greek Gods. His symbol is the Unblinking Eye. Pronounced CROH-nus.
- **Day Patrol:** Armed bands of human warriors that serve as police; they answer to the priesthood.
- **Gaia:** The Earth Mother. She created the Titans with her lover, Ouranos, the Sky Father. Pronounced GUY-yuh.
- **Gods War:** The final battle between the Greek Gods and Titans in which the Gods lost and were either killed or imprisoned in Tartarus.
- **Hades:** Greek God of Death and the Underworld, older brother of Zeus. His symbol is the bident (a two-pronged trident). His imprisonment at the end of the Gods War prevents mortals from dying, but not from aging or becoming diseased or injured (see zombie). Pronounced HAY-dees.

- **Losers:** A popular insult, and also the name of the lowest free caste in society. Most slaves live better.
- **Loserville:** Slang for the run-down, economically challenged area of East Othrys; its population are "Losers."
- **New Greece Theocracy (NGT):** An oppressive regime built on what's left of America after the Gods War destroyed much of the rest of the world. The NGT runs along what was the west coast, from Washington state to California. The Titans used their magic to transform its climate to match that of the Mediterranean.
- **Night Patrol:** Armed bands of human-hating monsters that enforce the after dark curfew. Mostly made up of centaurs and harpies.
- **Othrys:** Capital city of the NGT; named after Mount Othrys in Greece, birthplace of the Titans and their former capital on Earth. Previously known as Los Angeles. Pronounced AWTH-rees.
- **Ouranos:** The Sky Father. Lover of Gaia, the Earth Mother. Devoured by their son, Cronus. Pronounced OR-raw-nos.
- **Pankration:** A form of mixed martial arts practiced by the warriors of the NGT. It combines boxing and wrestling, with lots of takedowns, chokes, and joint locks.
- **Rich-O:** Loser slang for the wealthy caste.
- **Zeus:** King of the Gods, ruler of Mount Olympus, brother of Hades, and son of Cronus. His symbol is the lightning bolt. Pronounced ZUICE.
- **Zombie:** A person who should be dead but isn't, often with a traumatic brain injury. Zombies are doomed to wander in pain for eternity—or until Hades is freed from his prison.

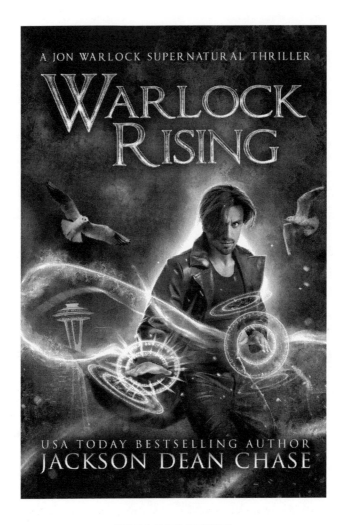

ACKNOWLEDGMENTS

DANIEL MIGNAULT: This book is dedicated to my loving family.

JACKSON DEAN CHASE: I would like to thank my friends, family, and fans, especially my street team, for their tireless support.

Additional thanks to my influences and inspirations, from late night sessions playing *Dungeons & Dragons*, to the time I watched *Clash of the Titans* four times in 1981 original. Thanks to the stop-motion magic of Ray Harryhausen, who filled me with wonder as he "unleashed the Kraken."

Writing a fantasy or science fiction book—and this book is both —is always a lengthy and challenging process. It involves a lot of world-building and research to get right. Not always real world accurate, but emotionally "right."

Everything, no matter how impossible in our reality, must make sense in the story world. It must be true to the characters, and by extension, to the readers as well. Hopefully, *Titan* achieves that. So I have one final thanks: to you, the reader, for taking this journey with us. Now go all the way with Book II...

Tartarus awaits!

ABOUT DANIEL MIGNAULT

Daniel Mignault started in the entertainment industry from a young age as an actor and model surrounded by worlds of fantasy and imagination.

As Daniel grew older, he found his passion change from being in front of the camera to creating the stories and characters he once played. Now a full-fledged writer, Daniel is ready to bring his stories to life.

Titan is his debut novel.

CHECK OUT DANIEL'S FILMS AND VIDEOS

Visit his IMDB page or visit his YouTube channel.

For more information:
www.danielmig.com
www.imdb.com/name/nm3693355

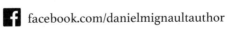 facebook.com/danielmignaultauthor

 twitter.com/DanielMignault

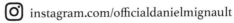 instagram.com/officialdanielmignault

ABOUT JACKSON DEAN CHASE

JACKSON DEAN CHASE is a USA TODAY bestselling author and award-winning poet. His fiction has been praised as "irresistible" in *Buzzfeed* and "diligently crafted" in *The Huffington Post*. Jackson's books on writing fiction have helped thousands of authors.

FROM THE AUTHOR: "I've always loved science fiction, fantasy, and horror, but it wasn't until I combined them with pulp thrillers and *noir* that I found my voice as an author. I want to leave my readers breathless, want them to feel the same desperate longing, the same hope and fear my heroes experience as they struggle not just to survive, but to become something more." — JDC

Get a free book at www.JacksonDeanChase.com
jackson@jacksondeanchase.com

THE GODS WAR—BOOK II

TITANS
WILL CLASH

TITAN
KINGDOM OF THE DEAD

DANIEL MIGNAULT
&
USA TODAY BESTSELLING AUTHOR
JACKSON DEAN CHASE

KINGDOM OF THE DEAD PREVIEW
READ THE EXCITING FIRST TWO CHAPTERS

THIS IS WHAT IT'S LIKE TO BE DEAD. It's funny, but it's true. I'm in the boat of Charon—just like a dead man, like a ghost, a ferried soul on its final journey. I hope this won't be mine. There are people I love, people I care for back on Earth. I can't let them down, just like I can't let my friends down: Mark Fentile and Hannah Stillwater. They're in the boat with me, my fellow fugitives from life, from death, from horror.

How we got here, to this place between worlds, is a long story. I go over it in my mind, searching for answers, searching for truth among the lies, the magic, the mystery. Maybe, if I can wrap my head around it, it will all make sense. Maybe I won't feel so lost or alone, though I don't know why.

I've always felt this way.

The River Styx flows, and we flow with it. Down, into the deep. Down, into the underworld, to Tartarus, the Kingdom of the Dead. But Tartarus is not just home to ghosts, it is home to monsters and to Hades, Greek God of Death. He has been imprisoned by Cronus, King of the Titans. Cronus the Immortal. Cronus the Cannibal, All-Devouring Father of the Gods: Zeus, Poseidon, and all the rest. Cronus, who is my father too.

My name is Andrus Eaves. I only discovered the truth of my birth yesterday... That I was born from a rock. The magic rock Cronus ate, tricked into thinking it was his son, Zeus. The rock that absorbed a fraction of my father's power. Power that flowed into me and *became me*.

In my former life, I was the adopted son of George and Carol Eaves. The Eaves are rich from oil—oil I found as a child in our backyard. That's another of my gifts, sensing the bounty of the earth. But my old life, my old esteemed position in society is gone. I wanted to join the Warrior caste and serve the New Greece Theocracy, the NGT that rules what's left of Earth. I wanted to put in my military service helping my fellow citizens before joining the family oil business. That's hard to do when you're on the run.

The NGT wants me dead.

That's because Cronus doesn't want any more children. *Especially me.* He likes to eat his spawn because, well, you know the story: Cronus worries they will grow up to challenge him. And he's right—I know I will. And I know Zeus did, and won, for a time. Only Zeus is dead. The Gods are dead: dead or fled, fled and gone. Only Hades remains, imprisoned in the depths of Tartarus. That's where Hannah, Mark, and I are going. To free her father.

To free Hades.

I look to Charon, the robed and hooded figure in black who guides our boat down the Styx. He's a living mummy, with parchment-thin flesh stretched tight over ancient bones. But he's not without a sense of style: his pointed beard is groomed into shape with cobwebs. And Charon's boat is just as ghoulish: long and narrow, like a gondola, decorated with the bones and skulls of the dead. Not exactly cheery, but at least it's consistent and exactly what you'd expect from the Ferryman of Souls.

I look to my friend, Mark Fentile, former priest-in-training. Mark, one step up from slavery, so poor he had to live in Loserville. Poor Mark! All he ever wanted was to serve the Titans and the Theocracy. That was before he realized how evil they are.

Mark has lost everything: his alcoholic mother, hung by the neck in their Loserville shack. Lucy, his beautiful blonde sister—*the girl who dared to love me*—lost to the clutches of our enemy, Inquisitor Anton.

Mark's mother is a zombie now, and Lucy, we don't know what happened to her. We only know she sacrificed herself wounding Anton, to buy Mark and I time to get to Hannah, and to buy herself revenge on Anton for raping her. I hope Lucy is OK, because if she isn't, she might be a zombie now too.

That's because the dead don't die. Not as long as Hades is imprisoned. Once King of Tartarus, now he is its prisoner, and a prisoner cannot force the dead to die. So the dead live on, in mindless agony, as zombies.

Immortality is the Titans' "gift" to humanity, the gift the Gods never gave, and now we know the reason why. It's a curse. You grow up, aging normally, then when you hit adulthood, you don't stop, but slow down—so slow, each year is like a decade, and that's great until you get too old to function. Then you slowly wither, yet horribly go on. That's because unlike the Gods or Titans, the human body isn't meant to live forever. But the bodies of immortals? Bodies like mine? We go on. We must go on until we are destroyed or destroy ourselves.

Like I intend to destroy Cronus—with Hades' help, and the help of my friends. Once Hades is free from his prison, then even Gods and Titans can die...

I look to Hannah Stillwater, the beautiful witch, the Demigoddess. She's thin, black-haired, and pale, wearing a purple cloak and toga. Almost eighteen, like Mark and me. Her dark eyes are tombstone gray and sharp with intelligence. Her raven familiar, Shadow, sits perched on her shoulder.

I look behind us, to the shores of the secret cave below Bronson Canyon. In the past, before the Gods War, the canyon was a place of magic and monsters. Hollywood filmed everything from *Batman* to *It Conquered the World* there. Under the NGT, it's a place of magic and monsters again, only this time, it's all real and nowhere is safe.

Moments ago, we barely got away from Captain Nessus and his

Night Patrol: centaurs and harpies. We'd still be fighting them if I hadn't used my magic to collapse the tunnel behind us.

So that's where my life's at. It's easy to look back, to other people, other places. It's not so easy to look to yourself, to gaze deep inside, but that's what I do now, and it all comes down to this:

I am Andrus Eaves.

I am a Titan, and I am Earth's last hope.

OUR BOAT GLIDES ON, through the murky darkness, through black, sluggish water. All around us is rock. Rock walls, rock ceiling. The Underworld. The Afterworld. Silent and eternal.

Tartarus is where your spirit goes when you die. It's not a place of punishment, it's just where the dead live. But just because you're dead doesn't mean you stop living—the flesh fails, but the spirit goes on. You're still you, only a ghost, and you go on doing the things you did in life. Sometimes good, sometimes bad. The difference is your mistakes can't kill you. You have eternity to learn and grow, to know joy or to suffer...

Hades ruled Tartarus once, and despite the Theocracy's propaganda, Hannah says he did a pretty good job. Now the Titans rule in his place. I'm not sure how things have changed, except there are probably more monsters. Monsters like harpies and centaurs need magic to breed, and there isn't enough of it on Earth. Oh, there's enough for short-term spells and the like, but long-term, sustained magic is hard unless you're a God or Titan. That's why monsters died out in the past. They're sterile on Earth.

Tartarus on the other hand, well, this place is pretty much *all magic*. It's below the Earth, but not really part of it: another dimension. You can only get in through gates, like the one we passed through back in Bronson Canyon.

The air down here isn't air at all. It's a deadly combination of sulphur, brimstone, methane, and other toxic things. As immortals, Hannah and I are immune. To me, the air has a strange, smokey flavor, but nothing too bad. But Mark is mortal, and shouldn't be able to breathe. He should be choking right now, strangling, becoming a zombie.

Only he isn't. He's wearing the ghost-mask Hannah gave him, a mask that makes Mark look like one of the dead, and allows him to breathe the gruesome gasses that fill Tartarus. "I can't believe it," Mark says. "We're really here, in the Underworld!"

Hannah shrugs. "It's not that special, priest. I grew up here. Personally, I couldn't wait to get out, but I guess every one feels the same about their home town. What about you, Rock Boy? You excited to be here?"

I bristle at the nickname. "I'm excited we're all in one piece. As for being here, well, it's better than being back there. I hope Ares is all right. Last I saw, Captain Nessus had his magic sword."

"Correction," Hannah says, "Nessus had *one* of his swords. You can bet Ares still has the other."

We'd left the God of War behind. Ares had bought us time to get inside the cave. I still can't get over the fact he was Mr. Cross, my gym teacher in disguise. No wonder he'd been so hard on me. He was secretly training me for this...

"You think we'll see him again?" I ask.

Hannah flashes a grim smile. "We're going to war, aren't we? War is kind of his thing. You can bet Ares will turn up sooner or later, don't worry."

I flash her a smile of my own. "Who's worried?"

"Don't try to play it off. You're worried as hell. We all are... Well, except this guy." She jerks her thumb back at the living mummy piloting the boat. "Charon's pretty chill, aren't ya?"

Charon bows his bony neck in a grisly nod. We sail on. Into the night. Into endless darkness.

I let the silence sink in, let it wash over me like waves. I reach out to the rocks we pass, taking comfort in them. Hannah's not wrong: *I am worried.* We're in danger: incredible, impossible danger! But we're also taking action. We're doing what's right. Right for us, and right for the world. Alone, none of us could, but together? We might have a shot.

"So what's the plan?" I ask Hannah. "You recruited us, remember?"

"Actually, I recruited *you*. I warned against involving Mark."

"I was already involved." Mark doesn't sound bitter, though he has every right to be. What he does sound is determined. "We're all in this together. I may be human, but I have something neither of you has."

"What's that?" Hannah asks.

"Brains."

She laughs. "Well, you're not stupid. I'll give you that."

"And you're brave," I tell him.

Mark shrugs. "I guess, but I'm not brave because I want to be. I'm brave because I have to."

"Not much difference in the end," Hannah muses. "We're all coming out of this heroes."

"Heroes or traitors," I remind her, "the biggest the world has ever seen."

She raises an eyebrow. "Oh, so you're bigger than Zeus now?"

"If we win, I am. If we win, Cronus is dead, the Titans are dead, and... well, I'm not sure what happens after that, but I'm sure it will be impressive. And we'll all be bigger than Zeus, not just me." I add that last part because it sounds crazy to put all this on me. Yet part of me, the newly awakened Titan part says, *Yes, I can defeat Cronus. Yes, I can save the world. I can rule in his place, because I should rule, only my rule will be just and strong and forever...*

Where is this coming from? I shake my head to clear it. I've had so many strange dreams, so many strange thoughts. It's my connection to Cronus. Through the accident of my birth, I absorbed part of his power, but what if I absorbed part of who he is as well? What if I'm no better than him and I just don't know it yet?

"The plan," I say, "what is it?"

Hannah shrugs. "To free my father."

"Yeah, you told us that, but how exactly? You do know where

Hades is, don't you?"

Hannah chews her lower lip. "It's complicated; the location is cloaked by magic. Magic no immortal can see through except Cronus, since it's his spell."

"And me?" I ask. "You think I can because of my connection to him?"

She nods. "That's what Ares and I are hoping."

"OK, so how do I do it?"

"Um... you just close your eyes, reach out, and look for him."

"I look for him with my eyes shut?"

"Yes, genius! Look with your *mind's eye*. The magic of Tartarus will enhance whatever natural ability you have... if you have any."

"You can do it," Mark says. "Have faith!"

"Spoken like a true priest," Hannah jokes.

He looks away. "Well, I don't know about that. I'm kind of between deities right now."

I apologize. "Sorry, man. I didn't mean it like that. I mean, I appreciate your confidence in me. Both of you."

"Charon too," Hannah adds. "He may not look it, but he's cheering you on."

I look at the grim, skull-faced ferryman. He looks back, with empty, unknowable eyes. "Thanks," I tell him.

Charon gives me a stiff, creaking nod, then returns to staring straight ahead. I watch his pole go in the river, propelling our boat forward. Pole in, pole out.

I try to time my breath with the pole. Breathe in, breathe out. *Slowly.* I close my eyes. Relaxing, going inside myself. I listen to the sound of the boat, the river, the rustle of Charon's robe.

I reach out, sensing water, sensing rock: *the river, the tunnel.* Forward motion: *slow, rhythmic.* Across the Styx, the River of Hate and Promises, and beyond... deep, into haunted Tartarus...

I sense the whispering presence of ghosts, but feel the physicality of monsters. Breath hot, muscles strong. Wild, animal, unnatural. *Magic.*

I feel other things too... brothers, sisters. *Titans.* Some monstrous, some fair, but all to be avoided. Unless... some of them want to rebel against Cronus? But no, as helpful as that would be, we can't risk it. Why should they follow me? I'm no one, nobody.

I pull away from them and keep searching, but it's no use. I don't know what to look for. I come back into myself, feeling drained.

"Any luck?" Hannah asks.

"None. Everything radiates magic, and I'm too new at this to know what to look for."

"The first time's always hard. Don't worry, you'll get better at it." She says it with a smile, but I can tell Hannah's not happy.

"I've let you down. I'm sorry."

"No," she says. "Not yet, you haven't."

We drift downriver, the only sound the creak of Charon's bones, the *slosh* of the pole dipping into the water. Maybe I can try again...

All of a sudden, Mark says, "Hey, wait! I've got an idea."

"Yeah?" I say. "What is it?"

"Maybe we're going about this the wrong way."

"Wrong way how?" Hannah asks.

"What if the problem isn't just that Andrus doesn't know what to look for, or that the whole underworld is covered in magic? What if instead of looking for the spell hiding Hades' prison, we should be looking for an area that *doesn't* look like magic?"

"You know I'm a witch, right?" Hannah reminds him. "I already tried that. I tried everything! I really thought Andrus might be able to succeed where I failed."

"Maybe it's impossible," Mark says.

Hannah snorts. "Really? That's a good attitude!"

"No," Mark says, "I didn't mean it like that. What if it's impossible for you, or Andrus, or anyone else to find Hades?"

"All right, maybe... but I don't see how giving up helps."

I've known Mark long enough to understand his moods, and how his devious mind works. "Hear him out," I say. "Go on, Mark."

He nods. "OK, so assuming Cronus's spell cloaks Hades' prison from immortals, what about mortals?"

"You mean you?"

Mark shakes his head. "No, not me. I mean monsters."

Hannah and I stare at each other, then Mark. "Even if that's true," she says, "the monsters are all on Cronus's side. They'll never agree to help us."

"I'm not talking about *any* monster," Marks replies. "I'm talking about one in particular. The one closest to Hades. The one guaranteed to be on our side and to know what to look for."

Hannah's face lights up. She leans over and hugs Mark, kissing him on the cheek as the thin boy blinks in surprise. "I love this mortal!" Hannah says, all trace of her bad mood gone. "Didn't I tell you it was a great idea to bring him?"

I scratch my head. "Wait, I don't get it... What monster are we looking for?"

"Cerberus," Hannah says. "We're looking for Cerberus."

THE GODS WAR, BOOK II: KINGDOM OF THE DEAD
available in ebook and paperback July 20, 2018

THE GODS WAR, BOOK III: GIFT OF DEATH
available in ebook and paperback July 27, 2018

SACRIFICE TO
SURVIVE

DRONE

BEYOND THE DOME BOOK 1

JACKSON DEAN CHASE

USA TODAY BESTSELLING AUTHOR

DRONE PREVIEW
READ THE INCREDIBLE FIRST TWO CHAPTERS

THEY'RE THREATENING to shut off our oxygen again. The final "pay up or die" vidmail came over the holocom this morning. It was read by a cheerful blonde who reminded us that failure to pay our bill by midnight will result in termination of service. Unfortunately, termination of service also means termination of us.

Mom says we'll get the money, but with late fees, the bill is more than any amount we can raise today, unless... But I'm not ready to think about that. Not yet.

I scrub my body with the last of the cleansing pads. Only the Elite use water to bathe, and we're anything but rich. My body is small and skinny, malnourished. Is it selfish that I want to be tall and strong? That I want to wear nice clothes and go to parties? It is, and it's also stupid.

The truth of my world is that Drones like me are bred to work in the factories. We don't have money to eat right or afford nice things. We don't have time for parties. We get up, go to work, get married, create another Drone, then die.

I take my time getting ready. The bathroom is the only place I ever have any privacy, so I stay in here a lot and pretend there is something more beyond these walls than the tiny, one-room apartment I share with my parents. Maybe I pretend more than I should. Knowing my dreams will never come true only makes reality hurt worse.

I haven't washed my hair all week, but I know I'll have to leave the apartment today. I've been holding back some of my water rations exactly for this purpose. I have to be careful not to waste a drop, so I plug the sink and fill it halfway from the ration bottle, then add a few drops of shamp-con. It foams, a million tiny bubbles stripping the grease from my hair. This is as close as I will ever come to feeling like a rich girl.

My hair is long and flame-red, which is unusual. "Gingers" have been almost extinct for a hundred years. Everyone thinks I get my color out of a box, but how could I afford that? My red is real. I like that it makes me different, but keeping it long requires a lot more work than the short cut my Mom wants to give me. She doesn't like me to stand out, says it's dangerous. Individuality attracts the wrong kind of attention. Not just from men, but the government.

"I'm not a terrorist," I tell her. "All I want is this one thing."

"Wanting one thing leads to wanting more," Mom insists. "You have to be satisfied with what you've got." Then she reminds me that my dispensation is running out in ten days. It's the exemption that keeps me from having to work because my parents need me at home to take care of them. They're both disabled. Me not being here will be hard on them, but my paycheck will have to make up for it.

Part of me wants to go to work. All my friends are already in the factories. They have been since they turned thirteen and graduated Worker Education. We don't see each other much anymore. Mandatory seven-day, twelve-hour shifts with only one state holiday off a month doesn't leave them time for fun.

Two of my friends are already married. They signed up for the factory marriage lottery, just like my parents. It's not required, but life's easier when both husband and wife work at the same factory.

I will never join the lottery. If I meet my husband through the workplace, that's fine, but I don't want my marriage to be random, forced to be with someone by chance. Still, the law says a Drone must marry by eighteen and produce a child by twenty-one, so I can't stay single forever.

My birthday is in ten days. Ten days until I'm sixteen and I start my job on the line at Foodtronix, the factory I will work in till the day I die—or the day I'm too disabled to do my job. Mom says the manager will make me cut my hair, and once I'm free of the one childish thing that sets me apart, I'll start to think like everyone else.

"There's safety in conformity," Mom says. "Your father and I only want what's best for you. We want you to fit in, to be normal."

But that's not entirely true. Once, when Mom was visiting the neighbor down the hall, Dad told me he loved my red hair. That everyone should have something for themselves, and he was glad I had something. When I asked him what he had that was special, he said he had me. I still remember that. I'll always remember that.

Mom knocks on the bathroom door. "Vikka? Honey, how much longer are you going to be? Breakfast is almost ready."

"Just a minute." I don't want to come out. I know what's waiting for me—not just at the breakfast table, but in the world outside. It frightens me so much my hands grip the edge of the sink until my knuckles turn white.

Staring into the mirror, I see the tired girl with the heart-shaped face and haunted green eyes. She is weak, crushed by the weight of her life. I tell her to be strong. The girl smiles—just a little—and some of the terror leaves her eyes.

"You can do this," I whisper. "You can do anything."

I change into my rags, a threadbare olive-green jumpsuit that's anything but flattering. "Rags" are what Drones call their government-issued uniforms: color-coded jumpsuits that tell which corporation you belong to. We get a new pair every year, but they aren't made well and start to fall apart after six months. My jumpsuit is nine months old and already frayed at the knees and elbows. I can't wait to replace it.

When I come out of the bathroom, Mom and Dad are at the kitchen table, looking miserable. I can tell they've been arguing about the oxygen bill.

"It'll be OK," I say automatically. "Right, Mom?"

"Yes, everything will be fine." Mom smiles, but it's strained, and I can tell she's only agreeing to keep Dad calm.

Ever since Dad was injured in the terrorist bombing at his factory four years ago, he's been depressed. He's blind, and missing all his limbs. The doctors said we should euthanize him. "It would be cheaper and more humane," they argued, but I cried so hard, I convinced Dad to live. Sometimes, Dad wishes he was dead, that he regrets being a burden to us. But he's not a burden. He's my dad.

Mom sets a bowl of sim-soup in front of him, placing a straw to his lips. It's not really soup, just water with a nutrient packet added. And it's imitation "beef," the same flavor we have every day. I hate it. There's a picture of something called a cow on the package, but there haven't been any cows since long before I was born. All the animals are dead.

Hands shaking, Mom places another bowl in front of me.

"Aren't you having any?" I ask.

Her stomach growls. "That's the last packet," she says. "You need your strength today."

I push the bowl toward her. "No, you have it. I'm not hungry. I should get this over with."

"Vikka," Mom says, "You don't have to do this! This isn't what we raised you for."

"I know, but there's no choice. We all know that."

I stand and kiss Dad's wrinkled cheek. His ash-gray beard scratches my lips. He's thirty-five, an old man approaching the end of his life. In five years, his genetic code will unravel and he'll be dead like every Drone who reaches forty. The corporations call death our "expiration date," and justify it by saying anyone older is a drain on society. But of course, those rules don't apply to them.

I hug him and say, "I love you, Dad."

He whispers, "Love you too."

I kiss Mom, ruffling her close-cropped brown hair. There is more gray in it today, or maybe I haven't noticed till now. She's two years younger than Dad, but her body is already breaking down. It barely fills her rags anymore, and I worry she's determined to join him in death.

I head for the door. "I'll be back with the money as soon as I can."

Mom rolls after me in her wheelchair, the stumps of her knees sticking out from under her blanket. "Vikka, wait! Don't do this. Let me go."

"No," I say. "You've done enough already. You can't go again."

Mom hugs my waist tight, telling me to be careful, how brave I am, and how proud she is to have a daughter willing to sacrifice for her family. "Don't let them talk you into doing too much," she says. "Just enough to pay the bill, OK?"

I don't answer.

"Please," Mom begs. "We don't need anything else. You'll start your job soon. We'll have more money then, plus you can get in the factory's marriage lottery. Adding your husband's income to yours will go a long way toward—"

I cut her off by telling her what she wants to hear. "Don't worry. I know what to do."

"Just what we need," Mom reminds me. "Don't be a hero. No good ever comes of it."

I pull my hair into a pony tail and slip on my breather—the oxygen mask required for travel. I check the tank. Half-full. Enough for an hour. I strap the tank on and turn to leave.

"Vikka," Mom says, "thank you for doing this. I love you."

"I know," I say. "I love you too." We hug again, and she isn't the only one reluctant to let go. I don't want to leave, but I have to.

WHEN I STEP out of the apartment airlock into the hallway, I'm greeted by graffiti on the walls, the same filthy garbage strewn everywhere. Thanks to the breather, I don't have to smell it.

I walk to the turbolift and hit the button, but it's broken again. That means I have to climb the service ladder. It's six floors to the lobby, and I almost slip when a loose rung pulls free. I watch it sail down the dimly-lit shaft, clattering off the walls.

When I get to the bottom, I discover the body of Widow Kenjins, crumpled and bent in her blue jumpsuit. She must have slipped. I check for a pulse. There's none.

I know I'm the first to find her because her oxygen tank and breather are still here. I unhook the tank and use my multi-tool to siphon her air to mine. I wrap the now-empty tank in her jacket and take it with me. The jacket won't bring much, but the tank is worth a lot on the black market. Maybe enough that I won't have to go through with my plan.

I exit the Liv-Rite Apartments onto McAuliffe Circle and head toward Armstrong Avenue, avoiding the open sewer and potholes. There are a lot of disabled on the Dronetown streets: people missing limbs, hobbling on crutches, or using wheelchairs.

I look above the plasticrete skyline to the encircling Dome. The gray roof is impossible to see through. It always is, but I keep hoping someday I'll see the sun, the clouds, or some kind of weather. Anything but the everyday normal of cold, crisp nothing.

As I step onto Armstrong, I notice a new holoboard has been installed over the intersection. The 3-D image of a stern man's face instructs everyone to "WORK HARD AND OBEY," then switches to a smiling woman saying, "EVERYONE CONTRIBUTES, EVERYONE LIVES." The man and woman are of indeterminate age, at least as old as my parents, but healthier, more youthful look-ing. It is hard to tell how old the wealthy really are, since they don't die off at forty. They just go on forever, living off us like vampires.

A boy on an expensive white jetbike swoops by, the only person on the street not wearing rags. The Elite wear whatever they want, and he's wearing black synth-leather. It's an expensive riding suit with white racing stripes. I wonder what he's doing in this part of Alpha City. His kind don't normally come to Dronetown. I can't tell what he looks like under his helmet, but when he slows, I know he's looking at me.

I get self-conscious, not just because he's a guy, but because he's rich, an air-hog. The Elite live on Mansion Row, in the tall part of the Dome with the most "sky." They're the families of the moguls and their corporate officers, the people who run Alpha City. Their air isn't rationed, nor are they limited to the one child per family policy of the government. The Elite don't care about trash like me. I've even heard stories about gangs of them snatching Drones for their parties, then dumping them in the gutter when they're done.

"What are you looking at?" I demand. The breather makes my voice harsh and modulated.

The guy revs his engine and speeds off. I'm relieved, but part of me wishes he'd given me a ride. It's another five blocks to the closest Trade-Mart, and every minute I save is more air to breathe.

Back in the Before Times, there were no domes. Air was free. The sun always shone, and there were real cows to eat. Everyone was happy. But there were too many people, and that ruined everything. Resources got scarce. Even the air became polluted. That led to wars, and whole countries fell apart. Governments couldn't be trusted. They started killing their own people.

The earth was dying.

The big, multinational companies banded together to form the New World Plutonomy, and the CEOs of these corporations became the moguls, the Council of Seven that rule us. They overthrew the old, elected governments and promised a glorious new future with food, shelter, and security for all. The NWP herded the willing into domed cities connected by subway tunnels so no one ever had to see the poisoned surface again. They said our only hope was to live inside the domes under their rules.

The NWP make the poor work in factories, telling us it's for our own good, and the good of the planet. The stuff we make keeps us alive, and allows us to trade with other cities for whatever goods we can't produce on our own. It also makes the moguls richer.

If we work long and hard enough, the NWP promises that some-day, things can return to the way they were in the Before Times, only better. We can all live outside again...

Only not everyone believes them. There were some who questioned corporate rule, who wanted to see what life was like outside the domes. They said the Council of Seven were lying to us. They formed the Resistance, staging protests and strikes, calling for unions and a Worker's Bill of Rights. But unions are treason and punishable by death.

After the NWP executed many of the Resistance leaders, the ones who got away reformed in secret, renaming themselves the Revolution. They're terrorists who use assassinations and bombings to disrupt the corporations. Dad's injury was caused by them. I may not like the New World Plutonomy, but I hate the Revolution.

———

The Trade-Mart is a pawn shop, and it's in the worst part of Drone-town. The owner, Trader Nox, is a fence with connections to the black market. It's the only place I know I can sell the tank without being arrested.

The neighborhood gets rougher, more ruined-looking with every step. This is where the Unassigned live—Drones who refuse to work and survive by killing, thieving, and whoring. Security rarely patrols this area, either because they're afraid or because they've been bribed. Maybe both.

This is the most reckless thing I've ever done. I clutch the hidden tank tightly through the jacket. As my anxiety grows, my pace quickens.

A tall punk with a blue mohawk leans out the doorway of an abandoned building. He leers and whistles. I cross the street to avoid him and run into a bald guy with a prosthetic hook for a hand.

"Hello, beauty!" he says with fake cheer. "Whatcha hiding under the jacket?"

"N-nothing," I stammer.

His hook taps the jacket, clanking the tank underneath. "Nothing, huh? Then you won't mind giving it to me and my friend, and maybe something else..."

The punk with the mohawk circles behind me. He has hungry

eyes and a crutch slung over his shoulder like a club.

I run. They give chase. If they catch me, I'm not just dead. *I'm worse than dead...*

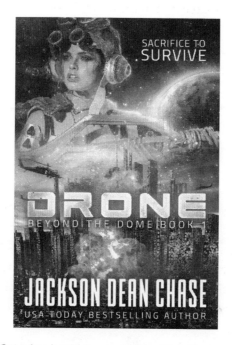

Get a free book at www.JacksonDeanChase.com

Beyond the Dome, Book 1: DRONE
available in eBook and paperback August 3, 2018

Beyond the Dome, Book 2: WARRIOR
available in eBook and paperback August 10, 2018

Beyond the Dome, Book 13: ELITE
available in eBook and paperback August 17, 2018

Beyond the Dome, Book 4: HUMAN
available in eBook and paperback August 24, 2018

31442695R00159

Made in the USA
Columbia, SC
02 November 2018